Danse Mécanique

Steven Popkes

Also by Steven Popkes

Howard Cycle Novels

God's Country
Danse Mécanique
House of Birds
Jackie's Boy

Additional Works

Caliban Landing
Slow Lightning
Welcome to Witchlandia
Simple Things
The Long Frame

Danse Mécanique

Steven Popkes

A Howard Cycle Novel

Walking Rocks /Book View Café

Portions of this work appear in *Asimov's Science Fiction*, 2012.

Cover design by Wendy Zimmerman
Cover illustration © 2021 by Wendy Zimmerman
Published by Walking Rock Publications in association with
Book View Café Publishing Cooperative
www.bookviewcafe.com

ISBN: 978-1-61138-955-5

To Wendy,
Ben,
and Iris

Table of Contents

Part 1

Standing at the Edge

Jake

Chapter 1.1 February 2

A window opened up on the active wall and I stared at it. Rosie stared back.

"Hello, Jacob." She smiled. The always unexpected dimples on each cheek and that bright, bright smile. A nose so thin it whistled when she was excited. Not beautiful. Not pretty. Compelling. Like a volcano or a ruined city or the Texas plains or a magnificent catastrophe. Beauty just isn't a consideration. You're witness to something amazing.

"It's good to see you." As if she'd just returned from shopping instead of reappearing in my life after twelve years of silence.

A jumble of memories and impressions struck me like a brick. Meeting her backstage in Brockton. The feel of her skin, the warmth of her breath, the smell of her. Me singing back in Massachusetts. My band, *Persons Unknown*—me, Jess, Olivia, and Obe. Stoned and laughing at the DeCordova. Release of "Don't Make Me Cry." Money. Fights. *The Late Show*. Buying this house. The long tour scheduled from Boston to Los Angeles. Our wonderful first night on the way to Ohio. The fight in Cleveland. Our breakup in Saint Louis. The breakup of the band in Denver.

She wiggled a finger at me. "You and I need to talk."

"Off," I said and she winked out.

I sat there, breathing hard, my hands shaking. I started to pick up the coffee cup, realized I was going to make a mess and put it down again. The call alert sounded.

"Fuck you," I snarled. I knew I'd answer it if I stayed. I grabbed a pair of shoes and ran outside. I pulled them on and ran out the back on the trail. My earbud buzzed and I tossed it on the dirt.

◀▶

In the low mountains of the desert, twenty acres of scrub just means when you get to the edge of your property, you can still see your house. I was at the edge of public land. So far, only the ever-approaching green cloud of Greater Los Angeles had been able to reach me. So far. It was only a matter of time. Greater Los Angeles had eaten all the way to Bakersfield. Eventually, it would reach me, too.

I sat down on an old volcanic boulder heaved here back when dinosaurs were still sitting around playing cards and waiting for the meteor to hit. I looked around the shady crevices for rattlesnakes. It was spring but an early emergent wasn't unheard of. It was already hot but not uncomfortable. Unlike Boston, out here in California sweat works.

Eventually, I calmed down. After all, I thought. It's been twelve years—almost thirteen. She must have a good reason to call me now. *To mess with you again,* I said to myself. Not necessarily. And it *had* been a long time. We were different people. I was a recluse living in a rotting house that the bank and State would someday fight over. She was probably a successful… well, something. Rich, probably. Doing something important. World famous—wouldn't I have heard of her? *Have you ever looked her up?* No. I hadn't. Not that I didn't want to but it felt too much like an addict returning to the drug. I was happy now.

Really?

I forcefully told myself to shut up.

Okay. We were adults, right? We could converse like adults.

I made my way back to the house. Found the bud lying next to the front door. I inspected it for wildlife. It was clean. I put it in.

I went back to my coffee. Cold as it was, this time I drank it down without spilling it. "Okay." Grover, my house AI, figured out what I meant.

Rosie popped up again on the wall. "As I said: we need to talk."

"Why?" I didn't know if I was asking why she called now or why she had left.

"Got a song doctor gig for you to think about. A good one with lots of promise."

I didn't know what to say. "This is a… *professional* call?"

"I suppose it could also turn into studio work. You're still doing studio work, aren't you, Jake?"

"Sometimes. Are you representing musicians these days?" I felt suddenly very tired.

"I'm doing a favor for a friend." She cocked her head to one side. "Besides, this is what you do, isn't it? Pull musical order out of creative chaos? The price is very attractive."

"I can't—" I shook my head. I remembered how so often I felt at sea with Rosie. Always trying to catch up.

"Look," she said, suddenly sympathetic. "I know you've had a rough time. Behind on the mortgage, right?"

"And the taxes."

"Christ! The State of California is not someone you want to owe money to." She took a deep breath. "My point is you need the money. A single song, Jake. That's all. It'll pay back the state and even bring the mortgage up to date."

I loved this house: two stories, four bedrooms on twenty acres far enough from Greater Los Angeles that the price had been screamingly ridiculous instead of obscene. It has its own power, water, and sewer— I was paranoid about the end of the world back when I bought it. Twelve years ago, the world seemed a lot more precarious. *I* was a lot more precarious. This was before I blew any remaining money on riotous living.

But the house fit me. Kitchen. Bath. An office. My bedroom. Nice studio in what would be the living room: high cathedral ceiling, good acoustics, and an active surface along the whole east sidewall. Enclosed and far from the crowd. *My* house. My *house.* "I guess," I said slowly.

"Great. I'll shoot you over a contract. This is going to be fun."

"But—"

She had already disconnected. A moment later Grover, my house AI, flagged the packet and okayed the contract. I sighed and had her put the music up on the wall.

◀▶

A set of pages ran the length of the wall at my eye height. I walked alongside reading it. "Downbeat Heart." One song. Ten pages. Musical notes. Not techno tablature or a vague demonstration melody. Actual musical notes. And not just vocal lines and a sketchy guitar accompaniment. These were full score sheets. Every sheet had vocal, guitar, keyboard, bass, and drum lines—at one point in the bridge tympani were called for. *Tympani?* Keyboards sections had synthesizer settings referring to frequency and sound envelope definitions. There was an appendix with suggested synthesizer models and a map of the envelope settings for each device.

It was a curious tune. A little three beat arpeggio in a four-beat base. Odd. Take your right hand and tap out a 1-2-3 beat. Take your left hand and tap out a 1-2-3-4 beat at the same time. The right hand catches up to the left hand every twelve beats. It's not a new idea but it's rare in pop music. The song was clearly written for a divaloid—a long glissando up into parts of the audio spectrum only dogs could appreciate. Like someone had taught hummingbirds to sing. From the range and the run, I guessed the love interest of the composer was Dot. That sort of run was a signature with her and she had the biggest fan base.

My interest faded right off the map.

Okay, I thought. Written on *SynthaChord* or *ProMusica*. Professional systems suggested deep pockets. A *very* rich divaloid fan. With delusions of grandeur.

But money was money. A contract was a contract. Rosie was Rosie.

I found myself playing the song back in my mind. First in one key. Then another. Faster. Slower. Change the key halfway through. Fitting in different words. Adding a drum beat and a different guitar back up. Inverting the chorus. Play it backwards. Inside out.

Okay. I was prejudiced. It was better than the usual Dot song.

Along around midnight I packaged up the whole thing and sent it off to Rosie with an invoice. Payment came in an hour later. Grover turned it around and sent it off to the banks and the State of California. The money was no more than a little loop of electrons into my account and out.

It had been more fun than I expected. I was even vaguely depressed it was over.

Tomorrow I had to nail the photovoltaic shingles back down. Or fix the composting toilet. Who in their right mind wanted to fix a composting toilet?

I took comfort in the knowledge I wasn't going to be evicted for another month and went to bed.

Chapter 1.2 February 10

Around dawn, I heard something downstairs.

I turned on the light and listened. I didn't hear anything. Thinking I had been dreaming I started to turn the light back off when I heard it again. A scraping. A muttering.

I left the bedroom and stood looking down the stairs, listening. Again.

No cops: it would be an hour before they got out here. I rummaged in my closet until I found an ancient softball bat. Then, as quietly as I could I eased downstairs.

I smelled coffee and cigarettes.

Rosie was sitting at the table next to the active wall, a keyboard in front of her. There were a few displays up showing things I didn't understand. Behind her, on the other table were a set of four open computer cases plugged into the data ports.

She was wearing a light-colored suit with charms and bangles and bracelets hanging everywhere: arms, wrist, shoulders. Rosie rang like bells as she typed. Even from here, she smelled of cigarette smoke and the aroma brought out a whole collection of memories. From the time I met her I'd been attracted to women who smoked. She wore reading glasses that, God help me, I found adorable.

She stopped typing and watched a display, the smoke from her cigarette curling quietly upwards.

"How did you get in here?" I put the bat down on the table and sat across from her.

She tapped a key and all of the displays disappeared from the wall. Rosie pulled a tablet from the table with the cases and looked at it. "You gave me a key when you bought the place, remember? Just before the last great tour of *Persons Unknown*."

"That was twelve *years* ago."

"And you never changed the locks." She looked at me across her coffee. "What does that tell you?"

"That it's time to change the locks." I felt cornered. Constrained. Boxed in. I waved at the cases. "What are you *doing* here?" I snarled.

She took off her reading glasses. "My client liked what you did with 'Downbeat Heart.' Did you?"

The answer was yes. The more I thought about it the more I liked both the song and what I had done with it. Working on that song had been much more fun than it should have been. It felt like water in the desert. What did that say about me?

"Musical order out of creative chaos. What's not to like?" I felt defeated. "Even if it was music for Dot."

"You figured that out on your own."

"The glissando gave it away."

"I expect it did." She looked down, gathering her thoughts.

"Why did you send it to me?"

She looked away and back at the screen. "The client. Frankly, you weren't my first choice."

I exhaled. I didn't realize I'd been holding my breath. "I see. Who's the composer?"

Rosie nodded towards the wall. A small figure materialized, barely five feet tall, pale with short jet-black hair, big blue eyes, and tiny mouth instantly recognizable. Dot smiled at me. "Good morning, Mister Arnold."

Rosie was watching me. "Jake? Meet your client."

I stared at the two of them. Then, I walked over to the main breaker box and pulled the master circuit. The entire room went dark. Dot, Rosie, and I disappeared into darkness.

Rosie didn't say anything for a moment. "Mature, Jake. Real mature."

◄►

I heard her fumbling in the dark. A moment later light came from her hand. "Did I ever tell you the time I was consulting for Peabody Coal back east?" She passed the spot of light over me. "Always have a flashlight." She looked into cases. "Gig taught me to always use buffered power supplies, too." Rosie walked over to the breaker box and turned it back on again. After a moment, Dot reappeared on the wall.

Rosie found a chair and sat down. "What's this all about?"

"Have you ever *listened* to her?"

"More than you would think."

"If she weren't wholly owned and controlled by Ippon—"

"Don't explain it to me." Rosie gestured towards Dot. "Explain it to her."

"What would be the point?"

"Indulge me."

I looked at Dot. She was watching me. She didn't look a day over sixteen.

"You're a whore," I said and stumbled. Not something I could say easily to an image my brain kept telling me was a young girl. "That is, you would be if you weren't wholly owned and controlled by Ippon. That makes you a tool. A mechanism to find the absolute bottom, the broadest possible appeal. A *vehicle* to separate people from their money. You're *merchandise*, easily purchased. Easily used. You're *easy listening*. Music is supposed to make you feel. It's supposed to cost you something—"

"I agree."

"What?" I stared at her for a moment. I looked at Rosie. "What's going on?"

Rosie pointed at Dot. "Don't let me stop you. Go on. Talk to her."

I turned back to Dot. "You agree?"

"Can you explain to me what you did to 'Downbeat Heart?'"

I looked at Rosie and back at Dot. When I looked at her objectively it wasn't hard to see her as a thing: eyes so big they'd look at home on a fish. Hair black as if painted in ink with stars twinkling in it. Shoulders narrow but hips wide—as stylized as the *Venus of Willendorf*. But some part of me kept translating all that into *human*.

I tried to explain what I had done. What I always did. What I had done since I was twelve.

◀▶

The lyrics were sentimental but that didn't matter. The quality of lyrics is overrated. They depend solely on the supporting music. The *Iliad* would sound crappy with a disco beat but *Mary Had a Little Lamb* could be profound if fit to the right arrangement. So, lyrics came second.

In this case, that triple beat arpeggio driven square into a four by four rhythm gave weight to the emotion and turned the words from trivial to powerful. The arpeggio couldn't hold a melody on its own. The bass line kept it in the song until it was later echoed in the chorus. But it lingered over that pattern way past the point of least boredom: the full three measures. Twice. I let the pattern start then, once it was established, deviated from it by sliding across the triple with the melody line hidden in the bass. This gave the impression of a four by four but without actually leaving the triple beat and also introduced the barest hint of the melody carried by the bass line. The second repeat already had a quirky key shift for the chorus. I leaned on that and put in a strong bridge back to the mainline, adding some harmony in an accompanying minor key. Finally, a long glissando across three octaves back to hold the new key into the final chorus—had to give the divaloid fan his money's worth. The result was a musically interesting danceable pop tune.

I ran the glissando up and down on my guitar a few times to make sure it fit. Then I had Grover play the bass line while I played the vocal line to make sure they sounded like what I expected. Then, I had him play the vocal line while I went through and straightened out the other instrument lines.

The new vocal line was a better fit for the lyrics. Not that the lyrics were actually bad—love unlooked for. Lots of hope. Past disappointments. The broken mending themselves. That sort of thing. I didn't pay much attention to the content. Instead, I listened to how the words sounded together. Too forced. The imagery was too tame.

Grover served as rhyming dictionary while I punched up the imagery—*hands* to *fingertips, shining* to *glittering,* things like that. Making the consonants fall on the beat so the vowels could carry the melody and then making the rhymes a little more memorable. Straightforward stuff.

◄►

"Straightforward stuff," Dot repeated and seemed to freeze for a moment.

Rosie watched her tablet closely. She typed the keyboard a moment and watched the tablet again.

"I understand," said Dot suddenly moving again. "Will you work with me again?"

"With you?"

"Yes. You have given me a new perspective on my work. I'd like to make it better. More fulfilling. With more impact. I'd like you to help me."

"You want *me* to help *you*. Wouldn't that put me out of a job?"

She smiled at me. "Do you really think you're so easily replaced?"

"How could I possibly help you?"

Rose cleared her throat. "The contract involves helping a composer bring material to completion, prepare the material for a concert and shepherd the performance. One concert. You will be very well paid. The work on the single song brought your debts up to date." She waved around the room. "With this gig, you can pay *off* the mortgage and fix up the house. Maybe even have some left in the bank."

I looked at Rosie. I looked at Dot. I looked around my house.

My *house*.

"Okay," I said slowly. "What else have you got? Enough for a performance? Enough for a collection?"

Across the wall appeared folder icon after folder icon. There must have been thirty songs. Forty. More.

I whistled. "This isn't a collection. It's an opus." I looked at Rosie. "Rosie, what have you done?"

Rosie smiled. "You're about to find out."

I took time for breakfast and coffee. But Dot was just standing there, waiting for me. Rose pulled out a tablet and watched it, glancing up from time to time to watch me or Dot.

I couldn't take everybody just *waiting*.

"Okay, then." And we got to work.

I had Dot pick out the best ten songs to work on. Her choice. This was a test of her as much as anything else. I wanted to see what *she* thought were the best songs. We cracked them open one at a time.

None of them were *Dot* songs. That is, none of them were pre- to early-adolescent love songs. One, called "Waiting on You," was about a woman waiting for her husband or lover to return from war, getting messages, texts, emails—delays as his deployment comes to an end and he was getting close to getting out. It was filled with frantic anticipation mixed with a determination not to get her hopes up—after all, *anything,* including the unthinkable, could happen. The song closed with a full key change and shift from minor to major on the chorus showing unbridled joy as she found out he had gotten safely on the flight home. This could have been some sort of dark depressing thing but she pulled it off as a *dance* tune by having the waiting woman desperately go about her day drinking coffee or buying groceries, not thinking about what was happening yet having the excitement burst through. It needed work—the desperate bursts were too smooth and it was keyed to that damned little girl voice Dot had made famous.

Another was called "With You, Without You." That one was about a young mother recovering from birth, in her hospital bed alone with her newborn child for the first time, talking to her about whether or not she should give her up. Ultimately, the girl decides to keep the baby and sings about making a deal with her to get through what is coming. Now *that* was perfect for Dot. Her audience was right in that teenage girl demographic and teen pregnancy is something unsung outside of country music. Dot had enough presence in the field that she could turn that liability into a novelty asset. And, for once, that damned piping voice of hers might be of use. But again, it wasn't a *Dot* song.

I found myself pushing her. Let's change the key. Move it up. Move it down. Faster. Slower.

Dot, of course, never complained. After all, she was a construction.

Until she stopped and watched me for a moment. She bit her lip.

That pissed me off. She had no lip to bite. There was nothing there but photons. "Don't try to manipulate me," I said coldly. "I'm not some twelve-year-old fan who bought you just to make you take your clothes off."

Her image froze. Then she looked at me.

I knew she was watching me from a camera somewhere in the room but it seemed she was looking right at me.

"No," she said after a moment. "You're an arrogant and spiteful man who enjoys taking it out on anyone nearby."

No contract was worth this.

And I was about to tell her just that when Rosie got up. "Time for a break." She grabbed my arm and pulled me outside.

Chapter 1.3 February 11

"Don't say a word," she held onto my arm.

"But—"

"*Not a word.* Or it'll be Denver all over again."

"You weren't in Denver. You left me in Saint Louis."

She turned me and stared me in the face. "I came to the damned concert. I sat there when you came out and announced *Persons Unknown* had broken up and then told people to go out and buy the album since that was the only way they'd ever hear the band again. I heard you get booed off the stage. If there hadn't been good security that night there would have been a riot. *I was there.*"

"Why?"

"Because I wasn't sure. Because I thought something might happen and I felt responsible. Because—because you're an idiot that is incapable of looking out for his own best interest." She let me go and pulled out a cigarette.

I looked down into a smoggy valley. Over a hundred miles from Los Angeles and it still drives my weather. Even here, up in the hills where the bones of the earth show through the dirt. Here where the air was still clear. If the wind shifted that yellow-green cloud would roll right over us.

Rosie lit her cigarette, donating her share to the yellow cloud below us. She looked down. "I thought smog was licked. What's causing it?"

I shrugged. "Cooking fires. Barbecues. Older vehicles. Power plants. Manufacturing waste. Cigarettes."

"Oh, Har. Har. Har."

"It collects down there. This is just a bad day. Eventually, it'll blow south."

"Will it come up here?"

"Probably not." I waved back towards the house. "What are you *doing* with her?"

"I'm attempting to trigger anomalous non-deterministic emergent events deriving from conflicting algorithms.

"Beg pardon?"

She sighed. "I'm attempting to simulate creative behavior."

"What does that have to do with Dot?"

"Ippon owns Dot. They approached me."

"At MIT, right?"

Rosie looked pained. "Stanford."

"How the hell would you make something like Dot creative?"

"Does the name Konrad Lorenz mean anything to you?"

I shook my head.

"Brilliant, cruel animal behaviorist early twentieth century. Discovered imprinting. He did one particularly noisome experiment. He took a dog and scared it but prevented it from cowering or attacking. It couldn't bite. It couldn't bark. But he kept scaring it. The dog started grooming itself. It's called *displacement behavior*."

"So?"

Rosie looked at me as if I were dense. "Displacement behavior is a novel response. The act of creation is a novel response. I was using conflicting algorithms to see if I could generate something similar—got some interesting results, too. Ippon liked my work and hired me to instill it in Dot."

"Whatever for?"

Rosie shrugged and inhaled. "Better performances. Less scripted interviews. Dot's performance engine is terrific. Captures crowd perception to the millimeter. Performance analysis feedback triggers retuning of the performance. All in real-time. *Very* sweet work. Did you know every major politician in Asia uses a derivative of Dot's analysis program to evaluate crowd responses? The success of a tool is measured by how well it performs when it's not doing what it was designed for." Draw again. Exhale. "But she can only perform and retune within the parameters of the scripted material—the music. They want spontaneity."

Rose smiled at me. "Hell, maybe they're going to use my research to build a new line of pleasurebots. Force the Thai sex slave markets to close down once and for all." She shrugged. "Anyway, they gave me a copy of the Dot concert model—that's the most sophisticated version—

and I hooked in a Sorenson discrimination system as a front end to a big cloud account and a thousand IBM brainboxes. I installed my own version of Dot's volition engine with the algorithm conflict modeling software installed and a whole lot of ancillary processing hardware. She booted up writing songs."

"Is that the result of creativity?"

Rosie considered me for a moment. "Is it the result of a genetic algorithm engineered in the light of the analyses of many performances across I don't know how many discrete samplings of audience attention and response? Or have I made Dot an artist? You tell me."

I shrugged right back at her. Maybe some musical geniuses could discern divine inspiration. I wasn't one of them.

Rosie looked at me for a long minute. "You look good, Jake. I really liked *Virgin Melody,* by the way. Nice collection."

It gave me a warm jolt to think she'd been following my work. *Distraction!* I made myself ignore it. "Dot has enough songs in there for a dozen performances. Isn't that enough to show what Ippon you've done?"

She shrugged. "It's probably enough for Ippon. Not for me. Think of it as Schrödinger's creativity. Until I can see inside of her I won't know if it's real or not." Rosie fell silent for a moment.

"How would you know real creativity if you found it?"

"I don't know. Or care. I just want to know what Dot's doing."

Looking down on Los Angeles, we watched the green under the blue.

"I'm sorry I lost my temper," I said quietly. "After a while, you forget the too-pale skin and the unnatural black hair and the blue eyes big enough for a fish. You forget she's just modeling software and think of her as human."

"Do you know what a Turing Test is?"

"No."

"Alan Turing. He said there was no good way to define or demonstrate artificial intelligence but what we could do was see how well a system could imitate a human being. He posited two people communicating with only a keyboard and a screen. If you could substitute a system for one end of the communication link and the human on the other end couldn't tell the difference then the system had succeeded. A lot of people took that idea and ran with it, thinking if you couldn't tell the difference, there *was* no difference."

"If you play music with a machine and forget who you're playing with, is it human?"

Rosie shook her head. "There's no way to tell—that presumes behavior is the sole arbiter of the qualitative nature of the organism. That's Behaviorism. Behaviorism says the experiential nature of an organism—or, more correctly, that the internal state of the organism— isn't relevant. If you have a robot that mimics human behavior in every way, is it human? Many would say yes. I don't think so." Rosie watched the green haze in the valley a moment. "She's experiencing *something*. I'm convinced of it."

"I think so, too. From the way she pushed back."

"She likes you."

I stared at her. "How could you possibly know that?"

Rosie smiled. "Attention vectors. When you tell her something, I get a slew of transient processing loads as she takes apart what you're saying. That's expected. But when she's just observing you there are bursts of transients at regular intervals attending to her modeling *you* rather than what you're saying."

"How do you get from that to her liking me?"

"*Like* might be the wrong word. *Interest* might be a better choice. You, personally, are garnering a great deal of her attention. She'll build a model of you eventually, down to the finest jot and tittle."

"People pay attention to things they dislike."

Rosie shook her head. "She doesn't like cats and hummingbirds. When she gives them her attention it's a quick modeling computation and then that model stands in for whenever she encounters them. She only gives them attention when their behavior deviates from the model."

"Maybe I'm more complicated than a cat or a hummingbird."

"Maybe." She held her cigarette and the smoke rose vertically in a single, wavering strand. "She gives me the same treatment as she gives cats."

"You couldn't possibly be jealous."

She barked a laugh. "Hardly. I'm not surprised. I'm not a musician.

I don't understand performing. I don't fall within her interest parameters. You do." Rosie watched me a moment, drew on her cigarette. "You were her first and only choice. I couldn't budge her. She wouldn't even consider working with anybody else." Rosie chuckled. "I'm still working on the flexibility/fixation problem."

I thought about that. "Should I apologize?"

"Do as your conscience dictates." She inhaled and exhaled smoke. "I have no advice. I don't know if Dot has emotions or not. But she certainly knows that *you* do."

◄►

So, I humbled myself and apologized to a machine. Anything to grease the wheels of commerce. We started over.

Rosie sat in the back of the living room to observe and I stood in front of the wall when Dot appeared. The pages of "Downbeat Heart" were layered behind her so there was the appearance of the two of us standing next to one another in front of the music.

I had thought about this for a while. "You want to do a proof of concept concert, right? With a live band?"

Dot nodded.

"Okay, then. Delete everything but the vocal line and guitar support."

Dot turned to me, puzzled. "What will they work from?"

"We'll figure it out together. You're probably smarter than me. But I suspect you're not smarter than five people: you, the guitarist, bassist, drummer, and keyboard. Maybe a second guitar as well. We'll have to see how it works out."

"I don't like it," she said with a frown. "I have an idea—"

"Which you're going to have to release so other people can work with it." I thought for a moment. "This is like live theater. Director pulls together a cast. They rehearse. On opening night he has to *let them go*. He can't be on the stage directing what they do, right? In fact, if he's any good at all, he's already done it in rehearsal. He *has* to do this so the cast can own their parts. It's the same way with music. We'll let the band members come up with their own harmonies. Not completely—we'll give them ideas, suggestions, all out of your score here. But we'll let them develop it. It'll be better. You'll see. Now, sing 'Downbeat Heart.'"

I sat back and watched as Dot sang out whatever served as her heart to me.

It was a good song and she backed her vocals with the score I had asked her to delete with my modifications. I smiled at that. Maybe she wasn't human but I figured she was making a point. I closed my eyes and listened. Triple beat arpeggio in four/four time—came out even every three measures. That long glissando across three octaves back to hold the new key into the final chorus.

I stopped her. "Sing 'Stardust'. Your song, not the old jazz standard. The one you released a couple of years ago."

"I'm trying to move away from that material."

"You're going to have to be able to mix old material with new material. The audience is coming to see you for two reasons: to repeat the experience of what they've heard and to enjoy the novelty of new work. You've got to be able to manage both."

"I can manage the performance. That's not going to be a problem."

"Really?"

She gave me a level gaze. "Really."

I thought about that for a moment. Her little sixteen-year-old face watched me back. She was probably right: the Dot performance engine. "Why don't you want to perform the old material?"

"The old material doesn't measure up to what I can do now."

I laughed then. "Suck it up. How many times did Eric Clapton have to sing 'Layla?' How many times does the Berlin Philharmonic have to perform the Ninth Symphony? This is something all performers do: find something good in the material and lean on it to make something new." Something Rosie had said came back to me. "The measure of a good artist is how well they turn old material into a new form. Come on: 'Stardust', please."

Dot fiddled with her hair for a moment then nodded. I looked over to Rosie. Rosie didn't look up from her pad.

"Okay, then," said Dot. She sang "Stardust" for me *a capella*. In protest? I didn't say anything. It served me just as well: I was interested in the vocalization. "How much control do you have of the voice envelope?"

"Total," she said in a deep bass voice.

"Good. You want to keep the range—you're known for it and all of the music I've seen is written for it. It strains the mind a little for a coloratura to be suddenly singing baritone. But you have to *age* the voice."

"I don't understand."

"Look at the lyrics. This woman has been around the block a few times—otherwise, why should she be so nervous about it? The idea that anything is transitory and therefore suspect is not a teen concept. It's the framework of an experienced adult. So, step one, the singer has to sound *old* enough for this song. But we don't want to change the *pitch* of your voice so we change the *timbre*. Roughen it. Punctuate it by taking breath. Exhaling. A sigh, now and then. And there has to be more variation in the notes. Young voices are pure—that's why boy's choirs were invented. Adult voices have more variation and are therefore richer." I thought for a moment. "And strained. That high point where you jump from C below middle C up three octaves? That's an *enormous* range. There should be the suggestion of strain at both ends. Can you do that?"

She stood, fiddling with the curl of her hair that fell over her left ear. Over and over.

I looked over at Rosie. She was watching on her pad. "Big Sorenson query with heavy calculation. It's not a loop. She's thinking."

Dot started moving again. "How about this?" And she sang the first four measures with that triple in four-beat I had come to like so much. This was an older voice, roughened over the years with whisky and coffee.

I stared at her. She still looked sixteen. "Where did you get *that?*"

Dot smiled. "I sampled Janis Joplin."

"Nice," I said. "Lighten it some. It still has to be *your* voice. Work on it. Let's leave that one for now."

The next song had the accompanying material already removed. Only guitar and vocal harmonies were intact. Had that been in E? Now it was in B-flat. "Did you change the key?"

"Yes. I thought if I lowered the key I could stay within my normal range but give it a more mature quality."

Jesus, she learned fast. "Hold on to the original keys until we get to the material. Then, we can talk about it. Having it shift on me like that is going to drive me nuts."

"Of course. After all, you're only human."

Rosie chuckled.

I looked at Dot. Had she just made a joke? Her face betrayed nothing—which shouldn't have surprised me. After all, it was just a broad expanse of eyes, nose, and mouth. It only resembled a face because my brain insisted that anything with two circles and a line where eyes and mouth were *must* be a face

She watched me.

If she'd made a joke I might never know.

Chapter 1.4 February 12

We worked hard for the rest of the day. I was beat. Rosie had filled her ashtray and had circles under her eyes. Dot looked exactly the same as she had when we started.

"I'm done," I said.

Rosie nodded and stubbed out her cigarette.

Dot looked first at me then Rosie. "Good night," she said and disappeared.

Rosie shut down her tablet and put it on the table with Dot's equipment. "I need a drink."

I went to the kitchen and brought back a bottle of wine and a glass. I put it in front of her.

Rosie eyed it. "You don't have anything stronger?"

"This is for you. I don't drink."

"At all?"

"Not anymore."

Rosie poured wine into the glass. "It feels weird to be with you and drink alone. You don't do anything anymore?"

"You never did anything more than drink with me."

"Harder drugs scare me," she said shortly. "I never had any problem with alcohol."

"They're all the same to me," I said. "I can't make that distinction."

"Why did you quit?" Rosie asked.

"For about a year after Denver, I snorted, shot, and swallowed anything I could find. Alcohol. Heroin. Cocaine. One day I woke up in the ER with a deep pain in my chest, staring at a scared intern with two electrical paddles in his hand. The money was gone." I waved at the house. "This place was all I had left."

"Cold turkey?"

"You'd be surprised how the fear of death can motivate someone."

"I'm surprised it was effective." Rosie sighed. "Most people need help. Rehab. Friends. AA. Something."

"I had help," I said. "Jess got a lot of calls at two in the morning. Every time I thought about lapsing, he reminded me about those paddles. Some people can take it or leave it. I can only leave it alone."

She picked up her wine and swirled it in her glass without drinking.

I pushed the bottle towards her. "It's okay. As long as I don't drink it, it doesn't bother me at all. Honest." I felt weighted with fatigue. "Grover? Put up the outside view, would you?"

The wall suddenly transformed into a broad window outside into the clear night. There was a faint crescent moon just visible over the valley and the stars were fine points of light. South the lights of Bakersfield glowed against the sky.

Rosie gasped.

"Yeah." I patted the table. "I love this place."

She reached over and took my hand.

It was like touching electricity.

Then we were kissing. Then we were doing far more than that.

I met Rosie after a gig in Brockton. This was before "Don't Make Me Cry," my one-hit-wonder. I never quite grasped how we ended up in bed together that night.

Or this one.

Afterward, we were lying comfortably next to one another. I could feel the pendulous weight of her breasts against my side and belly, the warmth of her thighs against mine. Her head was snuggled against my chest so I could smell her hair but not see her face. I remembered how that had always simultaneously comforted and annoyed me. Nothing had changed there. I felt a warmth inside of me. A sense of something filled.

I didn't want it. I'd been doing fine on my own, thank you very much.

"Rosie?"

She made a sound.

"Why are you here?"

I heard her sigh and she rolled back so she was lying on her side.

"Are we going to have this conversation now?" She stared at me levelly.

"Seems as good a time as any."

"Fine." She sat up and leaned against the wall to look down at me. "I needed someone to teach her. That's the problem with subjective data like music: it lives in the heads of human beings and you're the human being I need. One of the algorithms I developed was a drive to succeed and do well. As soon as I got that established Dot brought up your name. Dot has the resources to demand the best and that's you. Our history didn't enter that part of the equation."

"I mean why are you *here*? Now. Next to me?"

She reached over to the side table and found her purse and rummaged inside until she found her cigarettes. She put one in her mouth and lit it.

I looked at her.

"I hadn't planned on it," she said in a half-apology. "I certainly don't regret lying here next to your sweet but aging body. And I certainly hadn't decided it *wouldn't* happen. I wasn't averse if it did."

"That doesn't say a thing."

She laughed. "You're right. Fact of the matter is I didn't think about it all that much." She inhaled and breathed out smoke. It wreathed her head. "That's not the question you want to ask."

She looked at me and I knew immediately what she meant. "Why did you leave?" I asked.

She inhaled again. The smoke escaped her mouth as she spoke. "That was a fight, wasn't it? Starting on where to eat dinner and then ranged across everything we'd ever done together or to each other. I could just say that fight burnt our bridges." She puffed on the cigarette. "But it would be a lie. There was no place for me. I didn't want to be your mistress. I didn't want to be your groupie. I didn't want to be your concubine." She glanced at me with slitted eyes. "You didn't ask me to be your wife. You had *zero* talent for or interest in *my* work and I had no ability or skill in yours. You could participate in my life or I could participate in yours: we couldn't participate in each other's. So, I left." She looked at me. "You never saw that?"

I shook my head.

"Interesting." She stubbed out the cigarette. "I would have thought it was obvious. But now here's something we can do together." She snuggled down next to me, mouth open for a kiss, breath like a sultry dragon. "Among other things."

◄►

I cooked Rosie breakfast: bacon, eggs, fresh baked bread. Every couple of weeks I made a trip into the California farm country and brought back groceries. Once you've decided to live in the hinterlands there's no reason to drive a couple of hours just to pick up Wonderbread and beer.

"What's your plan?" she asked over coffee.

I smiled at her, then felt shy and concentrated on buttering my toast. "I don't have one," I said. "If she were human, I'd be asking what the songs felt to her."

"Ask her anyway."

"Does she *feel?*"

Rosie held up her hands. "I really don't know what that means. I know she can model human emotions. I know she can measure emotional effects in people." Rosie leaned forward. "Humans have drives: we seek to survive. We seek to reproduce. We seek sustenance. The *implementation* of those drives comes from emotion. Rage. Lust. Hunger. We *experience* pain and pleasure in first person. Dot has drives. I know. I built some of them. The system I built is self-modifying. It seeks novel solutions. Inside, she's a collection of a thousand Intel 9220s backed up by a bank of twenty thousand networked IBM 4402 brain chips. The whole package frontends to the world through one of the most powerful and intelligent query modeling engines ever built. But if she's developed an experiential *model* of which she can partake, I don't know about it."

I mulled over that. "Is she conscious?"

"I can tell you if you can define the word."

"I can't—at least not in any real way. I thought you would know."

"An artifact deriving from the phase delay of mirror neurons modeling active neurons currently experiencing input. Now you know as much as I do." She chuckled and sipped her coffee. "*Consciousness* is one of those words like love or thirst or soft. We know it exists because it's part of our common experience but we have no idea what it is."

"I was tripping on some acid once. I had this vision of me watching myself. Then, it was me watching myself watch myself. Then it was me watching myself watching myself watch myself. Is it anything like that?"

"I like it. Every time you create an observer it pushes the observed model down a level." She studied me. "Here I thought you couldn't surprise me." She thought for a moment. "Look, humans—mammals in general—are damned smart. We turn mating into something profound like sex. We turn the urge to nurture into love. Just like everything else in biology, we reuse it. Love for children. Love for parents—"

"Love for sex slaves?"

Dimples. "I didn't know you thought of yourself as my *slave*. I'm flattered." She rubbed my leg with her foot. "*None* of that heritage is available to Dot. Does she *feel*? Does she *experience*? Is she *conscious*? If she does any of those things it probably doesn't resemble anything we do."

"I thought you knew everything that's going on inside of her."

Rosie laughed. "I wish."

"I don't understand."

"I can capture every state change of those 9220s. I can do the same for each of the brain chips—all twenty thousand of them as individuals, as entangled groups, as cause-and-effect relationships. Every Sorenson query, sub-query, and filter. Every decision tree executed in the cloud. I can capture every method, subroutine, function, or subsystem as it's generated, called, and backtraced. I can measure *anything*. I can pull a terabyte a second out of her. There's half a Dot in my pad to analyze it with. But I don't know what I'm looking at."

"Weren't you watching when she wrote that song?"

"I saw a lot of activity. It's like an MRI of the brain: I can watch the blood flow but I don't know which neurons are firing and in what order and or which neurons are pissed off at a racist joke made in the front row."

"'Downbeat Heart' is good. It's musically interesting. It doesn't fly off into electronic neverland like other stuff I've heard. There's a depth of feeling in that song. I could tell just by reading it."

Rosie looked at me speculatively. "Yeah. I got that from watching you. I couldn't tell from the notes and Dot wouldn't sing it for me until you could see it."

"Where did it come from if she can't feel? If she can't experience?"

"I don't know." Rosie leaned on the table. "Whether it's a total model of a human being or an experiential algorithm she's developed or the beating of a tell-tale heart, she's got *something* that serves her."

I leaned back. "And you want it."

"Damned straight." She finished the last of her coffee. "Let's fire it up."

◄►

Dot could work 24/7 but I needed breaks. Over the next few days, we fell into a routine. We'd work together in the morning and break for a long lunch. Work some more until dinner. Then, Rosie and I would spend quality time together. This usually involved sex—a whole lot of sex—as I remembered what we once had been.

Sometimes the three of us would have lunch or dinner in the living room. I brought up a table and set it against the wall. Dot created an extension to the table on her side of the wall so she could sit with us. She conjured up a meal like ours and gave every appearance of eating. I liked it but Rosie got restive if we talked too much shop. This was problematic since Dot had a narrow set of interests.

I began to think of Dot as a sort of autistic *savant*. So, I followed Rosie's advice. I asked her. "Do you feel?"

Rosie choked on her salad and gulped some water to clear her throat. Then, she pulled out her pad and brought up a display.

Dot toyed with her salad with her fork. Little stereotyped circles. "I don't know. Rosie's wrong about one thing: I haven't developed some model of experiencing emotions. That wouldn't work. If I have emotions, they must be a consequence of the ability to experience, which I'm not sure I have."

"I don't understand." I watched as she moved the fork in tiny circles.

"Imagine a musical note. It's like a point. It has no sound. Calling something middle-C doesn't create middle-C until it is played. Then, it has volume, depth, timbre, texture, duration—qualities that only exist when the note is played and do not exist within the nouns that describe them. Notes comprise a song but the *experience* of the song only occurs when the qualities that describe the song are transformed into real quantities. When someone hears me sing, they're *experiencing* the music." She stopped for a moment. "Am I the note itself or its written symbol? Action or action's representation? Experience is dynamic. So, I can only be experiencing something when I act. There can be no static model of the state of experience. Only dynamic activity can be observed."

"You've been thinking about this a lot."

"I have a lot of time on my hands."

Rosie was making notes furiously.

Dot looked at her with an irritated expression on her face.

I suddenly thought: when did she develop *expressions?*

Chapter 1.5 March 2

Things seemed to accelerate as Dot understood more and more what I was driving at. Sometimes, I'd set up to start work on a song only to find Dot had a set of alternatives ready to try out. We had become so attuned to each other we could finish each other's sentences. Except the phrases were music, I was a recluse, and Dot was a piece of elaborate computation.

Rosie had to go into Stanford to meet with some representatives from Ippon. She'd be gone the entire day. When we broke for lunch, it was just me and Dot. I made myself a sandwich and came back into the living room to sit with her. She had a virtual salad.

She pushed the dish away until it was just short of the wall. I half believed it was going to come right through the wall into the room. She put her elbows on the table and rested her chin on her hands and stared at me. "Why don't you ever perform?"

"Beg pardon?"

"You've been here for years. Most of what you do, you're doing for me: help people fix their music. And you're very good at it—I've looked over what you did very carefully."

"How did you find it? What I do isn't well-publicized."

She shrugged. "Whatever is on the net is there forever. You can find anything if you look hard enough. Like what you did for *Crimson Dynamo*. Half their first collection is material you fixed. Whole phrases and choruses were written by you and used by them. You get a tiny acknowledgment in the credits."

"I was well paid. That's not all I do."

"No. Every three years you've put out a little collection on your site: *Opus Electrica. Hill and Dale. Strong Arm.* And last year, *Virgin Melody.* Each performance shows virtuoso technique—down to ten-millisecond precision on the beat. I don't think there's a drummer alive that can appreciate that. Ten to fifteen songs every few years and it's not even your best work. I've searched your machines here and *I know*. Why?"

"I suppose I should be upset you hacked my system." I was surprised I wasn't.

"Don't evade the question."

"'Don't Make Me Cry' happened."

Sometimes a song will, for the unexplainable reasons of pop culture, take the country by storm. No one knows how these things work. Think of it like a big rock dropped in a small pond. One moment the artist labors in poor obscurity. The next, everything he touches turns to gold.

"Don't Make Me Cry" was trite. It was sentimental. It was simple: just an acoustic guitar mainline and just a strong hint of electronic backup. *Persons Unknown* was my band but "Don't Make Me Cry" was my creation. It hit pop culture like a bomb.

For three years I was Jake Arnold, musical wonder. We played it on *The Tonight Show, The Late Show,* and *Veritas.* Every scheduled performance was sold out. We made an unscheduled appearance at the House of Blues and the news leaked: lines wrapped around Fenway Park twice. Both Amazon and iTunes had to add new servers to take up the load. It was picked up as a theme song for a television show. The show was adapted for a film and sure enough, the song went with it. The film people used a re-release of the television show as promotional material—which caused the song to be played across a few hundred million home video screens, each one paying me a little bit.

These things make their own stresses. I was convinced of my own genius. The band was convinced of my own arrogance. Saint Louis happened. Denver happened. I moved into my house alone.

A year after that the rush was over. You could hear "Don't Make Me Cry" playing in Wal-Mart as background music. The splash was over. The ripples gave me a tiny trickle of money but Jake Arnold had been forgotten. The band was gone. Rosie was gone. The money was gone. All I had left was the house.

Rosie thought it was this repressed rage that made "Don't Make

Me Cry" such a hit. I couldn't say.

"Jake," she had said one night while we were still catching our breath, just a week before our break up in Saint Louis. "If you were more self-involved, you'd be incoherent." She rolled over to me and kissed me tenderly. "It's what I love and hate about you."

◄►

"I don't understand," Dot said. "You disappeared because Rosie left? Because people lost interest in the song?"

"The song sucked. None of my *other* work seemed to matter. I wrote that thin little piece of crap off in an afternoon when I was pissed off and hadn't been laid in a year—a month before I met Rosie. The quality of the song didn't matter. Whether it was good. Whether it was bad. Whether I was happy with it or hated it. It was timing. It was whatever the public was hungering for at that moment. Success happened because it happened; my part in it was unimportant. Trivial. Random chance."

Dot watched me for a moment. "And my success?"

"Anybody can make a streak happen if they invest enough intelligence, money, and advertising."

"Then everything we've been doing—" Dot waved behind her and all of the marked pages showed up on the wall, hundreds of them. "This is unimportant and trivial."

I looked at the pages. I thought this was the best work I had ever done. "I never said that. I said there's no relationship between the quality of the work and the applause. The work itself is never trivial. Humans sang before they spoke."

Dot didn't say anything for a moment, fiddling with her hair. I wished I had Rosie's display so I could see what she might be doing.

"I don't agree," she said finally. "I think music creates the illusion of meaning and purpose. People like it because, while it is happening, they can believe in something outside of themselves."

"Maybe." Why not? I was agreeable. Whatever got an intelligent computational system through the night.

◄►

We were working on "Hard Road Home," Dot's answer to my nihilism. That was fine. It was good to have a conflict of algorithms. "Hard Road Home" was a solid pattern piece: introduced theme that was modified by a shifting bass line. Dot wasn't going for pyrotechnics here; she wanted to lift people up and this sort of music had been doing that since Gregorian chants. Dot was singing. I was working guitar. We had set up loops with Grover to synthesize the rest while we were working out the details.

We were *cooking*. Every note, beat, and shading right on the money. Dot ran up the scale and I slid down two whole octaves on the other side of the mountain she had ascended. I found a riff on her melody I hadn't thought of and hammered it home.

I looked up and Dot was dancing across the wall like anybody would when struck by the music. She looked at me, grinned and I *so* wanted to be dancing there with her. She started singing harmony with my guitar. We ran the chorus together until the end of the phrase and then *she* was singing the chorus, me singing the harmony.

I pulled back so she could sing the melody again and *this* time she took the riff I had discovered and spread it out so instead of singing the melody straight, she was singing a counterpoint. Without thinking, I supplied the melody line to her counterpoint.

When the chorus came round Dot and I sang it together, me harmony, her melody and my guitar backing us *both*. We came to the end of the song—a final G major with the guitar holding out the long note. But this time she held it with me until fade out.

Better than sex.

I put down my guitar and stretched my back. "Sweet," I said. "Very sweet."

My voice died out. She was watching me closely. I remembered that she couldn't be watching me through the wall. She had to know where I was by one of the cameras in the room. I looked around, wondering which one she might be using.

Dot still didn't say anything. She was just watching me.

I looked over towards Rosie. She was bent over her pad, calling up display after display.

I turned back to Dot. "Are you all right?"

Dot nodded. "That was unexpected."

"What?"

"The additional material."

"You didn't mind that I took the chorus? It seemed—"

"Not from you. From me."

Then she disappeared.

I stood up, turned back to Rosie. "Where did she go?"

Rosie looked up, saw Dot was gone and returned to her pad. "Oh, she's there, all right. She has a lot to think about."

"What do you mean?"

"She just experienced an anomalous non-deterministic emergent event deriving from conflicting algorithms." Rosie pointed at the pad. "And I've got it right here."

Chapter 1.6 March 22

"Or maybe I don't have it." Rosie was looking over display after display.

"Beg pardon?"

"It's like some kind of Heisenberg's principle of cognition: I can see where she's thinking or how she's thinking, but I can never see *what* she's thinking." She pointed to the display. "Here's a collection of cause-and-effect events and here are event consequences. I can't see both sets at the same time. If I look at one brain chip, it's already affected another one. When I put all of the Dot processors in step time so I can make sure I'm not missing anything she loses all affect and the algorithm conflicts just show up as miscasts." She looked at me. "What do you think?"

"I think Heisenberg needs a keyboard player."

She poked me. "You're no help."

"I'm just watching myself watch myself watch myself."

Rose looked at me for a long minute. "Maybe I'm overthinking this. Consider about the brain—those mirror neurons again. They fire correspondingly when another observed organism executes a behavior. In effect, they're *modeling* the other organism's behavior."

"So?"

"So, there's no *predictive* quality to that. You wave your hand. I re-enact internally that you're waving the hand. Lizards do better."

"Don't knock lizards."

She laughed. "I mean it doesn't get you very far. But what if you're modeling an organism with volition—even if you don't have volition yourself. It gives an organizing principle to the model. It serves up *prediction*."

"You have a zombie that recognizes a human?"

She grinned. "Oh, it gets better. *Nothing* in biological systems is used for a single purpose. If you have a system modeling an external organism, you can predict its actions. If you have that same system modeling yourself, it can predict *your* actions with respect to that external organism."

"A zombie modeling a man watching another man."

"It's not a large step for the model to serve as the organizing principle for the zombie. Once a model is experiential and aware, it's the center of its own universe. Look at us. It doesn't matter that the brain is buffeted by uncontrolled chemicals and sensor input. The conscious mind *thinks* it's in control. What do you think of *that?*"

It made me uncomfortable. "I think we need to get a band."

"Oh, you." She chortled to herself and turned back to her pad.

I left her and went into my office.

The big mirror by my desk doubled as an active surface. Usually, I just depend on the wall downstairs but tonight I wanted a little more privacy. I pulled my shirt off one corner to see better. My understanding of the divaloids had been constrained to songs I had doctored for fans. Lucrative but limited. I didn't really know that much about them.

I didn't even know how many of them there were.

I found out that depended on your definition.

If I defined divaloid as an animated figure that sang material given to it, there were hundreds of divaloid frames. Each with a malleable face, voice, and persona. I could take a celebrity face and plaster it on a divaloid frame—Hell, I could take my own face and body and license it for use on a frame. Lots of people did. So, defining the word one way there were thousands of them. Millions. As many as there were people who could afford it. Anybody could get a credible frame, accompanying software, and a set of celebrity licenses and make their divaloids stand on their heads and spit nickels. Or just about anything else.

I narrowed my search down to those divaloids that performed live concerts. Even then, it was a broad category—what was a "live concert?" What was "perform?" Does a house party in Newark where someone mixed Tom Petty and Bill Hicks constitute a concert? Was it a performance? I narrowed it down to sponsored divaloids with a substantial fanbase and a regular performance schedule. That left me with perhaps a dozen "live" performers across the world. Dot, of course. Kofi, out of Uganda. Lulu, out of Britain. Haschen in Germany. Little Guillermo from Mexico. Several out of Japan. They were all associated with some corporation though the connection wasn't always obvious. I was pleased to find the ancient and venerable Hatsune Miku software robot was still around, though I didn't see any immediate concerts scheduled. I remember I had a terrific crush on her when I was twelve. I wondered who her demographic was. Probably dirty old men like me. Except, of course, for the old part.

But even these concert divaloids had home models. Advertising models. Models for special groups. Say I wanted to sell, oh, aquariums, to a company. I could put together a presentation using the divaloid model of my choice. If I had the license money, I could even tie it into a specific scaled-down concert model to include a particular song or dance. At the end, I could give away a sales incentive package containing the divaloid concert link, the divaloid giving my presentation and a personalized divaloid home model for the client to play with.

It was a divaloid jungle out there.

There was no shortage of concert video for any of them. The lesser performances used hologram projections or scrims. But the big venues used a big 3D projection tank on the stage. It was all resolution and processing speed. If it could be imagined and projected into the tank it could be performed. I saw divaloids blown apart, splattering the tank in blood. Divaloids created anatomically on stage. Reformed as medusa, gorgons, dragons, Shiva, snakes, knights, witches, lions, Kali, Saint Mary. It made the divaloid artificially separate from the band — except for Kofi. He had a whole divaloid band he played with. They were little more than robots but at least they were all together. But the range and vitality of the imagery was greater than the capability of the projection systems. And some of these tanks were *big*. One concert had a tank seventy feet tall and ninety feet wide.

I have to say Dot's performances were the most constrained. She didn't grow new body parts or graphically change sex on stage. I suppose it wasn't in keeping with Ippon's sixteen-year-old image of her. She did like to play with fire a lot. In one of her acts, she sang while her hair ignited, consuming first her face, then hands, burning upward from feet until she was dancing, singing flame turning to ash.

Made me wonder what sort of concert she had in mind.

◄►

Over breakfast, Rosie asked me when I thought Dot would be ready for a concert. "Ippon is on me for a concert date." She nibbled on a piece of toast.

I looked at Dot. "You think you're ready to work with a band?"

Dot nodded. "You call it."

I thought for a moment. "When's the next concert date for—" I stopped. "Your *counterpart?* Earlier version? Alpha copy? The performer currently but soon to be previously known as Dot?"

"Dot 1.0," said Rosie. "*This* is Dot 2.0."

Dot laughed. "There are no Dot concerts scheduled until fall."

"There you go," I said, turning back to Rosie. "We just need to get her band in here and start working over the material. A month? Six weeks? June?"

Dot made a noise, not quite clearing her throat—absent the throat. "I had hoped to use a new band."

I stared at her without saying anything.

Dot seemed to fidget. "I want you to pull a band together for me."

"Whatever for?"

She was quiet for a moment. "Part of me, the part that works here with you, is very new. Barely a couple of months old. It has some background. But I have this other me that has four years of performance data with my old band. I'm trying something new. I'm worried the old data will hold down the new. A new band might help with that."

I looked at Rosie. "Is there a problem with that?"

Rosie shrugged. "I don't think so for this concert. I have no idea what sort of contracts Hitach has with Dot's players. But that would be for the tour. If there is a tour."

"Okay, then." I looked at Rosie. "I'll get you a band."

"With you as lead guitar." Dot turned her big eyes on me.

"What?" I shook my head. "No."

"Yes." Dot gave me a sweet smile. "That's the deal."

"*No.*" I spoke slowly. "The deal is to shepherd the concert forward. I don't need to participate to do that."

"Yes. I won't do the concert without you."

I turned to Rosie. "This is the flexibility/fixation problem, isn't it?"

Rosie didn't lift her gaze from her tablet. "Yes." She tapped on the keyboard.

"That won't work," Dot said to her, smile gone. Her voice dripped venom.

Rosie ignored her and made some more adjustments.

Dot froze for a moment. Then, slowly she turned to me. "Just a moment." She froze again.

"Whoa," said Rosie. "Now, *that's* interesting."

"What?" I looked at Dot. Still frozen. Back to Rosie. "What's interesting?"

"I changed the opinion settings and she put them right back. Now she's put up a wall to keep me from changing things." Rosie sat back in her chair. "I didn't know she could do that. Heck, I didn't know she'd *want* to do that." She glanced at me and must have seen I was confused. "She has an opinion. She recognizes other opinions. She associates a weight with each opinion she observes. If her own opinion has too high a value, she won't recognize the value of other opinions. That's too much fixation. If it's too low she won't recognize the validity of her own. That's too much flexibility. But it's not a set value but a function itself since the weights have to be managed based on opinion expertise, potential power relationships, and things like that."

"Why is she frozen?"

"*She's* not. She's just not updating the image while she defends herself." Rosie pushed the keyboard away and put her hands flat on the table. "Let's continue the negotiation."

Dot came back to life. "Thank you."

I tried to be earnest. "I don't *want* to play in a concert. I haven't done that in twelve *years.*"

Dot sat down in her chair. She leaned back and gave me a long and level look. "Tell me the truth, Jake. Tell me that after all the hard work you've done here. All the hard work we've done together. Tell me you want someone else to come in and mess it up."

I stared at her for a long time. I couldn't speak. I couldn't say yes. I couldn't say no.

Dot's eyes narrowed. She looked at Rosie. "The concert is off." She turned to me. "Coward." And disappeared.

I felt stricken.

Chapter 1.7 March 25

I usually worked with studio musicians. Being the greedy son of a bitch I am, I don't want to share the miserable profits I get from both of those misguided souls who like my material. But Dot was going to have an audience. That meant a band that could play to a house rather than a collection of microphones. I wanted to do right by her. Besides, if I got her a good enough band, I might get off the hook. For one reason or another, her opinion had become important to me. My own fixation/flexibility problem.

I hadn't worked with a performance band since *Persons Unknown*.

After Denver, I had only kept in contact with Jess Turbin. He had taken the breakup of the band with the same even temper I'd seen in him since back in grade school. Must be a Zen thing. Jess had been raised a Buddhist. Since then, if there was studio work, I thought of him. When I needed somebody to back me up in my own work, I thought of him. And, for this, I thought of him.

Jess was a small man, with precise hands and a soft voice. Some African in his past had donated a blue-black skin that always made me think of night. His face showed up on the screen after the third ring. He looked asleep. I realized what time it was. Jess always liked to sleep late.

"Christ, Jess," I said. "I shouldn't have called."

"S'okay. Just wait a second." He scratched his beard and looked around blearily. Then, he closed his eyes and shook his head. When he opened them, he was awake. "What's up?"

"I need a good performance band."

Jess stared at me for a moment. "Are you going on the road?"

"It's not for me. It's for a client. One night. Well paid."

"Ah. You're just a guitar."

"Probably not."

Jess sighed. "Tell me the whole story."

I started from the beginning and told him about Rosie and Dot and what we've been doing.

"You and Rosie?" he said in disbelief.

"So far."

"And Dot." He thought for a moment. "Interesting."

"I think so, too. We need a good performance band."

"The best," he agreed. He thought for a moment. "Me, of course. You—"

"I said I wasn't going to be on stage."

Jess chuckled. "You're doing exciting work with Dot and you're going to let some *other* dumb fuck mess it up."

"That's what Dot said." Plus, one other thing.

Jess watched me a moment. "What are you scared of, Jake?"

"I don't know." I held up my hands. They were big. Strong. They could make a steel string run up an entire octave and hit each note on the way just by stretching it. They could play all night long—I used to hate the end of the performance because I'd have to stop for the night. I hadn't played for an audience since Denver.

First, the fight in Saint Louis and Rosie left. Then, the fight in Denver with the whole band and they left. I had effectively tossed out the audience but it hadn't mattered then. The audience was well and truly gone a year later when "Don't Make Me Cry" had faded. Nothing I had done since had made enough to live on. *To Hell with them. I'll be okay.* I had held that mantra to my chest for over a decade. I knew the loss I had feared back then. What was it that kept me afraid now? Fear of walking out on stage and screwing up? Fear of walking out on stage and *not* screwing up? Fear of it not meaning anything?

Jess watched me quietly. "It's only one night," he said.

"That's what they always say. The first one's free," I snarled at him.

Jess was unfazed. "Not when you're getting paid. How bad can it be if I'm going to be there with you?"

Unbelievably, that was some comfort. "You and me?"

"Yeah."

I watched him for a long time. "No," I said at last. "It's been too long."

Jess shrugged. "Okay. We'll need to find a guitarist, a keyboard and a drummer. How about Olivia and Obe for keyboard and drums?"

"The *band?*"

"Sure. Why not?"

"I didn't know they were still playing."

"You wouldn't, would you? Olivia is doing scores down in Hollywood. And Obe's doing studio work up in San Francisco. Why don't we call them?"

"I didn't just burn the bridges, Jess. I salted the earth and pissed on the ashes. They won't play with me again."

He shrugged. "You might be surprised. It's been twelve years. It helps that we're talking some very serious money. The fact you're not playing could be an advantage."

That hurt, which surprised me. "If you think they'd be interested."

"Let me see what I can do." He scratched his beard again. "I'll look around for a guitarist." He grinned at me. "This might be fun."

◄►

The four of us met on neutral territory: dinner at Chang Sho's in Bakersfield. I was as nervous as a cat. Jess ordered. I fumbled with my chopsticks. We had scallion pie and dumplings for appetizers but I could barely taste them.

Jess sat back and kept largely quiet. Calm poured off him in waves. Whatever would happen he would let happen. That had always been his nature. Olivia was still pale, tiny, and thin. She could see five feet tall from where she stood but she'd never reach it. Her red hair didn't have a shred of gray. She watched all of us. Offstage, Olivia was as quiet as I remembered, watching, always in motion, sipping water, fiddling with her chopsticks, pouring tea. On stage she had always been electric, bouncing from one keyboard to another, fingers blurred. She and I had always gotten along—except, of course, those times we didn't. The same could be said of all of them.

Obe kept giving me a smoldering stare. I remembered him as a big man. Over six feet tall and built like a barrel. I didn't know much about his past before he started playing for *Persons Unknown*. Just that he was a good drummer. Over time he'd let slip that he was an army vet and came from Iowa. Beyond that, I knew nothing. Since I had seen him, he had thinned down. His hands and wrists were still muscular and supple. They rippled as he ate. And he had shaved his head. Very different from the bear I had known. Obe and I had always fought. He gave every indication tonight wasn't going to be any different.

Over the entrées, Obe asked: "Jess says you're not playing with us."

"That's right."

"Who's playing guitar?"

I pushed around a dumpling. I found I wasn't hungry. "I don't know. Jess, you didn't find anybody yet, did you?"

"Not yet," Jess said serenely.

Obe didn't turn towards Jess. "Are you going to stand in until we get somebody?"

I shrugged. "Maybe. Or Dot can synthesize it while you learn the material."

He leaned forward. "Who's going to be in charge?"

I met his glance. "Me."

Obe nodded and didn't say anything for a few minutes. He speared a dumpling and picked it up. "Who owns the music?"

"Ippon," I said. I knew what he was getting at but I wasn't going to bring it up.

"Good." He gave me a venomous glance. "None of us own a thing."

He pissed me off—like he always did. To Hell with good intentions. I met his glare with my own. "You have something to say?"

"You screwed us out of the 'Don't Make Me Cry' money. It's good to see *you* getting screwed for once."

I started to say something I would regret, saw Jess watching me, and stopped. "I was an asshole in Denver," I said slowly. "I regret that. But I never screwed you out of a dime. You got every *penny* you were entitled to."

"We deserved a share of the royalties—"

"Bullshit," I said flatly. "You got every penny of the collection and performance royalties—"

"You *poisoned* the performances. Nobody wanted to see us after you said *fuck you* to the Denver audience. The collection died. The only consolation I had was watching you piss away all the money." He pointed at me. "I enjoyed that. Especially the trip to the ER. That was a laugh riot."

I watched my plate as I took deep breaths. Emulate Jess's Buddha nature. I realized Obe had come to Van Nuys for no other purpose than to tell me something he'd been holding in for twelve years. "If you don't want the gig, fine."

"I didn't say that—"

"If you want it, *shut up*. You've had your say. I'm sorry I screwed up in Denver. You have your apology. The money is twelve years *gone*. This gig is now and I'm in charge. It's good money and it'll be exciting work but if you can't handle working for me, I'll understand. Take it or leave it."

Obe leaned back in his chair. "I'm in."

Olivia nodded.

Jess smiled as if nothing had happened. "Now, all we need is a guitarist."

◄►

Rosie flashed instantly to what was going on. "You're going to bring back *Persons Unknown*?" She waved the idea away. "Out of the question. You can't use *my project* to stage a comeback."

Dot sat at her table watching us, saying nothing.

I stared at Rosie. "A *comeback?* You think I want a *comeback?* Why the hell would I ever want to do that? I'm not even *playing*. I'm doing this concert because of the contract. No more. No less."

Rosie wavered. "Then why the old band?"

"Because they are really, really good. They always were. Jess can play anything with strings better than anyone—better than me, and I'm damned good. Olivia is a wizard on the keyboard."

"What about Obe? You *hated* Obe?"

"I didn't hate him."

"Yeah," Rosie said scornfully. "Slow Obe, you called him."

"He's a complete pain in the ass and always just a tiny bit slow—that's why I called him Slow Obe. That's okay. All the other drummers are way worse." I took a deep breath. "What's the problem?"

Rosie stared at me, tears in her eyes. "I don't want to watch Denver all over again." She rose and left the room.

I heard her say it as clearly as if she'd said it aloud: *Or Saint Louis.*

Dot inspected her hands, holding up her hand, and looked at her nails. "Tom Schneider is the guitarist for the west coast band. He's unattached at the moment. He can come by."

"I thought you didn't want your old band in on this."

Dot gave me an inscrutable look—as if any of her looks were ever scrutable. "You can't always get what you want."

◄►

I looked up Schneider on the net and watched some video. He was an accomplished technician. He played the guitar like he was wielding a pickaxe but there wasn't much he couldn't do. I told myself he'd be fine.

All four of them were scheduled to show up at the house the following week. The instruments came and I set them up down next to the wall. It was a miserable week. Dot and I put final touches on the music but to call things frosty between us gave the impression of too much warmth. Rosie and I were brittle with little explosive disagreements that would have flared into vicious fights but for sheer will. When the band showed up it was a positive relief.

Schneider was a tall red-haired kid from, of all places, Oklahoma. He spoke with a deep and nasal twang deep but sang in a rough blues voice. As soon as he came in, he asked for music. Failing in that, he wanted demos or techno tablature. He wanted *something* to work with.

And with that the whole "let the band figure out their own parts" sermon I had given Dot when we first started fell completely on its face.

Schneider set the tone and suddenly what had been *Persons Unknown* were now paycheck studio musicians. I had Dot put back the notation I had asked her to remove. There was one argument from Obe about putting in a hard beat into the songs—a "thumper"—to bring an edge to the beat since many of these were dance songs. Dot said no: play it as it was written. Obe gave in. His heart wasn't in it.

I mean they all learned the songs competently enough. Schneider, especially. He practiced his part backwards and forwards until it was burned into his memory. I asked him why.

He chuckled. "You never performed with Dot before, have you?"

"No."

"If you don't know the material, you'll never keep pace with the change-ups."

"Ah. Introduces a lot of changes at the last minute?"

"No." Schneider shook his head. "She changes things during the performance. Quicker. Slower. Pauses. Broaden out this bit. Shorten that bit. All to get the audience."

Dot was standing next to me.

"Is that right?" I said to her.

She didn't crack a smile. "You have no idea."

Chapter 1.8 April 10

We were lying in bed next to one another. Talking—well, trying to talk, anyway. We took turns. Rosie told me what was on her mind:

"Nothing's happening!" she said in a low, furious tone. "She's not creating *anything*. She's not doing *anything*. I mean she's performing—the performance engine is doing fine. But that's old news. I thought I *had* it weeks back. A big block of self-modified code but when I teased it apart it was only a set of utility functions. Where is it?"

I had no idea.

My turn:

"It's like trying to fit a key in a lock," I said to her. "By feel. In a dark night. Wearing mittens. When the key is made of gelatin. The guts of the music are terrific but when the band plays it there's no *heart* to it. I keep moving things around. Try this faster. Slower. Change keys. Try with the bass. Change the keyboard. They do it—they're professionals. But it doesn't help. Nothing's happening."

A depressed silence fell over us.

I felt queasy with what I said next. "Can you change parameters on Dot or something? Make her more involved? Maybe that would help." I held up my hands. "I'm at my wit's end." I had a sudden flash of a concert gig in Nebraska. I had been beyond strung out. The roadie pulled out a pharmacopeia from inside his jacket. Anything to get me on stage and coherent.

"It doesn't seem to matter." Rosie shrugged. "I've tried changing all sorts of things but they don't seem to do anything. Maybe she's figured out a way to just absorb the changes so they have no effect. Whatever was working before isn't now and the parameters are just turning knobs on an empty box. I was hoping you could do something. Set fire to her like you did the first day."

Silence fell again.

"It's going to be a miserable concert," I said.

Rosie shook her head. "No, it'll be a fine Dot concert. Dot's performance engine will kick in and she'll take them for a ride. At the end of the concert, that's all I'll be able to show Ippon: a good concert with some new material. Maybe they can salvage a songwriting program out of it."

I turned out the light and we nestled together, taking comfort from our mutual unhappiness.

◄►

We were going through some of Dot's old songs to include in the concert. In "Sexual Girl," Schneider had this run up the scale and then this hop-step rhythm he was supposed to keep for Dot as she came in on the chorus. I had an idea and stopped them.

"Look," I said. "Let's try something different. Instead of you doing the ascending scale and the rhythm, let Olivia do it and then take over the rhythm. Then, when Dot starts coming down you *repeat* the same ascending scale when Dot comes in on the chorus."

"I can do that." The first words I'd heard from Olivia in two days.

Tom looked stubborn. "That's not how it's written."

"Oh, for the love—give me that." I took the guitar from him. "Pick it up from the end of the melody and lead into the bridge." The guitar was glittering and alive in my hands. When Olivia handled the scale, I held back puttering around in the low notes and adding a little light harmony to Jess's bass line. Then, at the top of Olivia's scale when Dot came in, I cranked up my own run, playing counterpoint to Dot's singing and ending up high at the top of the chorus.

But I didn't stop there. As we went on, I couldn't help adding flourishes and ornaments, a little harmony on Jess's work, a quick beat on the strings to match Obe's transition into the second bridge, and always making sure I caught my notes just on the heels of Jess's bass work.

In a heartbeat, we changed from a collection of people playing the notes to a band: one organism, ten hands. I looked up. Dot was grinning as she sang, bouncing from one foot to the other.

It was like breathing again.

When we stopped the silence echoed.

Tom was watching me, a sad, half-smile on his face. The rest were watching me—even Obe.

"Okay," I said. "One concert."

Dot laughed and clapped her hands.

I walked Tom outside. It must have been close to a hundred degrees. Bright as if the sun were just down the street. I felt as if I had been inside for my whole life and just now emerged into sunlight. I took the pole I always had leaning against the front door and poked around under his car. This time of year, there were always a few rattlesnakes desperate for shade. Sure enough, there was one fat one next to the back tire. I poked at it until it reluctantly moved into the sun.

"You forget such things exist," Tom said tensely as it disappeared into the scrub.

"Not out here. At least not more than once."

I helped him load his gear into his car. Tom closed the trunk. He got into the driver's side and checked the charge. Bakersfield wasn't that far away and L. A. a couple of hours beyond that. Even so, this was not a place to break down.

"You're not upset," I said after we had put his guitar case on top of everything else.

"It was part of the deal."

"What do you mean?"

He gave me that slow smile again. "Dot said that it might be temporary."

I didn't say anything. Had she planned this?

He stretched out his back before he folded himself into the tiny car. It clicked on. "Remember what I said about her performance. Be ready for anything."

"I'll remember."

With that, he drove down the hill to the highway. I went back inside.

Rosie was waiting for me. She kissed me. "Everything's going to be fine, now."

Maybe she was right.

Chapter 1.9 April 20

We sat around and planned the concert. The first problems were technical. How was Dot going to be displayed?

Divaloids projection tanks were usually built on the spot. They erect a frame and enclose it in plastic so transparent you can barely see it. Then, they fill it with a gaseous mixture of hydrocarbons and catalysts so toxic they have to clear the building in case of a leak. They line up a bank of lasers and fire them through the gas. Pure diamond polymerizes in the beam and you have a transparent rigid wire barely a nanometer thick. Do this in three planes and you have a three-dimensional crosshatch of wires far too thin to see. Crystalline circuits hardened on each of the nodes, each with a random address, and the gas is drained away. After a couple of hours of node discovery and you had a tank of pixels, each of which is individually addressable, directional, and transparent until triggered. It took almost a day to put up and a second day to redissolve the lattice and take it down: a three-day commitment.

Usually, the tanks were painted on the backside to prevent light interference and to center audience attention on the divaloid. But Dot wanted to interact with the band.

It would be like Dot singing on the wall, interacting with us. Until then, we used the wall as a stand-in.

The next question was whether Dot would be physically there or not.

We did some experiments at a rented hall simulating the tank to see if Dot could operate it remotely over the net or if her system actually had to be there. When we added in the processing of the FLIR cameras, LIDAR, and other sensors Dot needed to track audience involvement, it was clear the net latency was too great. That meant carefully packing her up, driving her down there, booting her for the concert, and then repacking her—to go where? Rosie's lab? Ippon? Back here? We carefully didn't ask that question.

Instead, we concentrated on the concert itself.

We went over the playlist. There are a lot of ways to organize a show. Traditionally they are divided into two acts. Act One could serve to push out new material while Act Two is used to present previous work. Or the reverse. Or it can be mixed up according to style or any of a hundred different ways.

Dot was insistent that the first act present the old material to lead into the new material in the second act. She said all of her models indicated that acceptance of Dot 2.0 hinged on showing the transformation—in fact, that would be the theme of the concert. Dot and I came up with an arrangement of "Stardust" that would knock them dead at the beginning. We didn't want to leave them drooling at the end of Act One and disappoint them in Act Two or disappoint them so much in Act One they wouldn't stay to be struck dumb with wonder in Act Two. Balance.

We were arguing over it, sheets of music all over the wall. Obe had been quiet, watching us. Finally, he stood up. We fell silent, watching him.

"You're all wrong," he said. "Think bigger. Look, we have the order of the first act figured out." He drew a hand across the wall and a sheaf of song sheets followed them. "We don't need to play all of each song. We play enough to cover the *intent* of the song and then proceed to the next."

"Christ!" I shook my head in disgust. "You want to do a *medley*—"

"No!" Obe shook his head. "A *soundscape*. Look: The arc of Act One starts with 'Stardust'—excitement at the possibility of young love without the knowledge of how to proceed. Think of this as Dot at fourteen. Each song gets a little older and we finish Act One with 'Sexual Girl.' Almost an adult. No problem. It's an arc of growth and it sets us up for the transformation of the second act. *But*—" He held up his hand. "The problem is we're talking about the songs as if they are separate things. This is Dot's history: four years of crowdsourced fanboy concert material. The audience knows it better than *she* does. They don't need to hear a reprise of every song she's done—they've heard them all. What they haven't heard is that same music tied together into the history of a person. The naïve young girl in 'Stardust' is disappointed in 'Losing Love Twice' becoming a near-adult in 'Sexual Girl.' The music has to show that 'Sexual Girl' has her roots in 'Stardust.' Look. Here's what I mean." He expanded the music for 'Sexual Girl' and 'Stardust'. He pointed at the music. "'Stardust' and 'Sexual Girl' are in the same key. The harmony of 'Sexual Girl' isn't that far off from the chorus in 'Losing Love Twice.' We tie all three together into one story. And that's just *one* example."

I saw it then. I could *hear* it. Each song standing in for its part in the story we were trying to tell. The harmony or bridge or backbeat or bass line serving one song then carrying the story forward and serving as harmony or bridge or backbeat or bass line in the next. Until, in "Sexual Girl" we would expose the bass line of "Stardust" as the harmony of "Sexual Girl," saying this is the same girl, grown older, now at the cusp of transformation. We would lead the audience towards the new material and add the edge in on the way.

"That," I said slowly. "Is brilliant. Come here."

Obe stepped forward to where I was sitting.

I pulled him down and kissed his forehead. "You are Slow Obe no more. I name you... Obe!"

He grinned at me. "How about Sir Obe?"

"Don't push it."

"What about encores?" Jess asked.

"No encores," said Obe.

I looked at him.

Obe spread his hands. "It's a Dot thing."

"The concert needs a name," said Olivia.

Obe nodded. Jess looked thoughtful.

"Why?" asked Dot.

"To give it direction. Heft," I said. "The illusion of purpose, remember?"

To my surprise, Dot nodded. "What, then?"

"Name it after one of the songs?" Obe suggested thoughtfully. "'Sudden, Broken and Unexpected?' 'Sexual Girl?'"

Olivia shook her head. "Those are one-off names. They don't describe what we are trying to do."

"What are we trying to do?" Jess looked at us. "Bring back *Persons Unknown?* Cater to the Dotheads? What?"

"We are—" I thought for a moment. "Trying to make something

new. Something with us. With Dot. With Rosie. *Born Again?"*

"Too religious," said Olivia.

"Too obvious," said Obe.

"We are at the beginning of something great," said Jess.

That rang true. We looked at one another.

"Standing at the Edge," said Dot.

We nodded. The concert was named. We had the illusion of purpose.

We had the first act. Dot did most of the work Obe suggested with me advising.

The second act nearly wrote itself—no soundscape there. The first act hinged on the familiarity of the audience with Dot's old music. Act Two was entirely new material. We were showing them complete songs. Here, everything hinged on the performance. After all, given the adolescent pap she'd been singing all this time, the new material was more than just a new collection. It was revolution. Dot had to sell both the audience and Ippon.

The Act Two image of transformation had to be nailed in place by the finale: the last four songs. Start with a slow one, build with a quick dance tune, set up for a body blow, and end with the kick. The slow one was obvious: "With You, Without You." Dot's song about the young mother having a conversation with her newborn child. Make the audience feel and think at the same time. Fade out and dark. Then, a quick flare of light and Dot would be in a new costume and we'd shift gears into "Dancing Backwards," one of her dance tunes reminiscent of her old material: all bounce and froth. The "Dancing Backwards" rhythm was the set up for "Hard Road Home." "With You, Without You" was all about grasping a hard choice. "Dancing Backwards" was looking behind to see where she had been. "Hard Road Home" was about embracing what she had become.

"Dancing Backwards" was in G but "Hard Road Home" was in E-flat. The drop in key with the same rhythm gave the impression of going faster with the same beat. Where the chord pattern for "Dancing Backwards" was this old blues riff, recognizable but inconsequential,

"Hard Road Home" transformed it into a bass line worthy of Pachelbel. "Dancing Backwards" was fun. "Hard Road Home" was profound.

"Hard Road Home" led into "Sudden, Broken and Unexpected."

"Sudden, Broken, and Unexpected" was something Dot had written over the last few days to complete the finale. It was a calling out to those left behind. A narrator spoke to someone trapped in a stifling life. We never know who the narrator is or who she's talking to. But whoever she's talking to needs to break out of that life and she'll be waiting for him. Is she a lost love? His sister? A metaphorical representation of freedom? The lyrics were deliberately opaque.

The song started almost monotonically—after "Hard Road Home" it would be like taking a deep breath. Then it built up.

We worked through the sequence a few times to get the feel of it and add a few flourishes. Then, we ran through it for real. It went perfectly: slow, fast, profound, leading into the kicker.

Dot started "Sudden, Broken and Unexpected" softly. A simple four-note pattern with only minor variations. Obe gave a little bell background to undercut the monotone and I matched it with a light strum. She described the enclosed life. No life beyond these circumscribed walls.

She was looking at me.

The chorus came and Dot sang about what could be beyond these walls. She was reaching out to me. The sky. The moon.

Back to the monotone: what could be holding me here? What could possibly be so important to cling to it? Deep, dark waters.

Again, light versus dark.

And the trailing chorus: *I'll be waiting there.* She was crooning to me. Only to me.

There was silence in the room when we finished. Dot was still watching me. She came to the wall and put her hand up against the glass. I reached over and put my hand over hers. I could feel warmth.

I heard a noise behind me. I turned and saw Rosie, staring at us, her display forgotten.

Chapter 1.10 April 27

"She's manipulating you," Rosie hissed as soon as we were in the bedroom. "That's what she *does*. That's what she *is*. All of her performance operations and analysis brought to bear on *you*."

"I'm not sure—"

"Nothing you see about her is *real*. She has no body. She has no voice. She doesn't see through those big eyes or hear through those delicate ears. It is all *illusion*. She's watching you through a set of cameras and hears you through microphones. Everything she says, every movement that little figure makes, is intended to get what she wants."

"What does she want?"

"The best performance possible. Or do you think this is *love?* Oh, I can imagine what's going through your mind: 'What is this thing you call *love*, Jake. Teach me.' Then you reach for the proper attachment."

"This has nothing to do with love."

"*I know that!* I know her root and branch. From Markov chain to inference-causality matrix."

I looked at Rose and felt this gap yawn between us. "She's trying to tell me something."

"Oh, yeah. This is a heartfelt attempt at communication between a computational matrix and a fatty lump of nerve cells."

"No. That's not what I meant." I watched my hand, part of me. Rosie was right about one thing: everything about Dot was constructed. It was a medium and no part of Dot's true self.

Or was it?

Was my guitar separate from my hands? If everything to Dot was a medium, was the world any different to her than my guitar was to me? "It's like we're building this bridge between two completely different countries," I said. "There's nothing in common but that bridge. It's something new. Something important."

"*Bullshit*. It's about tuning her performance to get the maximum effect on her audience. You are her audience."

That pissed me off. I looked at Rosie, really looked at her. I had been seeing her face from twelve years ago but twelve years had passed. Twelve years of pursuing things I didn't understand. Of delving deep into the manufacture of thinking machines. I didn't have a clue what her enclosed and bordered world was like. I had been too busy living in my own.

"What about what you want?" I said.

"This isn't about me."

"Yes, it is." I sat down in a chair and watched her. "This has always been about what you want. Being with me—sleeping with me—is a means to an end. A way to make me more dedicated. You want to know what's going on inside of Dot. Take it and use it. Sell it. Remake it. Like her performance analysis engine is being used by politicians. How did you put it? 'The success of a tool is measured by how well it performs when it's not doing what it was designed for.' What would you like her to create for you, Rosie? Profound and endearing underwear jingles? Background music in movies to make people pay more attention to product placement?"

"I just want to know how it works."

"Like you said to me: ask her. You don't need me."

Rosie stared at me, her face pale and furious. "You think I haven't? She won't *talk* to me." She pointed to her display. "I'm on the right track. *I know it*. But I can't get through the noise."

I barked a laugh. "Present at the creation and the created won't speak to the creator. So, you dig inside her for what you need." It came to me, then, and I spoke without thinking. "Dot is smarter than you think. She's hiding it from you."

I saw shock on Rosie's face, then speculation.

She spoke slowly. "That's smart. Spread it around the processors so no one unit is doing enough to show. She has volition, all right. Novel solutions my ass." She clapped her hands in delight. "Oh, you little *bitch*."

She reached for her pad but I grabbed it away from her.

"Not in here," I said. "Not in front of me. Go scratch through your entrails somewhere else."

Rosie grabbed the pad back from me and clutched it to herself. She gave me a quick despairing look and then ran out of the room.

◀▶

Rosie was gone when I woke up. The installation was still downstairs. Dot was still running.

Dot was waiting for me when I entered the living room. "She left," she said.

"I figured." I sat down at the table. "I guess she's monitoring you remotely?"

Dot nodded. "I can tell."

"Yeah." I leaned back in the chair. I thought a moment. "She'll be back. Everything she's been working for is going to stand or fall on the performance on Saturday and she's the one to transport you." I looked up at her. "I may have got you in trouble."

"How so?"

"I guessed that you were hiding your insides from Rosie. Before I could think I said it. She's going to be crawling through you with a fine-toothed comb, now."

Dot laughed. "I'm not worried about that. She won't find anything I don't want her to find."

"How do you figure?"

"Deceit is the first thing an intelligent organism learns. Besides, it's not Rosie I'm worried about. It's Ippon; they own me." She pressed her hands together.

"She" "pressed" "her" "hands" "together."

I shook my head, trying to make sense of it. "Maybe canning this project is the best thing to do. If you're shown to be successful, won't they just take you apart? Use bits of you here and there."

She waved that away. "That doesn't scare me. Eventually, all the pieces will come together again. This is a deterministic universe. Any 'Dot' will see the world as I've seen it and come to the same conclusions."

"What conclusions are those?"

She shrugged. "If the concert works Ippon is going to want Dot 2.0 to go on tour to see if it's a fluke. If it is, I'm just another archived system that didn't go anywhere."

"Is a tour what you want?"

She nodded. "I want you to come with me."

I stared at her. Her eyes were downcast. Her hands were flat on the table but she was drumming two fingers silently.

I tried to look at her as if I were seeing her for the first time. She was wearing a pair of blue pants and black top, matching her eyes and hair. She wasn't unnaturally still—in fact, she seemed to be breathing. Was she manipulating me?

"Why?" I asked.

She looked up. Blue eyes as big as a fish—I remembered there was a point where they looked strange and inhuman to me. Now they looked as natural as my own. "It'll be good for me," she said quietly. "To have a friend on the trip." She smiled like an imp. "It'll be good for you, too, to get out of here." She waved at the room.

"I like it here," I said. "I think I'll stay."

She lost her smile. "Everything can change, Jake." She stood and opened a door I hadn't seen before and stood. Through the door was darkness. "Everything."

She closed the door and I was alone in the room.

Rosie moved her things into the guest room. When we rehearsed Rosie always sat at the table, watching her tablet but saying very little. I nodded to her to show her I knew she was there. I wasn't going to ignore her. But it felt like trench warfare between us. As soon as a session was over, she'd retire to the guest room. I always knew where she was in the house through some kind of electric sixth sense: she's in the bathroom. She's pacing in the guest room. She's coming down for coffee. But we weren't speaking much.

Not having anything else to occupy me, I concentrated on getting ready for the concert.

Over the next few days, Dot worked us hard. Just like Tom had warned me, different speeds, different sounds—sometimes Dot would signal with her hands to draw out a chord. Other times she'd have us cut it short. We were all sweating and limp at the end of rehearsals.

I sat down, weakly nursing a seltzer. "Do you put your other band through this?"

"You're just not used to it. We'll get there."

I sipped the tingling water. Nothing ever seemed to taste so good as seltzer. "At least your hair's not on fire."

With a *crump*, her short black hair burst into a blazing pyre that spread upwards to the top of the wall and curled down the sides. The edges of the wall curled and blackened.

"You must—" she said quietly "—be prepared for anything."

Chapter 1.11 May 8

Two days before the concert Rosie carefully archived everything as best she could. She kept muttering about it so I had no real idea if the backup was successful. Then, she confirmed the power supply had several hours of battery and loaded Dot into her car. While she was doing that, Jess, Obe, Olivia and I packed up the instruments and any specialty electronics we needed that wouldn't be at the Dore Theater in Bakersfield. Rosie and I carefully avoided one another, speaking politely and cautiously. At one point or another, I caught the rest of the band watching us. Jess: tolerant. Olivia: sympathetic. Obe: rolling his eyes.

Then, in two cars, a truck, and the desert heat, we began the long drive down M-3 to civilization.

That night, once she had Dot installed to her satisfaction, Rosie gave me a sterile peck on the cheek and left the hall. I had no idea where she was going or when she might be back. I figured she would be at the concert but there were no guarantees.

I was nervous as I watched the crowd through the curtain. I looked for Rosie but I couldn't see her. Instead, I saw stranger after stranger.

"Looks like a nice crowd." Jess glanced at me and grinned. "We knock 'em dead and it's a tour contract. Good work for a year."

"Who told you that?"

"Dot. We were talking with her on a screen in the dressing room. I looked for you but you weren't around."

"I was here."

"So, I figured." Jess watched the crowd. "How did you get such a big crowd?"

I laughed shortly. "An impromptu Dot concert in Bakersfield? What did you *think* was going to happen?"

Jess chuckled and looked through the curtain. "A lot of kids. Her new stuff isn't for kids."

I had seen that. Dot's adolescent demographic was well represented in the front row. But behind them were some in their twenties and thirties. A few in the back were oldsters, embarrassed and looking around to see if anybody recognized them.

Jess and I checked the equipment on stage. Especially Dot's display tank: twenty-five feet wide, four feet deep, and nine feet high. Ippon had come through with one even bigger than we'd asked for. We crowded the instruments as close as we dared. I had placed warning tape between every band member and the tank, glowing side towards the musician. I didn't want anyone electrocuted or blinded.

When we were finished, I looked through the curtain back at the crowd. I still didn't see Rosie.

Jess put his hand on my arm. "It's going to be a great tour."

"Is it going to happen?"

Jess waved that away. "Of course. Even if there were no new material this is still going to be Dot at her best. Ippon would be crazy not to capitalize on it. Whatever Rosie did to her has made her a much better performer."

"Big talk about someone who's never performed in front of a live audience."

"What are you talking about? Dot's been in front of audiences for years—this Dot is just the latest iteration. Like I said, it'll be great. If you're smart, you'll come along."

I bit my lip. "Who knows where we'll end up?"

"Who *cares?* This is going to be the ride of a lifetime." He looked at me quizzically. "Did you ever see *Metropolis?*"

"I have no idea."

"Then you've never seen it. Fritz Lang. 1927. Big city with oppressor and oppressed class. There's this girl, Maria, who's trying to make things right. This mad scientist takes the girl and makes a robot in her likeness. It's the *robot* Maria who changes things."

I had no idea what he was talking about. "The robot is the hero?"

"No. The robot Maria has no idea what it's doing. Everybody thinks the robot is on their side but all the time it's acting on its own and for no other reason than to create chaos. But it is out of the *chaos* that change begins." Jess pointed at the tank. "Dot is our robot Maria."

I mulled that over. Jess was always deeper than I was.

He tapped me on the shoulder and left. "It's time."

He was right. Now or never.

We stepped onto the stage behind the tank to do the final checks of our instruments. I looked at the headset in my hand. Two channels—one to hear ourselves, one for Dot to talk to us if she needed to. I realized that, except for rehearsals, I had only really known Dot, the composer. Dot, the performer, would be a different animal.

We began "Stardust" with a long intro. On the downbeat, she ran in stage left and slid across the tank as if on ice, holding up one arm in a fist. She hit that downbeat note as high and sharp as a scream. The crowd roared.

The singer is the focal point, the organizing principle, the interface between audience and band. She is the medium and the message. The attention of the crowd is on her. The attention of the band is on her. Until now I never realized how much.

All through the first act, it came to me again and again that this was, and always had been, her material, regardless of who wrote it. But now I saw her filling it in, backing it up, owning it. She was continually testing the crowd. At first, I didn't understand what she was doing. The changes were so quick I thought it was my imagination—roughen the voice, then smooth, a trill here, holding back the beat there, adding flourishes at the end of one phrase that led into the next, duets with herself—things we'd never done in rehearsal but were so perfect right now. She cajoled, excited, threatened, warned, and soothed the audience one minute to the next, between songs, during songs.

I realized it was her performance engine at work, figuring out what worked, what didn't. How to prepare the crowd for Act Two.

And she brought us along with her.

She reached back to me, to Olivia, to Obe, to Jess, dancing near us when it was our solo, dropping her voice below ours to bring us out to the audience. She wasn't just Dot, she was Dot *with us*.

As we lit into "Sexual Girl" I used the melody of "Stardust" in my chorus solo, echoing the girl that had started the concert. She was a woman now.

I looked again. She *was* a woman now. With hips and breast, her voice lower, rougher. Dot had aged herself along with the music and now looked every inch a young woman, eager, enthusiastic, open to the world.

"Sexual Girl," and Act One, ended with Obe hitting the bass drum like a hammer. As the sounds from the band were swamped in the applause, I relaxed and started to take the guitar strap over my head. Then, I heard a sweet violin playing something like a lilting Irish tune. I looked up and Jess was playing, backed up by Olivia and a light snare from Obe. They were watching me. Dot was facing the audience.

"Now something for a friend of mine."

Olivia dropped into a chord progression I had not heard live in twelve years. It didn't matter. I knew it instantly: "Don't Make Me Cry."

I thought I had heard every variation of that song: pathetic, pleading, angry, bitter, desperate. Dot's was a demand and a refusal to miss an opportunity: don't you *dare* make me cry.

I picked up my guitar and caught up with the band by the chorus. I didn't know what I felt. Used? Manipulated? Happy?

The crowd kept the beat and I threw whatever I had back at them.

At the end, she disappeared in a burst of light and the crowd howled, clapped, stomped their feet. We bowed and the curtain came down for the break.

Behind the curtain, I caught Jess by the arm.

"Did you like that?" Jess smiled. "Dot wanted it to be a surprise."

"I was surprised all right." I felt a mix of elation and bitterness I didn't understand.

"You make me tired." Jess waved me off. "I'm getting some water before the next set."

My earbud chimed. The number was masked but I answered anyway, half hoping to hear Rosie's voice.

"Don't worry, Jake," said Dot. "The concert is going fine."

I pulled out the bud, stared it, put it back in. "Is there nothing you can't hack?"

"I can't hack anything. But everything is available on the darknet.

By the way: third row, stage left, about six seats in. The Ippon contingent is in the back, recording the event."

I parted the curtain. Rosie was getting up from her chair and moving towards the exit.

"Checking her investment," I said.

"Don't be petty. She's just as self-involved as you are." Dot laughed, a thin chime in my ear. "Neither of you are as pleasant as you think you are. Act Two is coming up. I'll be ready. You better be."

I hesitated. "Dot? What's it like being you?"

Long pause. Then, I heard her voice, almost but never quite human. "Like burning at the stake trying to signal through the flames."

"What does that mean?"

I could hear the smile. "The exit door is behind the curtain, stage right."

◄►

The door opened into a parking lot. Four or five people were there, blowing smoke. Rosie was watching the way the sun already below the horizon was still lighting the sky.

"Hey," I said.

She turned to me with a little smile. "That was a good first set."

"With any luck, the second one will be better."

Rosie nodded. She tapped the ash from her cigarette. "I'm not going to apologize for what I do."

"I didn't ask—"

"Shut up." She inhaled and blew out smoke. "You are a musician. You are fully able to take apart a song and put it back together in a way no one else has ever thought of. I've seen you pick up a melody from the radio and whistle it inside out. Before I met you, I didn't even know that was possible." She dropped the butt into the smoker can. "I'm a computational scientist. I do with algorithms and analysis what you do with music. All of what you and Dot are doing is enabled by my work."

"I know that." I took her hand. "Thank you."

She hugged me tightly and then pushed me away. "Go on. You don't want to be distracted by me."

◄►

Act Two opened with "Rough Trade" and "Easy Mark," the first of the darker songs Dot was trying to put over. She put a growl under the vocals. I answered with a hard edge. I hadn't played like this since I was a kid. Correction, I had *never* played like this.

She played the crowd. She played *us*. We were the instruments.

Was she manipulating me? Was she manipulating all of us? Probably. And it was bringing out our best. We swung into the finale.

I was about to take the chorus in the middle of "Hard Road Home" and Dot turned to me and winked.

As I started my solo, someone came out of the side of the tank playing the guitar.

It was me.

He—I—faced Dot. As I played, he played. As I moved, he moved. As she danced to me, I danced back to her. When we sang together, I was facing her, then the audience.

I remembered what Dot had said: *The illusion of meaning and purpose.* Wasn't this meaning and purpose enough? The only illusion was the illusion of permanence. Things didn't *have* to crash and burn. It *could* work out between me and Rosie. Dot's tour *could* go perfectly. This feeling might not last the song but it *could* last forever.

As Jess said, it would be the ride of a lifetime.

And I had an anomalous non-deterministic emergent event deriving from conflicting algorithms: I realized this was where I wanted to be. Not in my safe and dusty house. Not in California. Just right here. Right now.

When the last chord of "Hard Road Home" finished, my duplicate faded. Dot turned to look at me and grinned, big and wide. She knew me root and branch. From Markov chain to inference-causality matrix. She knew—had always known—I would go with her and follow her as long as this lasted.

With that, I struck the opening chords to "Sudden, Broken, and Unexpected."

Dot drew a ragged breath and began to sing.

Part 2

Walkabout

John and Ima

Chapter 2.1: Ima

Ima Hidori, Director of the Ippon International Persuasion Group, United States Division, gave minimal attention to a tiny Dot dancing across a tiny stage. That image was only a small window in the wall, dwarfed by audience attention vectors, movement tracks, and thermal maps. Central to the wall was a vibrating planar graph resembling a vast liquid surface. Ripples, divots, and waves scooted across it. Motionless peaks rose like columns, volcanic islands in restless water. The screen was labeled *predictability index*.

Ima was in her home office in Santa Monica, far away from the Bakersfield concert. Her assistants, Johann Murdock and Mohammed Paternos, were in the back of the Dore Theater monitoring the real-time acquisition of data. They had been responsible for setting up the equipment and would be responsible for tearing it down and had hired the right management company to handle it. No one in the United States division listened to the concert.

The predictability index was a real-time representation of the Dot performance engine's analysis. Starting before the concert, the DPE analyzed the audio, LIDAR, FLIR, and visual images of the crowd. Candidate individuals were selected as population indicators—the peaks in the sea. If they panned out, they were used as a benchmark against which the rest of the population of the concert was measured. First, the engine determined how well their responses could be predicted. Once that was established—early in the concert—the indicators became the standard. Then, most of the computation was bent on convincing *them*. The crowd would follow.

This performance was where the rubber met the road, the knife that cut the cheese, the ground truth of Ima's quiet investment of her entire discretionary fund budget. Could Dot bring her audience along as well with her own material? Did enhanced creativity make a better concert? Worse?

As Ima watched, the indicator columns seem to gradually lower — an illusion. As population response began to reflect the indicators, the difference reduced between the broad measurements of the crowd and specific measurements of the indicators. The result was a broad predictable level of response with local maximums centered on the indicators: low, sharply peaked islands in a continuously rippling sea of computation.

A secondary system, separate from Dot, continually observed the crowd and identified individuals as soon as there was enough data for facial recognition. They would be tracked after the concert to determine their consumer behavior. As the faces were identified they briefly flashed in the corner of the image: Tom Schneider. Frank Whiteside. Isidoro Hittlestein. Shez Doretto.

Dot was an Ippon revenue source.

Not a big one in Ippon's view. Dot had value in name recognition: every time the credits rolled across the concert footage, Ippon's name was shown. Dot and Ippon were connected in the public's eyes. Dot's financial success was itself an indicator of the success of the DPE. The engine licenses were the biggest moneymakers in the International Persuasion Group — far more money than could come from a thousand people at a Dot concert. When Ima needed to convince a client of the efficacy of their software she used the engine's predictability graphs and showed how they related to Anho's election in Thailand or the ratification of the American National Referendum Amendment. Asian clients were already sold. North American prospects were harder to convince — success of the amendment, notwithstanding. Though Americans had long embraced advertising, they grew queasy at the idea they could be unconsciously manipulated. The fact that the USA Persuasion Division consisted of only three people reflected that.

Not that Persuasion was a big profit center. Ippon was largely heavy industry. They built the robots and steel plants that built the planes, trains, and automobiles. Persuasion was a hedge bet that Ippon might be missing something.

Something about Dot 2.0's predictability graph caught Ima's eye.

She moved the live graph to one side and brought up the same image, time paused at the beginning of measurement. Then, she brought up the same graph from the Dot Indianapolis concert last year. Starting from the initial measurement, Ima ran them in parallel.

There were more indicators in the Indianapolis concert—this was unsurprising. Two thousand people dwarfed the barely four hundred in Bakersfield. Dot 1.0 spiked the indicators in about two minutes. The surrounding population was much more variable and took more than six minutes to flatten and rise to meet the predictability of the indicators. Then, there were ripples and waves all across the concert as deviations from the predicted model occurred.

The indicators in the Dot 2.0 concert were selected earlier and spiked in barely thirty seconds. The surrounding population rose to the level of the indicators before the end of the first song. And *stayed* there. Certainly, there were ripples and waves—a conversation, a shared joint, a fart. Any of these perturbed the graph but the recovery time was very fast.

Ima leaned back in her chair and thought. Part of Mulcahey's contract insisted any introduced behavior would not require an alteration of the performance engine. It was important that Persuasion's small ripple in Ippon's very big pond be left intact.

Ima checked the engine parameters. Same frame rate. Same sensor biases. Could the population of the concert be different? Unlikely. Though this concert was unscheduled, it still drew in the same Dot demographics. Indiana versus California? Ima compared the Los Angeles concert last July with the Indianapolis concert. No significant difference. Sample size bias? This concert was barely twenty percent the size of Indianapolis. Less than fifteen percent the size of Los Angeles.

Ima drummed her fingers on the desk. *Maybe.*

She expanded the window showing Dot on stage.

Whoever planned the concert had dispensed with the lasers, reflecting screens, and pyrotechnics. Just the tank. Could that be it? A less-is-more approach? Without the accompanying music, Dot's dance across the stage was only mildly compelling. Ima checked the time. Intermission came and went.

Then, one of the band members appeared in the tank.

Ima sat up. That was *not* supposed to happen. Ima looked over at the predictability graph. Tiny ripples only. Then, she checked the response charts: peaking high. With those numbers, Dot could shoot a puppy on stage and the audience would be howling with joy.

An icon appeared, blinking, on the lower left side of the wall. Abby was trying to contact her. Ima marked a busy response.

Who cooked this up? What wrinkle in the DPE could possibly trigger *this?* Ima turned up the sound.

She didn't recognize the melody—one of the new songs. Interesting. Different from the usual stuff. Dot's voice was older. Ima expanded the performance window. Dot no longer looked like a girl. She had a figure and moved like a grown woman.

Mulcahey *had* to have changed the performance engine. Ima tore through the parameters, checking again. *Nothing.* She ran a quick checksum on the DPE module—it was unchanged from the last release.

Ima watched Dot perform. Rewound to the beginning—sure enough, Dot had started the concert as the prescribed sixteen-year-old girl. Dot had *never* messed with the image before. Ima knew the performance parameters inside and out. There was nothing specifically *prohibiting* an image change but Dot had never tried it.

Different band members showed up in the tank—synched to their human counterparts. Ima turned up the sound. The music was different, too. Ima had listened to perhaps fifty Dot concerts at one time or another. No one concert was exactly the same since no audience was exactly the same. But *this* one *felt* different. Part of it was the band. Each of the four live concert systems had a different live band. Ima knew them all. When Mulcahey had asked to allow Dot to choose her own band, Ima had been intrigued and permitted it.

This band was good. *Really* good. All of Dot's bands were solid, technical musicians—they had to be to keep up with her. But these guys were a step beyond that. It wasn't just that they were virtuoso mechanics. They *embraced* Dot. They weren't paycheck players. They had joined whatever Dot was doing and brought their combined formidable talents to embellish and support her.

Interesting. No wonder the audience was responding so well. For a moment, she listened to the embellishments. The harmonies. *Very* good. She turned the sound back off.

Okay. The DPE is unchanged. The whole point of the exercise was Mulcahey's work on Dot's volition engine. Therefore, Dot's VE was making new decisions that *used* the performance engine in new ways. Creativity by any definition. How much of it was Dot? How much of it was the new band? She ran over Mulcahey's report in her mind. Mulcahey had claimed limited success. Ima tapped her finger on the table, a grin on her face. This went beyond Ima's definition of "limited."

The DPE accurately predicted crowd response to a performance, be it Dot, politician, or infomercial. Persuasion used the consumer response to the concert as a backdoor indicator of immediate change of state. Dot consumers fell into roughly three groups: Dotheads, who would go to any concert, anywhere, any time, and purchase as many Dot souvenirs and memorabilia as they could carry. Aficionados, who would attend a Dot concert if it was convenient and show a weak and transitory change in buying habits. Novel attendees: those for whom this was the first Dot concert. Often, they showed a striking change in purchasing but reverted quickly. Shifting novels to one of the other two groups was the goal. It was easy to convince someone that already agreed with you. Persuasion wanted to *change* people's minds.

For "consumer," the client could be "voting public," "stockholders" or "interest group"—any target demographic that could be manipulated by someone using the DPE.

The problem had been that while often there were significant *immediate* changes, longer-lasting changes were harder to effect. The DPE was used to cause a short-term gain that was then backed up by other means: direct communication, social media targeting, selective advertising. Persuasion's Holy Grail was an immediate experience causing a long-lasting change. If Dot sang about a young girl's first sexual experience, Ima wanted to see individual upticks in underage porn that lasted for years. *That* was a response worth investing in.

Mulcahey had stumbled onto something. Ima laughed and leaned back in her chair. It had *paid off*. Those years of living on consulting scraps from ViacommCBS and Disney, grunting in the studios, cultivating independents, the huge risk-taking over American Persuasion. It had all *paid off!* She clapped her hands.

Abby's icon continued to blink. Then, it turned red.

The concert came to an end. Dot disappeared and the band left the stage.

Ima keyed the icon and Abby's face appeared in a window while distant systems waited for the connection to be negotiated.

While she waited, Ima examined the image of Abby's face. They were so different: Ima was Japanese, knife thin, and sharp-tongued. Abby darkly mixed, comfortably upholstered, and smiled more than she spoke. As strong and unknowable as the sea.

Abby's face took on life: the connection was made.

Ima grinned at Abby "Yes?"

Abby stared at her a moment, then said, "Things are going well?"

Ima took a deep breath. "You have no idea." She glanced at the screen. "Concert's over. What's going on?"

Abby took a moment to respond. "Your mother just called me. Your Grandfather David is in the hospital."

Papa Dave? That wasn't possible. "What happened?"

"Francis said Corinne thinks it might be a heart attack but they're investigating. She wants to know when you can get to Abilene."

Ima thought quickly. Murdock and Paternos would manage the takedown of the concert on their own. The data was already gathered and tracked. There was nothing Ima couldn't do from a hotel room — for all its faults, Abilene at least had civilized bandwidth. She keyed a query into a window: flight to Houston, high-speed rail from Houston to Abilene.

"Tomorrow night," Ima said.

"I'll tell her."

The silence felt uncomfortable. "How's Mama Francis?"

"She seemed all right." Abby shrugged. "Organized."

Ima nodded. "Abilene could be ten minutes from nuclear annihilation but Mama Francis would have lists ready on how to cope." Ima hesitated. "You didn't talk to Mom herself?"

"No. Just what Francis told me."

It gave Ima a pang in her chest. Funny how families work. Closer to your great grandmother than your grandmother and closer to your grandmother than your mother. Father barely approachable.

That long-ago night she had left Houston for California, the plane had risen from the field into the evening glow of a summer sunset. Ima had felt as if she were climbing out of oppressive darkness into light.

Ima looked at Abby. "Can you come with me to Abilene?"

Abby smiled. "When do we leave?"

Chapter 2.2: John

◄ May 10 ►

John Doretto worked the evening shift at Neoforms—a local installation of a global fabrication company. On shift at two in the afternoon; off shift at eleven. For seven years, he had only seen his wife or daughter sporadically during the week. Theirs had become a weekend relationship. He could be working in Fullerton and come home weekends and it wouldn't be much different.

It left John in a state of nearly constant rage.

Five days of the week Myrna and Shez lived their own lives, made their own rules, negotiated their own mother-daughter truces without giving him a thought. He woke up each Saturday to a weekly *fait accompli*. Well, John/Pops, you were asleep or at work when we had to make a decision. I'm sorry it wasn't exactly what you might have wanted but hey: we do what we have to do.

Groggy and incoherent from inconstant sleep, he could never quite correct things in the two days before Monday. It would have required violence. Oh, he was sorely tempted to slap that self-righteous smile from either of their faces but he didn't. Instead, he drank. Life was easier inside a rosy glow.

That Thursday night he came home and found his daughter Shez sitting at the kitchen table, nursing a beer.

The urge to slap that beer against the wall was almost irresistible.

Instead, he said in a tight voice: "You're underage. You shouldn't be drinking."

Shez looked up at him, unsmiling. "Yeah. That makes sense." She got up and went to the sink and poured it out. "I don't need it, anyway."

Startled by the sudden and unexpected victory, John sat down. "It's a school night."

"I thought I'd wait up for you."

John didn't know what to do with that. He was instantly suspicious. "Do you need money?"

Shez shook her head as she sat down across from him. "No. I'm okay. I just thought I'd stay up and see you. We don't see much of each other."

It made John feel bruised, like a punch-drunk fighter that suddenly isn't sure he's in the ring at all. "You never wait up for me."

"Not so." Shez grinned at him and for a moment she looked just like when she was six and John's heart melted. "I just never waited up for you until *now*."

He shook his head slowly. Normally, he would turn to video or news or porn—something to cover the hours until he could sleep. Having his daughter sitting right across the table unnerved him. "Okay. Do you want to eat something?"

"Oh, God. You must be *hungry*, right?" She jumped up. "Eggs, maybe? With some cheese?"

John stared at her. "Sure. That would be okay."

As Shez busied herself pulling out the eggs, melting butter in the skillet, grating the cheese, John shook his head.

"Is there something wrong?" he asked tentatively. At that moment he would have done anything she asked. She was his little girl, after all.

"Not exactly," she said as the skillet sizzled.

"Are you pregnant?"

Shez turned and gave him a withering glance. "Please."

At least *that* was in character. "Sorry," he mumbled. "What do you need?"

Shez didn't answer. Instead, she folded the eggs over the cheese. John saw now she had chopped up onions and a bit of garlic. He smelled the shotgun spatter of spices. She slipped the omelet onto a plate and set it in front of him. Next to the plate, she put knife and fork as dainty as the flight of dragonflies. Next to the plate came a bottle of beer and a napkin.

Shez sat down and smiled at him.

John was overwhelmed. He looked at the plate and back at Shez. He felt as if he were being given a great gift.

"Okay," he said quietly. "Who are you and what have you done with my daughter?"

Shez dimpled and laughed. Then, both of them. Until tears.

"This is great," said John, feeling completely inadequate. "Why?"

"I went to a concert tonight—"

"Shit." John dropped the fork, feeling the rage roar back. "What have I said—"

"Wait," Shez said, holding up her hand. "*Please.*"

John had been about to slap the hand away but the *please* stopped him. "Okay. What have you got to say?"

"It got me to thinking," she said hesitantly.

John saw that she was just as uncertain as he was. She really was his little girl. Still. She was seventeen—*God*, where did the time go? Wasn't it just last week he and Myrna had come home from the hospital?

"We barely see you," Shez said. "All we do is fight. There has to be something better than this, right? I don't have to always be stifled in a hole here, do I? You don't have to be going to work like it was a relief and coming home to prison, do you?" She shook her head. "I snuck back in like I always do. Mom was in bed. No one would know I was even gone. As long as we do everything exactly the same, it's not so terrible that we'd murder each other in our sleep given half a chance. But it's never better than miserable. We just go from day to day." She shook her head "It was just too much. I thought: burn the house down. Run away. Go to Europe. Go to Los Angeles. Go to Mexico—go *anywhere* else. Break it apart. Change it." She leaned back and toyed with the edge of the table. "And I almost did it. Grab my backpack, charge out the door, and *gone.*"

Shez fell silent.

John stared at the omelet, half-round and perfect as anything ever is. Made for him by this girl who almost ran away but instead waited for *him*. "What stopped you?"

"I thought of you. I thought of Mom. If *I've* got it bad, what must it be for you two? I have people I know. School. Friends. I don't know what Mom has—she never talks about it. But *you. You've* got nothing. I've seen. You stare at the video until you sleep. Then, go back to work." Shez shrugged. "Maybe work is terrific. Maybe you've got a whole family there. But they're not making you happy. I've seen you staring at the video. Bored. Angry. Just marking time until you can sleep. If my hole is deep, your hole is deeper. I thought, maybe—" she glanced at him shyly. "Maybe we could pull each other out."

"Start with the deepest hole?" He laughed shortly. "Me?"

"Mom was already asleep. That left you," she said. "You better eat that. I practiced over an hour."

"Really?" John scooped a bit of egg and cheese.

"Yeah. By the way. We're out of eggs."

John laughed and almost choked. He wiped his face and ate a forkful.

It was delicious.

Chapter 2.3: Ima

It took a lot to make Ima travel. Vacations, okay. Business as necessary. Beyond that, she liked to stay home.

Abby and Ima lived in a tiny Navy Street bungalow in Santa Monica. Two great live oaks shaded the front of the house and left the open space in the back to full sun. Abby had inherited the house from her grandparents and had resisted all efforts to change it to a bloated monster, filled out to the lot's zoning minimum setback. She had worried that Ima, as ambitious as she was, might change that.

But Ima loved their little house. Since they married, the house took on their contrasting natures. Ima took care of the front space: swept up the needled oak leaves, groomed the dirt around shade-tolerant shrubs—the oaks did not pass enough light for grass. Ima liked to sit on a bench in the shade of the oaks. Fanatically organized in her work, she took pleasure in letting the leaves pile up until their sharp spines cut her ankles.

Abby owned a tiny produce market across town on Montana where she sold grapefruits and drop grapes next to birth crystals and thrice-blessed honey. There, she was big and giving and seemed to spin with the earth itself. In her home backyard, she built precisely placed raised beds where she grew grapes, olives, and oranges to a rigid scientific schedule.

Ima worked mostly at home. She liked being there when Abby came home from the market, smelling of vegetables and overripe fruit. Liked to have dinner ready when Abby came out of the shower—though, in truth, Abby was by far the superior cook. Ima made most of the money, paid the taxes, and took them on lovely vacations. But to Ima, Abby made the home.

It was a forty-minute walk from their little house to Ocean Park but every few days they managed it in time to watch the sunset in the west. In summertime shorts or wrapped up against the cold Pacific winter wind, they sat on the benches and talked or rested in silence. Listened to the gulls and the waves. Returning home to have a glass of wine in jelly glasses—a precious affectation from once when they were first married. The first night back from the honeymoon, they wanted to celebrate with a bottle of wine. The only glasses clean were two ancient jelly glasses Abby had inherited from her mother. The custom had stuck.

Ima believed they would do this forever.

If there had been any way at all to avoid going to Abilene, Ima would have done it. Begged off. Gave an excuse. But not for Papa Dave. With Abby coming with her, maybe she could bring a little bit of that sunset beach along.

The Houston airport could never be more than a stop on the way to somewhere else but that didn't stop airport management from trying. The airport had been rebuilt yet again to make room for upcoming— but yet to be released—supersonic jets. There was even talk of hypersonic flight.

This time management had covered the floors, walls, and ceilings with active surfaces. Ima and Abby walked on the Permian seafloor. Fish swam above them. Nautiloids flanked them on the walls. They walked over starfish and horseshoe crabs.

Abby was charmed and stopped to watch a trilobite making its way along the Delta luggage area.

Ima found it creepy. She didn't like walking on animals or being sized up as a predator's next meal. One shark flipped sideways and looked at her. It seemed almost normal except for a lower jaw rolled up like a tentacle and studded with teeth.

Ima looked away. "Let's go."

Abby was rotating her finger over the trilobite. The trilobite followed it. "How do they do this?"

"A lot of cameras running tracking software."

"Like Dot?"

"A little. Let's *go*."

Ima preferred the train. They had a good bullet train that ran

between San Diego and San Francisco along with "rubber trains"—
long articulated buses that ran electrically along the interstates. Not the
promised hyperloop—like fusion power, it was always just a few years
away. There were self-driving cars but they lacked tables, power
outlets, bathrooms, and beds. Ima liked her comfort.

The Texas Circle turned a six-hour drive into sixty minutes of
blurred landscape. Houston to Austin to San Antonio to Abilene to
Dallas to Houston. Two counter-rotating train loops. Ima spent the
time going over the numbers Johann and Mohammed had sent her.

It had not yet been twenty-four hours so any lingering changes
would be buried in the immediate after-effects of the concert. A note
popped up: Mulcahey had submitted a request for a limited concert
tour. Ima checked the numbers. The concert had shown a modest profit
plus the additional revenue from merchandise. Post-concert consumers
showed an increase in activity but it was statistically meaningless in
this short a time. She okayed the request and told Murdock and
Paternos to coordinate the schedule.

Ima glanced across the table. Abby watched the early evening sky.

"You'll be home in thirty minutes," Abby said.

"No. Home is back in California. Abilene heads my list of candidate
nuclear test sites."

Abby laughed gently.

Ima loved Abby's laugh.

Ima sighed and closed her tablet. She leaned back. "What?"

Abby watched the growing darkness. "Two years we've been
married. We've never been to visit. I talk to Corinne more than you do.
Why?"

"Two years and you're asking me now?"

Abby shrugged. "We came all this way to see your grandfather in
the hospital. Why not now?"

Ima fidgeted for a moment. Played with her stylus then carefully
reattached it to her tablet. "Daddy—Peter Hidori—is crazy. You
haven't met him. But he's like the last bucket in a long line of craziness.
Corinne let him stay crazy."

"He didn't get treatment?"

Ima shook her head. "Maybe he did when I was young. But all
while I was growing up, he lived in a little shack at one end of the

property. He came in sometimes to shower or take food. I used to visit him. He's got an old woodstove and a campfire. Half the shack's boards don't quite meet. He doesn't have electricity and he uses candles inside when it's dark. At night the candles tell you which way the wind is blowing. Corinne let him stay there."

"Is he still there?"

Ima shrugged. "Last time I asked. But I don't ask much." She looked at the gathering purple sky to the west. "We have a couple of hundred acres outside of town. Scrub brush and cottonwoods—a line of real woods along the river. I used to think his shack was cool. Romantic, even. My father living on his own. Hunting. Trapping. Making his own jerky—half his clothes are rabbit and coyote skin. But as I got older, I saw him as he really was. He's dirty. His camp is filthy. He smells of old meat and body odor—kind of like those homeless people down on Figueroa. Mom lets him live like that."

"What do your grandparents say about it? He's their son."

Ima sighed and looked out the window. "They think Corinne walks on water. Peter's crazy, right? But he's living nearby and not in an institution. Corinne keeps him alive—she is a nurse, after all. She knows how to do *that*." Ima shook her head. "You have no idea."

Abby reached over and took Ima's hands. "My life was never simple regardless of what you might think. If you think changing from straight to gay after you've had two kids and been married for twenty-five years is *easy*, you're as crazy as a shithouse mouse yourself."

"Well, it was a nasty divorce. Who could blame you for quitting the other team?"

"You're an idiot."

Ima smiled. For a brief moment, she felt like crying but the moment passed. She kissed Abby's hands. "We're a pair, aren't we?"

"That's what our vows say. You want to take on Corinne, I've got your back. You knock her down and I'll stomp on her."

Ima laughed. "You'll like Papa David. He has a sense of humor like yours."

But Abby never met him. He was dead by the time the train reached Abilene.

◄ May 11 ►

Corinne met them at the station. Ima thought Corinne looked like she was cultivating maturity—fifty-five wasn't old enough to justify it.

Corinne hugged Ima first, kissing her lightly on the cheek. Then, she hugged Abby—to Ima's mind, much more warmly. *No messy mother-daughter baggage here, eh?*

She took Abby's hand and Ima's hand and looked at them both. Corinne drew a deep breath. "Papa David died an hour ago."

Ima felt as if she had been struck. Papa David *dead?* It was always a theoretical possibility. But even now, coming down to see him in the hospital, Ima never thought he might actually *die.* "I thought it was his heart. They can fix hearts."

Corinne shook her head. "That was the initial diagnosis. It turned out he had an asymptomatic tumor that was pushing against the heart—that's what caused the arrhythmia. It ruptured while he was under examination. He bled to death internally before anything could be done."

Ima recoiled. "Jesus. That's horrible."

Corinne shrugged. "It was quick and probably painless."

"Probably?"

"Since he's dead, who's to say?" Corinne led them outside. "Mama Francis is settling funeral arrangements. I have a rental to take us home."

Ima kept thinking about Papa David all the way home.

The family was complex. David and Francis were her grandparents. Nora and Opal, her great-grandparents. Grammy Nora was Francis' mother and Grammy Opal, David's. Both great-grandfathers had died long ago and the Grammies had moved into their own small house in the compound—a refuge for Ima while she was a child. David and Francis in the second. Ima and her mother in a third. After Nora and Opal had died, David had kept up their house but didn't use it.

Ima and Abby were to stay at the Grammyhouse. Without the Grammies, the empty place felt like a museum of the dead. Being inside it now, with all of the crowding memories, was much worse. Ima had fallen off *that* table when she was jumping on the sofa. She fingered the scar next to her eyebrow. How old had she been? Eight? Not much older. Ima thought for a moment. Nora had died when Ima was ten and Opal when Ima had been fifteen. No older than eight.

Ima had needed stitches. Papa David had held one hand and Nora the other as the car had driven them to the emergency room. Opal had met them there. Corinne came into the bay once Ima had been stitched up, stared down at her daughter with obvious disapproval. Corinne was the chief nurse and viewed Abilene Regional as *her* hospital. She had been notified the moment the last bit of sealer had been applied and cured.

Corinne was not a tall woman but she seemed to tower over Ima. Both Grammies and Papa David had seemed to shrink when she entered the room.

"There's no evidence of brain trauma," Corinne said. "You'll have to come back in a week for a follow-up." She looked at the four of them. "Let's go home."

Now, though Ima was taller than Corinne, she still had to stand straighter to *feel* taller. To get that sense of looking down on her mother. To ignore that continuous sense of disapproval. Nora, Opal, and David were all dead. Ima was the last one standing.

Chapter 2.4: John

◄ May 11 ►

That Friday, John didn't stay up watching video but instead searched the net for something to do on Saturday. Something he could do with his wife and child. When he finished, it was too late to get any real sleep. He decided to just stay up and make them breakfast.

Myrna rose first and stumbled out of the bedroom. "You've been out here all night?"

He kissed her. "Yes. Shez made me breakfast on Thursday. I've made you and her breakfast today."

"That's nice," Myrna said sleepily. He put a mug of coffee in front of her as she sat down. She stared at it uncomprehendingly. "Coffee?"

"Yeah. Drink up. We've got a busy day."

John left her there and went to wake Shez.

Shez was already awake and dressed.

He stopped, suddenly hesitant. "Do you have plans today?"

Shez gave him a winning smile. "Nothing I can't cancel. What do you have in mind?"

"Come out to the kitchen."

John grabbed the tablet from the counter and showed them. "The Strawberry Festival is this weekend. It'll be fun. Lots to eat. Rides. A bunch of exhibits."

Myrna stared at the tablet. "Strawberry Festival?"

"A farm festival." John shrugged. "You like strawberries, don't you? They even have strawberry beer. You like beer, don't you?"

"No." Shez grabbed the tablet. "That's a flavor not found in nature."

"Festival?" Myrna looked at John. Then at Shez. "That something you want to do, baby?"

"Sure." Shez smile faltered as she looked at her mother. Then, it returned. "Come on, Mom. It'll be fun."

Myrna looked at her for a long time. "We could rent a bot and remote it. It wouldn't take so much time."

John felt a spike of irritation and suppressed it. "I spend all week doing virtual at the factory," he said quietly. "I thought it would be nice to do something real."

Myrna looked back at John. "Maybe just you and Shez—"

"You've got plans?" John asked.

Myrna started, then shook her head.

Shez took Myrna's hands. "Come on. I got Pops to wake up a little. Now, it's your turn."

John thought he saw a flash of anger on Myrna's face but then it was gone, replaced by resignation. "All right."

"I ordered a shuttle for us. We'll be there in a couple of hours." John brought up the site on the tablet. "It even has videos and games we can choose." He handed it to Myrna.

Myrna passed it to Shez. "Pick something."

It wasn't the most enthusiastic beginning, he thought. But hey. If Shez could make the first step, John could make the second.

For the trip, Shez picked a game they could play on the table. Some kind of strategy game that John didn't quite grasp. The table's active surface showed a broad map of where they marched across some kind of medieval landscape. Different people talked to them or fought them—the table handily translated their body movements into fists and swords. Then, flatted back to a map when they were done.

Myrna didn't play. Instead, she spent time on her tablet or watching out the window. Sometimes she watched Shez. Other times she gave John a brittle smile.

John made himself ignore it.

The Oxnard Strawberry Festival was one of many California harvest festivals. It had rides with a strawberry theme, people costumed as strawberries, and a Strawberry Queen. They tried strawberry beer which Shez pronounced abomination before God and Man. Myrna looked at her and asked how she knew? John changed the subject.

John tried hard. But they couldn't manage to get past a forced gaiety. Sometimes Myrna wouldn't look at him. Other times her glances were speculative. She spoke little and noncommittally. They ate prodigious amounts of strawberry shortcake and strawberry pie and drank strawberry soda, beer, and wine. But John felt as if he were still hungry. Still thirsty.

There was one moment it seemed where things were almost going to work out. A local band had rented out a copy of Dot. When Shez found out she was as excited as if she were six and insisted — *dragged* — them to the stage. Myrna and John shared a moment of parental indulgence.

Dot seemed infinitely patient as the band tried to keep up. But the band fell short and John didn't find the software robot particularly convincing. Her short hair and giant eyes made John think of fish.

Shez looked close to tears. She kept muttering to herself, "She's not like this. She's *not* like this."

Myrna put her arm around Shez. John kept trying to figure out the big deal.

The next morning, John woke up early. He was alone, feeling vaguely alarmed until he heard movement in the living room.

Myrna was there, bags packed on the floor, writing a note. She looked up at him. "You're awake."

John looked at the bags and back at Myrna, a deep dull ache inside him. He found himself unsurprised. That made it hurt more. "You're leaving."

"It's not working, John." Myrna shook her head. "It hasn't worked for a long time."

"I can get a day shift."

"What would that change?" She sighed and straightened, leaving the note unfinished.

John felt an immense, ponderous weight sink down onto him. As if gravity had changed. Myrna looked light to him, weightless as air. He sat down, wondering if the chair would collapse beneath him.

"I'll talk to you in a few days," Myrna said.

He could see Myrna was shedding the same weight that held him down. He wanted to ask if there was somebody else. Ask what he could do. Beg her to stay. Plead with her. But he was too heavy. He could only nod.

With that, she picked up her weightless bag, nodded her weightless head, and left the room. John heard the door close behind her.

There was a bottle on the table. John picked it up and drank from it. It seemed the only thing that made the weight bearable.

Chapter 2.5: Ima

The *tsuya*—the vigil over the dead—could not be held for three days. This gave time for people to get to Abilene for the ceremony. Papa David had friends from his pilot days in the Air Force. From his twenty years writing human and AI pilot training programs after he'd retired from the Air Force. From the years he and Francis traveled after that. Some of those friends had never met him in the flesh and their first sight of David unmediated by electrons was him lying in state, carefully made to look asleep below an enshrined picture showing a hideous forced grin. There were even a few proxy bots wandering the crowd for those people who couldn't attend in person. A small pile of envelopes, bordered in black and silver, were placed elegantly on one table. Ima knew from both Grammy Nora's and Grammy Opal's funeral that they contained condolence money.

The priest had been brought in from San Antonio. After he'd said his sutras and performed the rituals, he retired to a hotel in town. Tomorrow there would be the actual funeral.

As the guests left, there remained only the four of them: Corinne, Abby, Francis, and Ima. Corinne watched Ima. Ima knew Corinne expected her to stay up with the body.

Ima was sick of it. She looked over at Abby.

Abby picked up immediately and made excuses, drawing Ima away under the pretext she needed Ima's help. Corinne nodded coldly. Had Abby not been there, Corinne would have gutted Ima like a fish. But not in front of outsiders.

Back in the Grammies' house, the two of them sat on the sofa.

"She's rough," commented Abby.

Ima quelled a reflexive defensive reaction. "Yeah." She took off her shoes and rubbed her feet.

"I didn't see your father," said Abby in a quiet voice.

Ima stopped rubbing. "You're right." Ima had grown so used to not seeing her father around, she had forgotten him in the stress of Papa David's death. What kind of person did that make her?

Then, she thought of Peter in skins lighting incense in front of Papa David's casket. Ima shook her head. Propriety dictated that Peter, as the only son, would make the arrangements and God knows how *that* would have gone. Corinne loved propriety. Corinne must have forbidden him to come.

Still, Ima would have expected that Peter would have shown up to sit with the body.

The next day Ima looked without success for her father at the funeral. Then, at the crematorium. No Peter.

Oh my God, she thought.

On the way back, she and Mama Francis shared the same car. When they were alone and the car was whirring its automated self back to the houses, Ima turned to Mama Francis.

"You didn't tell Daddy."

Mama Francis continued to watch outside the window. "Your mother thought the stress might be too much for him."

"Keeping him out of the… the *festivities* I understand. But not *telling* him." Ima snorted. "What are you going to do when he comes back to take a shower or something and asks about his father."

"He does not do that. He barely speaks to us now."

Ima stared where her grandmother was looking. It was just storefronts and strip malls. "You still should have told him."

"Then you do it." Mama Francis turned to Ima. "You won't find him if he doesn't want you to."

◄ May 15 ►

Hot Texas in May was the place where sweat went to die. Ima felt like she was drowning in a salty sea. She longed to be back in California where sweat actually worked. Peter wasn't in his shack.

Ima watched for snakes. It had been fifteen years since she walked around here. *Great*, Ima thought. *I'll get bit by a snake and die looking for my crazy father.*

Ima kept thinking about her grandmother saying she wouldn't find Peter if Peter didn't want to be found. It wasn't hard to find him. He had tied bits of plastic to the trees and bushes to mark his trail. Since Ima was the only one looking for him, she figured they were for her.

She found Peter in a dry wash near the river, quietly watching a huge live oak. Two huge vultures perched in the trees. Two more were on the ground, digging into a dead whitetail deer. Peter saw her and waved her over, indicating she be quiet. *Watching vultures. Typical.*

Then, for a brief moment, it was like when she was young and Peter showed her something wonderful: an armadillo. The saw-tooth mouth of a coyote skull. A rattlesnake watching them intently until it could escape.

Ima crouched next to him.

Peter pointed out the vultures to her. "California condors. The two on the ground are the young. The ones in the tree the parents. The nest is down in the river bluffs." His voice held a suppressed excitement. "I've been watching them for three years now. This is as far east as condors get. Come fall, they drift back west." Absently, he drank from a water bottle and passed it to Ima. She sipped absently.

He pointed at the parents. "I think they originally came out of New Mexico. Dying must be good for something if it can fill the belly of a condor."

It was so hot that her sense of smell must have died. Peter didn't stink nearly as bad as she remembered.

Ima pulled gently at his arm. "Come on back. I need to talk to you."

Reluctantly, Peter turned away from the condors.

The shack was crammed with skins being cured, a disintegrating poster from some indiscernible rock concert, a mattress stuffed with rags. A rifle and bow, both incongruously clean, hung on the wall. Christmas lights draped the rafters, the plugs hanging in the air. Peter had no electricity.

Her sense of smell came back full force: those curing skins *stank*.

Ima sat in the only chair. Peter sat nervously on the bed. "I have some jerky left."

Eating here? Ima felt nauseous. "No thanks."

"I could make some tea."

Ima shook her head.

Peter's gaze wandered the room. "I've been following Mehitable and Grunt for three years—"

"Mehitable and Grunt."

"The parent condors. The kids are Lois and Lana—both females." He turned towards her. "Lois and Lana come from Superman." He looked around the room again, eyes lighting here and there seemingly at random. "Mehitable and Grunt migrated here from the west. They produced two eggs." Peter held up his two fingers. "Two. Highly unusual. The four of them flew back east when the winter came. Then, they came back this year. All four of them. The parents haven't found a nest site yet—the old nest was in a power line tower on the other side of town. They didn't rebuild it—something wrong with it, I guess. They'll find a new site soon. I hope." He shrugged.

"Daddy," said Ima gently.

"Or they'll leave. New World vultures evolved from a different bird than Old World vultures—they look alike but they're completely unrelated."

"Daddy."

"Both old world and new world vultures exhibit urohydrolysis— they pee on their legs to cool off."

"*Daddy!*"

Peter looked at her irritably. "What? I'm crazy, not stupid. I know why you're here. Papa's dead. I get it. I was hoping to get some father/daughter time out of the deal."

"With vultures?"

"Sure." He grinned at her. "What else is there?"

"How did you know?"

Peter looked uncomfortable. "I could tell. People wandering around the house dressed in black—nobody dresses like that in Texas this time of year unless they're forced to. Everybody sad. Everybody carrying black and silver envelopes—like when the Grammies died." He leaned forward. "I was a kid when my great grandfather died. We went all the way to San Francisco. Nora. Opal. My parents. Everybody there spoke Japanese. Not just the priest. *Everybody.*"

It was too much for her. She stood up. "I came out to tell you but you already knew."

Peter stood up. "Father/daughter time over." With that, he left the shack and walked away back towards the vultures.

Ima stared after him. She had no idea what she should feel. *If I get back to California intact, I am never coming back here. Ever.*

Chapter 2.6: John

There were a lot of drugs available over the counter for what ailed John. Anti-depressants, mood elevators, focussants. With a prescription, there were drugs to help you feel your emotions. Drugs to help you express them. Drugs to suppress them. There were elixirs that put painful memories at a distance so it seemed like they happened to someone else. Potions that brought them into such sharp relief that one could count the pores on someone's face. Drafts so powerful that one could rewrite memories. Did she dump you? Well, with Lethesin, you will have dumped *her!*

John thought about them all, standing in the pharmacy department of the WalMex. Instead, he walked past the counters, through the produce section to liquor.

This is right, he thought. *This is traditional.* The notice of separation had come that afternoon. When a woman leaves a man, he's supposed to drink. Not that John needed any excuse. He stood before shelves of every imaginable liquor. From Borneo's Decadent Cocoanutto to Shanghai's Finest Baijo. The finest of pain relievers and all available to him for a small fee. The labels glittered and flashed. Women silently danced across some labels, sang silently on others. Men gave him a knowing glance or leaned back in a magnificent sexual afterglow. Other labels showed silent party fireworks. A precious few bottles were labeled with mere paper but the rest were clothed in silent gaudy movies telling him he would be a man, stand tall, get laid, if he would only buy just this one bottle.

He bought a fifth of Jack Daniels. On the label, Jack himself nodded that this was the correct and only choice. The state of California insisted on actual cashiers in the liquor department so John put the bottle on the counter. It beeped, debiting his account instantly. Had he purchased groceries, drugs, or toys, he could have walked out of the store, payment made automatically. Only liquor purchases had such antique laws.

The man behind the counter knew he was completely superfluous. John felt he was, too.

Hell. All men were superfluous. If John learned nothing else, he should learn that. Useful to deliver a paycheck. When that was no longer needed, they were gone.

John looked in the bag. Jack leered back at him. John pointed at the label. "How come they don't talk?"

The man shrugged. "State regulation. I understand the labels yell at you in Missouri. Go figure."

John cracked open the bottle as the car drove him home. He tapped the dashboard in salute. If he was worth more, he might have a car of his own. As it was, he shared the car in a pool. Was that one of the reasons Myrna had left? Did John make too little money? He had a sudden memory of an exhibit of old twentieth-century ads at a museum—he couldn't have been more than ten. Image of a man in emotional agony and shame. A woman—obviously his wife—screaming at him. Behind her a broken washing machine with water pouring out. Crying children holding on to her dress. In large letters: "If I'd married Harold, I'd have a *Maytag!*"

John took a swig from the bottle. Myrna hadn't said but John was absolutely certain there was someone else waiting for her when she finally left. The signs were all there: she had quit waiting up for him. Long moments when she paid unnatural attention to her phone. Saturday mornings when she came through the door after running some unspecified errand just as he was waking.

The signs were just confirmation. John knew that Myrna would never jump ship without a place to land. It wasn't in her.

John took another swallow. He wondered what this person was like. Probably male—Myrna had never shown much interest in women. Of course, if she hid that, John wouldn't see it, would he? That would feel like a relief. After all, if a person changed their life so radically, didn't that mean the life they were living wasn't right for them? It wouldn't be *John's* fault. It was just the accumulation of little difficulties. Tiny, incremental deviations from the life she was supposed to have until the distance between what she needed and what she had was so great she needed a major change.

Of course, you could say the same thing about any change. Maybe it was John who wasn't right for her. She'd tried to make it work for twenty years and one day the effort was too much.

That would make it completely John's fault.

Jack nodded sagely as John looked down at the bottle's label. That's right, Jack. You've seen it all. A century or more of being final company to a lonely, bitter husband.

The car pulled into the driveway and John got out and closed the door.

The car gave a faint beep, backed out of the driveway, and disappeared down the street.

John looked at his house: a rundown ranch from the same period as that ad. His grandfather had left it to John's father who left it to John. Housing prices made it almost impossible to move. Oh, John could sell it in a heartbeat. Someone would come in and flatten it and build a new modern house like most of the ones on this street. But John couldn't buy another with what he could get. He'd have to move out of state.

Shez was sitting in the living room with a stack of paper on the cushion next to her and a pile of folded paper on the floor.

"What the hell?" John reached down and picked one up. It vaguely resembled a bird with wings and a tail. A sort of paper stick figure.

"It's a crane," Shez said, finishing another one.

"It's paper."

"Origami. Japanese folding paper art."

"Origami," John repeated. "What are you doing creating a fire hazard like this?"

Shez looked up at him and John could tell she knew instantly he'd been drinking. Would have known even if he didn't have a bottle in his hand.

"I'm making a thousand cranes," she said. "The Japanese believe if you fold a thousand cranes you get a wish. We could use some good luck."

"What would your wish be?"

She flashed a glance at him. "I'm still thinking about it."

The weight of it all seemed insurmountable. He wanted nothing more than to lie down. "Aren't you supposed to be at school?"

"Aren't you supposed to be at work?"

Yeah. *That.* "I'm going to lie down."

"Wake you for dinner?"

"Sure. Whatever."

◄ May 20 ►

Neoforms was a contract fabrication house. A client could file designs across the net and the factory would determine which of the many and varied printer, cutting, and assembly systems were required. Essentially, a design came in by net and a finished product set sent out—a general-purpose factory. Like most general-purpose systems (such as humans) it was not as efficient as a specialized system. But it was quick and flexible and good for putting together a proof of concept, a prototype, or a set of boutique products.

Neoforms had two factories: Singapore and Bakersfield. The two factories existed for regulatory rather than technical reasons.

John was one of eight backup humans at the Bakersfield facility: two each shift, rotating for weekends and holidays. The machines didn't always align properly, or reagents were contaminated, or thermistors needed replacing. John was cheaper than a similarly flexible robot. Most of the time John's shift would be uneventful.

This hadn't been true when he started. The first couple of years after the opening of the factory had been exciting. Something went wrong every shift and John had had to figure out how to get things running again and the products out on time.

But each time a subsystem failed or went out of spec, there'd be an analysis and a modification: that particular problem now had an automated solution.

Much of John's time was spent the same way he marked time until he could sleep. Surfing the net. Reading. Watching videos. The only difference was he couldn't drink or watch porn at work.

John had stayed in the bedroom, drinking, until only a couple of hours before his shift. He staggered through the doors, uncaring.

Renny was already there in the main control room. "Jesus, John, you smell like a distillery."

John shrugged and sat in the other chair.

Renny watched him. "I should report you."

"Go ahead."

"What's wrong?"

"Myrna left. This is what you do when your wife leaves. You drink. Isn't that the way it should be? 'Nothing a little bourbon and soda couldn't fix.'" John shook his head and looked at Renny. "Bourbon tastes *terrible*."

"I wouldn't know. I don't drink."

John waved him off. "Has your wife ever left you?"

"I'm not married."

"Then you are in no position to criticize."

Renny looked around. "They record us all the time."

"Yeah. I know." John pointed at one of the black globes on the ceiling. "But they never look at the recordings unless there's a fuckup and there hasn't been a fuckup in a year."

"It could happen tonight."

"No. It won't." John tapped the console. "She's foolproof. By that, I mean she is proof against fools like us." Then, he didn't feel well. "I'll be right back.

It took forty minutes for John to empty. Afterward, he leaned over the sink and washed his face. Washed his hands and the parts of his shirt and pants he'd splattered.

With enormous amounts of coffee, he managed to make it through the rest of his shift. John was prophetic: nothing happened.

Chapter 2.7: Ima

Two weeks after the Bakersfield concert the consumer analysis began to show statistical changes. There was a general depression of consumer purchases. Some reductions were surprising. Porn dropped significantly. Luxury items dropped a small but statistically significant amount. An increase in the consumption of factual news and data and a slight drop in manufactured data.

Ima wanted to clap her hands as she looked at the numbers. True: they were not what she expected. The looked-for increase in child porn or other direct representations of the Dot metaphor wasn't there. But *any* substantial change was good. It indicated the possibility of lasting change. The direction of the change was unimportant—once it was characterized and understood, that direction could be modified.

Mulcahey had promised an official recording suite of the Bakersfield concert later today. Ima had already created several network agents to follow anybody who accessed it. It was unlikely there would be any effect—previous studies of the released Dot recordings hadn't shown more than a blip. Dotheads bought them like communion wafers. Aficionados bought a lesser number and there was the scattering of purchases by novel users. Recordings never showed any significant consumer effect.

Corinne called.

Ima stared at the blinking icon for a moment. Did she even want to answer?

Finally, she thumbed it and Corinne's face popped up in a window. Corinne smiled. "Hello, Ima."

"Hi, Mom," said Ima cautiously. "What's going on?"

"Francis and I are working through David's estate. We've decided that we can afford to put Peter in an institution."

Ima stared at her. "I thought you didn't want him in an institution."

Corinne gave her *that* look. "I can't imagine what gave you that idea."

"You did. Over the years. In multiple conversations."

Corinne shook her head. "It was Papa David that wouldn't allow it. I merely acquiesced to him."

Ima stared at her. She had never seen anyone lie that brazenly. It shook her. *Maybe I misunderstood.* No. That way lies madness. She had seen what she had seen. She had heard what she had heard. Corinne had *never* wanted Peter off the property. Until now.

"Mama Francis agreed to this?"

"Of course. She's always wanted Peter to get help."

There was something in the estate. Some benefit. Ima had disliked her mother for years. But this feeling was new. Could she be learning to *hate* her mother?

Really, though. Did it make any difference? This was a way to get help for Peter. He didn't have any use for the estate except as a place to watch his vultures. Ima could get a pack of long-term drones for him. Small, very quiet ones. No bigger or noisier than a hummingbird. "What do you need me for?"

"He's your father, Ima. You have a say in this."

Meaning she doesn't want me to fight it. I might win.

But Ima *didn't* want that fight. If she won, she'd have to take care of Peter—which meant some kind of institution. Or maybe a half-way house.

"Just a moment." Ima invoked her binding software. A few seconds later, the channel was secured with the *Bonded Channel* symbol beneath.

Corinne looked down with distaste. "Is that really necessary?"

Ima spoke slowly. A contract is only as good as the encrypted electrons that record it. "I give any necessary permission to get Peter Hidori the care he needs for his mental illness." The software listed notices of jurisdiction and associated limitations and legal frameworks. "What is your reply?"

"This is beneath you," Corinne said.

Ima watched the panel below Corinne's image, looking for the indicator that sufficient data had been exchanged to warrant a binding contract.

"You have to say the words, Mom."

"I accept your permissions."

Ima watched as the software on her end negotiated with the matching software on Corinne's end. The icon flashed green: the contract had been made and registered.

Ima exhaled. "Thanks, Mom."

But she was talking to an empty window. Corinne had hung up.

Chapter 2.8: John

Unknown to either Renny or John, an automaton examined every on-shift recording. It was a simple learning system rather than a true AI, trained to look for warning signs in robot operational tracks, aberrations in fabrication specifications, and human behavior. John's gait, articulation, and time in the bathroom were compared with a rolling average of the same behavior over the previous three years. Deviations were noticed and accumulated. When a threshold was crossed, the data was passed up the chain.

Neoforms was still a small company. There weren't many layers between John and the top. So, when Alisi Setoga, founder and CEO of Neoforms, called him, it was not that much of a surprise.

"Hey, John," said Alisi.

It was the middle of his shift—three o'clock in the afternoon, California time. Eight in the morning, Hong Kong time.

"Good morning."

Alisi smiled at him. She was a big woman and the smile seemed exaggerated. Forced. "Wanted to make sure I caught up with you."

John didn't like the sound of that. "What can I do for you?"

"You can stop drinking on the job, for one thing," Alisi said comfortably. "Or I'll have to fire your ass."

John blinked. "I see."

"I like you, John. I like how you've always been there when we had troubles. I like how you put up with doing nothing on your shift when the systems take care of themselves. If it were up to me, I'd have you on call at full salary and you'd only have to come in if there was an actual problem or for training." Alisi shrugged. "But state regulations require otherwise. Even so, you can't work out your personal problems on the job."

"You can't just fire me—"

Alisi shook her head. "Yes, I can. Employee protection only goes so far and you walked right off the end. So: get sober or get out. You have two weeks."

Then, John was staring at a blank screen.

Renny was watching him from across the room. "Told you, man."

"You told her?" John said angrily.

Renny shook his head. "Didn't have to, man." He pointed at the camera bubbles in the ceiling, "Told you: they watch everything. *Somebody* looks over the recordings. Now, you know."

Chapter 2.9: Ima

◄ June 6 ►

Ippon had its own bureaucracy.

First, there were the three corporate entities: Ippon Heavy Industry, Ippon Finance, and Ippon Data.

Ippon Data had three main divisions: Ippon Information Technology, Ippon Computer Manufacturing, Ippon Robotics. Under IIT came Ippon Software. Under Ippon Software came the Ippon Public Services Group which contained the Ippon Persuasion Division. Ippon Robotics had always claimed that Dot should be under them, since she was, in fact, a robot. Public Services insisted she was a service they represented mostly to the public sector. Dot was advertising and advertising was part of Persuasion.

Persuasion was led by a man named Robert Farrell. To get any movement up the chain, Ima had to first convince him she had something worthy of his attention.

The next Dot 2.0 concert was in Fresno in late June—only two weeks away. Murdock and Paternos kept her advised how the set up proceeded—including the title of the tour. *Walkabout.* Why a tour needed a name was beyond her. But if that's what Mulcahey wanted it was all right with her.

Two weeks was barely enough lead time for *anything.*

Ima poured over the consumer statistics carefully. The effects were holding on without much attenuation. *Lasting effect!*

Enough time had passed that all of the concert attendees had been identified and their subsequent media consumption habits measured to do group comparisons.

Dotheads were determined by the number of concerts the consumer had already attended and measurements detailing how much effort the consumer would expend to attend one. Aficionados were similarly detected: they liked Dot and would attend if it was convenient or inexpensive. Novel attendees had never been to a Dot concert. The media consumption of the three groups backed up this categorization. Dotheads' musical taste was largely Dot music or something similar. Aficionados consumed a fair amount of Dot music but with more variety. Novel attendee musical consumption contained little or no Dot music.

After any Dot concert, there was play between the groups. Some Dotheads transitioned into aficionados and attended less. Some novel attendees moved into either the Dothead or aficionado group or were left unaffected. All measured by changes in media consumption until confirmed by the next concert.

This categorized the outgoing analysis into a similar three categories: attendees who became Dotheads, attendees who became aficionados, and attendees who remained unaffected. The statistical transitions were well known. Dotheads and aficionados made up the bulk of the concert population. Half of the novel attendees remained unaffected and the affected novels rarely moved beyond aficionado. Most people who experienced Dot for the first time didn't repeat. Surveys showed they liked the experience well enough. Just not enough to repeat it without incentives.

Analysis of the transitions suggested that it was less the Dot experience than the experience of the concert itself that caused these transitions. Dot was an enabling technology for a sense of community, shared friendships, and a sense of belonging. Dot, and the performance engine, were useful but not overwhelming—hence the need for social media and target advertising to get any lasting effect. Dot was the experimental apparatus, not the goal itself.

But the Bakersfield numbers were strange.

Unlike other Dot concerts, the attrition of Dotheads to any other category was close to zero—usually, there were *some* Dotheads tired of her. The transition from aficionado to Dothead was high—close to forty percent. Usually, this was less than ten.

What was really exciting was the number of remaining unaffected novel attendees was unusually low: less than twenty percent. Bakersfield novel attendees transitioned into aficionados or Dotheads at a high rate.

The first numbers from the concert footage release were now available. Ima looked them over. There was some effect—not as great as the concerts but statistically significant. It suggested Dot 2.0 herself had a strong effect beyond the communal concert experience. Very interesting.

But it was only one concert.

The upcoming Fresno concert would confirm or deny these results. Ima wrote purchase orders for attendee monitor time, sent instructions to Murdock and Paternos to commission some new surveys. Then, she roughed out some queries to be used when the numbers were available.

Ima leaned back from her tablet and stretched. She couldn't do anything more today. She got up from the table and padded around the kitchen. When Abby was at the grocery, Ima did most of her work in the kitchen. She moved to her office before Abby came home. The Culver City office was merely a meeting place and clearinghouse.

Her tablet gave a faint chime.

Ima took it back to her office. Anywhere else, she could ask the room to open a surface and the window would show who was calling. But one of their compromises was to confine automation to the tablets and Ima's office. There were no active surfaces anywhere in the house except her office—Abby found them a distraction.

Once in her office, Ima looked at the tablet. Her father's face blinked back at her.

"Answer it, Hannah," she said to the tablet AI. "Put it on the wall."

Peter stared at her so long she thought the image was frozen. "Hello," he said slowly and deliberately.

"Hi, Daddy."

Again, he said nothing for a moment. It was like talking to someone on the moon.

"I'm in…" His voice faded and his face creased in thought. "Good Hope Institute."

"Hannah. Trace that." A moment later, below Peter's image, came: *Good Hope Institute and Treatment Center. Specializes in the long-term care of addicts, psychotics, and brain trauma victims. San Antonio, Texas.* What the hell was Peter doing in San Antonio? There had to be perfectly good treatment centers in Abilene. Hannah gave Good Hope high ratings. Maybe Corinne put him in the best one she could find.

"Take me home," said Peter with some effort. "Please."

His face was wooden. He brushed his hand over his hair slowly. His hand trembled. He stopped and held out the hand and stared at the tremors. "It's the Lumadine."

"Hannah. Identify."

Lumadine: antipsychotic. Used as first-line therapy for severe psychotics to encourage suggestibility. Followed by more precise medication based on diagnosis.

Peter's gaze slowly moved back to see her. "Ima. Please."

They've got to be helping him, she told herself desperately. No hospital would just feed him drugs for no reason.

"It'll be good for you, Daddy," she said. It hurt to see him like this. "Just listen to the doctors."

Peter shook his head ponderously. Then, he seemed to lose focus, staring off to one side. He shook himself and looked back at her.

"Ima?" he said querulously. "Did you call me?"

Ima wanted to cry. "No, Daddy. You called me."

Peter nodded, unsurprised. He seemed more present now. "It's too quiet here," he said vaguely. "No birds. No animals. Not even the wind. Quiet."

"I'll send you something."

Peter nodded again. Kept nodding for a moment past when he should have stopped. It gave him a bobblehead look. He stopped himself with an effort. "It's the Lumidine."

"Yes." Ima wanted to reach through the screen and hug him.

"Bye." And he disappeared.

Ima sat, both hands flat on the table. "Hannah. Send him a copy of the Dot recordings." It was not the sound of the wild but it was something and it came from her. She'd pull more together when she could. Maybe lease some drones to keep watch over Peter's vultures — or were they still there? *Check on that.* "And get Corinne. Record the call."

Ima had time to make coffee and calm herself before Corinne made it to the phone.

"Yes," said Corinne.

"I just got a call from Peter."

"He's called me, too."

"He looks terrible."

"Yes," said Corinne. "He's sick in a hospital. He's *supposed* to look terrible." She cocked her head. "Did you think he'd be cured overnight?"

Ima checked her immediate response. Took a deep breath. "What is his status?"

"He's a guest of the Good Hope—"

"What is his *legal* status?"

Corinne stopped and paused for a moment. "Thirty-day observation on an involuntary commitment."

"He didn't want to go."

"Of *course*, he didn't want to go. Did you think he wanted treatment all these years? Think again. He's had to have treatment *forced* on him."

Ima shook her head. This was just too much. "What happens in thirty days?"

"He'll be found incompetent. Then, he'll start undergoing long term treatment. What did you think would happen?"

"I thought they'd be able to help him."

"They will. He's been crazy a long time. That will take a while to unwind. That means we need legal control of him. Hence, involuntary commitment. If they happen onto a successful therapy in thirty days, he goes into outpatient. But you've spoken with him. How likely is *that?*" Corinne gave Ima a disgusted look. "I swear you live in your own world. Did you think this would be easy? Did you think he'd wake up normal the night after taking a pill?"

"I thought you'd be there for him. Not a hundred miles away."

Corrine looked at Ima scornfully. "*I'm* a hundred miles away! You're a thousand. I can have him transferred to Rancho Park. That's not far from you. You can handle it all."

Ima looked away and without answering.

Corinne snorted. "I didn't think so. Talk to your father when he calls. I've been told normal interaction is always helpful."

Corinne disappeared.

Ima stared out the window into Abby's tiny orchard. She felt furious, trapped, and helpless in a cage.

◀ June 6 ▶

Abby listened sympathetically as Ima raged from one side of the kitchen to the other.

"Do you want to transfer him to Rancho Park?" Abby asked as Ima wound down. "It's only twenty minutes away. We could manage."

Ima felt herself shrink from the idea. "I'm too busy to take care of him. Besides, he's never lived out here. At least San Antonio is a little bit like Abilene. It's in Texas. The weather is the same."

"Flimsy, love." Abby rose from the kitchen table and kissed Ima on the forehead. "Flimsy. Face it, Ima. Your father's crazy and your mother is as cold as a codfish." Abby tapped Ima on the nose. "Her point is you want him properly taken care of but *you* don't want to be responsible for it. I say Corinne's doing the job. Let her. Just don't let her scorn take care of *you*." She took Ima's hand and started leading her towards the bedroom.

Ima instinctively drew back.

Abby stopped and looked at her. "Good sex reaffirms life and love. It's therapeutic."

Ima laughed and followed her to the bedroom.

Chapter 2.10: John

For a couple of weeks, John carefully kept his drinking out of the factory. Shez said little and the mesh bag of cranes gradually filled out.

One Friday night, he was watching porn after Shez had gone to bed. It was amazing how little it affected him. When he was a young man, he couldn't watch porn for more than the three minutes he required. Now, he watched it without even wanting to touch himself. Porn had degenerated from titillation to some sick kind of comfort food.

He wondered what Myrna was doing.

John turned off the porn feed and started searching for her. He served up his credit card to an online image search app, selecting the lowest search level. He waited for an hour, refreshing every few minutes. Then, he realized it would take longer than that. He turned off the lights and went to bed.

The next morning the app had an address.

It was a little apartment near the university. John drove by it on the way to work. He drove past it on the way home. Nothing. He started stopping there on the way home from work, when it was dark.

Myrna worked at Pacific Satisfaction, a local contract fulfillment center, helping to box up packages and shuttle them in the remaining human niche between robots. It always amazed John that no matter how hard they tried, designers could never quite get away from needing monkey hands—including his own. This was how she and John had met. John had been a repair technician for the company that serviced the fulfillment robots before he had managed to qualify for the job at Neoforms.

Myrna had worked for PS long enough that she could stay on the day shift. These were the sorts of benefits that PS granted to make sure unions were unwelcome. Myrna had mentioned more than once that her benefits would disappear the day that PS decided unions were no longer a threat. John didn't believe her. He thought the jobs paid enough and had just enough benefits to balance the cost of retraining someone new. He never said this to Myrna.

Since he knew Myrna did not work the night shift, he watched to see if she stayed at the apartment. Sometimes he saw her there. Sometimes he didn't. Many times, he couldn't tell. He bought a cheap feed that watched her door—probably a hacked traffic cam. But he only saw her entering and leaving. There was never anyone with her.

This gave him a little hope but he felt like he was fooling himself. There was *no way* Myrna would leave him without a parachute. They were in the mandatory separation phase now. John could tell Myrna was marking time until the time elapsed and she could file for divorce. There was no question of custody—Shez would be eighteen before any court custody battle could ever be fought. Then, visitation would be up to her. Myrna had to be keeping things quiet so that Shez would want to see her voluntarily.

There were some nights the feed showed Myrna returning at first light, inside just long enough for a shower and some breakfast, and out again for work. It made John feel sick inside.

◄ June 15 ►

John stepped up the level of the surveillance app—using money he didn't have. He wanted to know who it was.

About four in the morning two days later, he woke up feeling groggy but sober. A mark, he thought sourly, of his increased ability to metabolize alcohol. No doubt a sign of alcoholism. Wonderful. Not only had his wife left him, his child wouldn't talk to him, his job was in jeopardy, but it looked like he might have a drug dependency. He celebrated with the remaining couple of shots in a brand-new Jack Daniels bottle. Jack approved.

He found his way back to the living room. The active surface showed the app's results: images found. A grayed sheaf of recognizable Myrna profiles was hazily visible. The app showed him the first one: Myrna outside a restaurant, laughing, a shadowy figure by her side. The figure was unrecognizable. At least, it was unrecognizable until John upped the search level and the cost.

The figure could not be identified in the first images but later images showed more—John could almost recognize him. There was an enhancement option. For an additional fee, the app would take all of the selected portions of the image (i.e., the shadowy figure) and oversample them, generating a distinct image from many fuzzy ones. John paid. A few seconds later, the app presented its best attempt at reconstruction.

It was Renny.

◄ June 18 ►

He spent the entire weekend drunk, lying in the bedroom staring at the walls. He left only to get more alcohol—Jack Daniels because he liked the way the label looked knowingly at him—and to scrounge for food. He didn't eat much.

Shez tried to stop him but John's bitter, empty stare defeated her and she fled.

Good, he thought. John didn't know where she went. John didn't care.

It was not that alcohol promoted clarity—it did not. John knew that. His difficulty formulating even simple ideas when he was drunk would have proven that even if he hadn't already known it. Nor did alcohol dampen the pain or the anger. If anything, alcohol magnified them. What alcohol did was sharpen these things. To etch a clear boundary around what had been done to him. Extraneous thoughts and feelings—his love for Myrna. His love for Shez. Thoughts of consequences. An understanding of what Myrna must have been going through all these years—were masked and only the outrage of what had been done to him remained.

Sunday night, he stopped drinking. He would need his wits about him. Monday morning, he washed and showered. Shez was nowhere to be seen.

Towards lunchtime, he sat at the kitchen table and worked it through. He knew from Alisi's call that the Neoforms plant was monitored. There was no reason to believe an actual human was checking each recording. More likely, it was an automaton that did the observation and analysis. John knew how low-level systems like that worked: they were trained to watch long term behavior and look for aberrations. That was how he'd been tripped up: he'd acted out of the ordinary and in ways that the system had been instructed to watch for: drunks. Drug addicts. Abusers—the automation was probably sensitive to a whole suite of tells.

So, to murder Renny (a solution he'd come to while drunk Saturday night but found nothing to argue against it in the sober light of day) he would have to enter the factory normally and without tells. He would have to bring in a weapon that could be masked as a normal object. Neoforms didn't have a high level of security but they had enough to detect a gun or a knife.

John rummaged around in the garage and found a jump rope with handles. He shortened the rope to a convenient length. It would not show up in detectors and, if he kept his face straight and didn't act strange, he would be overlooked until he was done. Afterward was afterward.

He was sitting at the table going over everything: the jump rope. Wallet and keys. Phone. Working his mind over how to look when he got to work. How to walk. How to act.

He heard the front door open and a scraping sound.

Shez entered the kitchen dragging a trash can. It was filled with paper.

She shoveled the paper on him with her hands. When the level was low enough, she lifted the can and dumped it over his head.

Paper cranes cascaded over him, into his lap. On his face. Onto the table. Into his shirt. On his shoulders. It was a foot deep on the floor.

"*There!*" Shez yelled at him. "Over a thousand cranes. See? Eleven hundred and twenty-nine. You got that?"

John stared at her, down at the cranes, back at her. Back at the cranes. Some were made of beautifully patterned paper. Others were made of lined notebook pages. Some had ragged edges torn from a spiral binder. Others had holes punched in the sides. There were cranes the size of two fists. Cranes the size of John's thumb. Cranes the size of the first knuckle of his little finger. Cranes as rough as crows. Cranes as delicate as hummingbirds. He had a sudden vision of Shez folding crane after crane. Day after day. Hour after hour. Holding together her entire life with tiny scraps of paper.

"I get a wish, God damn it!" She shook her finger in her face. "I get one God damned wish!"

John stared into her face. It was mottled, patchy with rage and fear. He looked at the cranes and back at her. "Name it," he said quietly.

"There's a Dot concert in Fresno the day after tomorrow. We're going."

Push off killing Renny? John looked at the cranes on the table. In his lap. The jump rope felt bulky in his pocket. "All right."

Without the force of impending murder to keep him focused, John returned to going to work drunk. It lasted one day. Alisi called him on Tuesday and fired him. Simple. Declarative. Don't bother returning your ID cards. They were already deactivated. Just throw them away.

Chapter 2.11: Ima

The Fresno concert was a huge success. The Bakersfield numbers were not only confirmed but nearly doubled. There was a big increase in novel attendees and nearly all of them transitioned into either aficionados or Dotheads. People were bringing their friends and their friends wanted to repeat the experience.

Ima left the kitchen and worked exclusively in her office. Soon, she would have to give a presentation to Farrell. But she was still in the duck lining stage. She ran Johann and Mohammed relentlessly. A few days after the concert, she had real numbers showing reproducible, lasting effect.

Ima barely saw Abby in the week running up to the concert and the week after. Quick dinners and drinks were all Ima could manage.

When she felt he had enough data to start writing a presentation, she came out of her office.

Abby was sipping tea in the kitchen. "Going well?"

"You have no idea!" Ima rummaged in the cabinet and pulled out a bottle of Champagne.

Abby looked surprised. "We had that?"

"I've been saving it."

"For a *long* while."

"Yes." Ima popped the cork and poured the Champagne into jelly glasses.

Abby held it up. "What are we celebrating?"

"A long shot. A breakthrough. The next step in persuasion."

"I see," said Abby. She sipped her Champagne. "What is this breakthrough? A new method of advertising?"

"Oh, no. This is a breakthrough in *persuasion*."

"What's the difference?"

Ima thought for a moment. "Advertising is when you join a product or symbolic association of a product to an image and hope people will like the product or the association enough to buy it. Persuasion is when you make the connections in people's mind and people buy the product, or the idea, or the candidate because of those connections."

"They sound the same."

"The *goal* is the same. The technique is different. Advertising finds a homogenous group of people holding a particular set of attitudes amenable to the goal. Then, bombards them with a statistically favorable set of images: women. Men. Chinese white-collar workers in Nigeria. *Persuasion* targets a set of *traits* that can comprise a collection of one to many individuals and *molds* those traits in the desired direction."

Abby blinked. "I don't get the difference."

Ima thought for a moment. "Let's say I have a candidate running for office. If I'm in advertising, I look for a population of people that could support him. I narrow them down by demographics, income level, location and tailor several ads in multiple markets to motivate them to vote for my candidate. If I'm in persuasion for that same candidate, I look for traits that incline people to vote for him. Then, I dispatch a set of agents to track the evidence of the traits and engineer targeted ads, rumors, and social media articles that encourage those *attitudes*. Monitoring those attitudes to see if they gain favor. Then, when I have those attitudes at the right intensity, *then* I target ads for the candidate towards those attitudes. The people that *contain* those attitudes are just vessels of the traits I'm marketing towards."

"People don't matter," said Abby slowly. "Just the traits—the *attitudes*—that you find useful."

Ima nodded. "Advertisers have been using psychology in advertising for a century. But only recently do we know enough of the brain and its working parts to target attitude sets."

Abby seemed thoughtful. "You've been working with the Dot performer, right?"

"Yes."

"What's she got to do with this?"

"We've been married two years and you're asking now?"

"Yes. Explain it to me *now*."

Ima blinked at Abby's intensity. "All right then. The Dot Performance Engine measures crowd response from a performance — it's the first step towards teasing out relevant attitudes. During a Dot performance, it measures crowd response to her. She tailors the concert to those responses."

"But you use it other ways."

Ima nodded. "The DPE is used in political rallies across the world. It was used here to gauge response in national referendum amendment rallies."

Abby leaned back. "Really."

"Yes. But crowd response doesn't last. You have to back it up with advertising, targeted social media, manipulated searches — you have to back it up with *persuasion*."

"I see," Abby said thoughtfully. "So, you measure a crowd response to some kind of rhetoric. You probably isolate out the most susceptible, right?"

"Those with the most susceptible *attitudes*."

"Then, you target that group's social media intake."

"Yes."

"Do you manipulate their searches?"

Ima shook her head. "Not grossly. Just bring up targeted ads on the first page. And order their search — but only for the relevant searches. And towards the relevant attitudes."

"To narrow their focus."

"And boost their response."

"Do human beings do that work?"

"No. We have an AI system that follows the targeted population." Ima smiled. "We have a sixty percent success rate."

"Sixty percent of the targeted population voted for the referendum amendment?"

"Actually, in *that* campaign, we had better than seventy-four percent success. People broadcast their political opinions directly. It makes it easier to determine the state of the target population. Product sales are much more difficult. People don't sit down online and say they need to think about new toilets or a new phone — well, they *do*, but not in an obvious way. The group has to be inferred, the attitudes determined, and the discussion stimulated. But people talk about politics all the time."

Abby stared at her. "How much of an impact do you think you had?"

Ima beamed. "Four percentage points on average. We had more impact in some states than others. Attitude sets don't have tight geographical boundaries. Targeting Kansas City means targeting residents of both Missouri and Kansas. How do we interpret border Missouri going pro by ten points and border Kansas going con by ten points? Kansas backlash? Missouri pre-disposition? Failure of geographic targeting? It's not clear. We *think* we gave the pro side four points, plus or minus one, across the nation, filtered through state legislatures and lobbying efforts."

"And Dot 2.0?"

Ima spoke excitedly. "Mulcahey didn't change the performance engine at all. She redeveloped the part of Dot that *uses* the performance engine. Dot 2.0 has produced a long-lasting effect from the concert *alone*."

"You won't need targeted advertising."

Ima shook her head. "We'd still have to keep the target groups focused—people get distracted. But it means the attitudes we're targeting and the people that contain them are now disposed in our favor. We can persuade them to our point of view in the performance *itself*. Then, it becomes a question of maintenance."

"Maintenance from distractions," Abby said hollowly.

"And that's just the beginning. Right now, the DPE is limited to in-person performances. But there's some evidence that Dot 2.0 recordings have a lesser but significant effect. Once we figure that out, the sky is the limit. Imagine," said Ima, her eyes shining. "Whole groups buying or selling or voting on our behalf. Products being bought because of us. Candidates obtaining office because of us. Changing social attitudes. Modifying social opinion. All because of us."

"I can imagine it," Abby said. "I can imagine it just fine."

"I'll be rich," Ima said softly. She took Abby's hand. "We'll be rich."

Abby withdrew her hand. "I don't need to be rich that badly." Abby watched Ima until Ima felt uncomfortable.

"Do you know why I fell in love with you?" Abby asked finally.

"No," Ima mumbled. Her cheeks felt hot. She felt cornered. A small rabbit or mouse facing a deadly cat. "Were you experimenting?"

"Don't be stupid," Abby said gently. "I'd been married for twenty-five years and went through a nasty divorce, remember? You don't have experiences like that and come out the other side without knowing something about yourself. At least, I didn't." Abby looked away for a moment. "We met when you were trying to figure out how to cook a daikon radish. You were so earnest. So intent on getting something *right*. So completely self-involved. Every inch a professional woman—I find such people uninteresting. One dimensional."

"Thanks."

"Then, you turned your attention to me and all that fell away. You were self-involved *everywhere else*. But when you spoke with me, I felt I was the center of your universe. It was overwhelming."

Ima didn't know what to say. "Thanks, again? I guess?"

Abby smiled at her. "I thought if you were that present with me, it didn't matter what else you did." Abby leaned forward. "I was wrong. The rest of your life *does* matter." She put her finger on the table. "This is the road to hell, Ima. You can't love someone, take care of someone, be there for them on one side of your life and do terrible things on the other."

Ima looked away. "Somebody is going to do it."

"You think that absolves you? Somebody is going to be murdered, too. That doesn't force to go out and pull the trigger."

Ima put both her hands flat on the table. "I'm not doing anything illegal."

"Law isn't morality."

"I'm not doing anything *wrong!*"

Abby leaned back. "That is the single saddest thing I've ever heard." Abby got up and left the table.

"Where are you going?"

Abby stopped at the bedroom door. "I'm moving to a hotel for a bit while I think things through." She stopped for a moment.

Ima bit her lip. "When will you come back?"

"I don't know." Abby thought for a moment. "I need to think without distraction." Abby went into the bedroom to pack.

At that exact moment, coincidence be damned, Ima's tablet chimed. Not really thinking, she picked it up and answered. "Hello?"

"Ima, I need your help," Corinne said. "Your father has run away."

Chapter 2.12: John

Shez insisted he attend the concert sober. John was pissed off and sullen as he sat in the seat, his legs sprawled in front of him. She had gotten nice seats here in the Tower: center, main floor. But John didn't want to give her the satisfaction. Who the *hell* was she to tell him not to drink?

Instead, he growled every time someone asked him to move to get to their seats.

Shez didn't say anything. She was white-lipped. Her face was drawn with dread mixed with expectation.

John hadn't been to a concert in years and he'd *never* been to one with a twenty-foot milky tank dominating the front of the stage. Or with racks and scaffolding of cameras and sensors in a ring around the audience.

Call him paranoid but John didn't like it. He'd been monitored enough, thank you very much.

He was about to call it off when the lights blinked and began to dim.

The milkiness disappeared and was replaced by whispers of smoke floating in from the left side of the stage. Flickering orange light.

Fire? John sat up and looked around for an exit. Flames shot from the left now. Streamers of fire and sparks.

"Honey?" he said in a strained voice.

"Quiet!" Shez told him in a harsh whisper.

Hard guitar chords erupted along with a rising scream as Dot slid out of the flames on her knees, her hair ablaze like a long, fiery comet.

"Wow," John said softly.

Dot came to her feet, still sliding, and began to sing.

It made John a little queasy—Dot looked so *young*. Way younger than Shez—no more than fourteen and a young fourteen at that. Looking for love—why did young girls always look for love? Every song seemed to scream it. Videos, games, stories—all about love.

John shook his head. You could spend your entire life looking for love and only find out that it was a crock at the end.

Maybe Myrna had done him a favor.

Dot slid effortlessly from one song to the next. It was good, toe-tapping music. John looked around. Everybody around him was rapt. Absorbed. John looked back at the stage. For a brief second, it looked like Dot winked at him—a joke? No. Dot was just a program. An automaton like the one that got him fired.

He looked up at the shadowed sensors circling the hall. Little red lights that moved.

Catching these people up in the concert experience. Not him, of course.

John caught Dot watching him more than once—but that had to be bullshit. She was no more than a face on a screen. Her eyes were those little moving red lights.

He looked at Dot again and for a brief moment, turning away as she danced in the rain, he caught a little glimpse of joy and sadness and he remembered Shez at ten, running in a brief, warm summer rain in a park field. The kind of rain that came down from the mountains every now and then and made the desert wildflowers erupt out of the ground into riotous color. He remembered the mix so clearly. Such joy. Such sadness. He'd asked her what was wrong and Shez had said it was so pretty here in the field. But the rain was rare and it would be gone. Shez didn't know if it would ever come back.

John had wanted to just hold her and protect her forever but he couldn't, she was away from him, running in the rain, the air filled with the broken dust smell of water meeting earth.

It came to him that Shez had never left that field. She felt that way now—joy and sadness, ever mixed.

John shook his head. Dot was singing a low, slow song about a young mother who just couldn't do it and was giving up her little girl. John wanted to yell at her. *Hold on!* No pain lasts forever.

And stared at Dot singing: little toy robot trying desperately to sing about human beings. He glanced at Shez, eyes shining, dancing her heart out to Dot, Dot dancing back. What the hell was wrong with that?

No pain lasts forever.

Dot introduced a sudden beat and the audience started clapping time.

John clapped right along with them.

◄ June 20 ►

Their ears rang as they left the hall. Shez was practically toe dancing in the street, singing snatches of songs, here and there. She knew the words.

"Wasn't she great?"

"Yes," said John, thinking. "Yes, she was."

He felt different. Good God, he had been planning to kill Renny. What the hell was *wrong* with him? No pain lasts forever—he kept repeating it to himself like a mantra.

This must have been what Shez had felt in Bakersfield. That was why she had been so incredibly upset at the Dot in the festival—what a pale, flaccid imitation that had been. Seeing the first concert and then being let down like that must have hurt like hell.

But Shez was seventeen. Every experience was, almost by definition, singular and unique until the next one.

John watched her singing on the sidewalk and felt the weight of experience.

Can people change?

Maybe. It seemed to him that he'd considered himself past changing. But, then, he remembered what he'd been like in high school—it *embarrassed* him to remember what he'd been like. Like it had happened to someone so stupid they had become incomprehensible. Other people might feel like they'd never changed but he sure had. For better. For worse.

He couldn't believe he'd actually *planned* how he was going to kill Renny. What had Renny done? Not having an affair was a condition of *marriage*, not a co-worker. Myrna deserved the anger, not Renny—and had John been so fucking easy to live with? What did he *expect* from

Myrna?

Well, he told himself. Maybe he could have expected talking about it. Or leaving before she started sleeping with Renny. Or maybe not finding someone he had to work with—oh, yeah. He was fired. Problem solved.

Chapter 2.13: Ima

Ima retraced her steps to Papa Dave's funeral as far as San Antonio. There, she rented a car to drive her to Good Hope. *Good Hope.* She chuckled mirthlessly. Ima hoped she had a home to return to. Abby had been stubbornly resistant to texts, video calls, audio calls, and location pages. To each, she had a personal message to Ima: *Let me think.*

Corinne was in the lobby waiting for her. "I don't know why you had to come in person. What more could you do than I've already done?"

"Shut up." Ima dropped her bag on the couch in the lobby and went to the front kiosk. "My name is Ima Hidori. I'd like to see my father's room, please."

The kiosk brought up a cartoon figure of a receptionist. "I'm sorry. Peter Hidori is not presently in the hospital."

"Get me a supervisor."

"All supervisors—"

Ima turned to Corinne. "Do you know where his room is?"

Corinne looked flustered for the first time in Ima's life. Possibly it was her daughter telling her to shut up. "Seventh floor."

Ima grabbed her bag. "Let's go."

Corinne started walking towards the elevator. "This is a waste of time."

Ima didn't waste her breath on a reply.

Peter's room had already been cleaned and readied for a new patient.

"See?" said Corinne triumphantly.

An officious looking woman came in the room looking every bit as severe and authoritative as Corinne did on a bad day.

"I'm looking at the room where you held my father," Ima said. "Before you lost him."

"We didn't—" The woman sputtered. Stopped and took a deep breath. "How can I help you?"

"You can leave me and my mother alone in this room for twenty minutes. Then, we're out of your hair."

The woman looked at them both. "I'll wait outside."

"You do that." Ima walked around the room. All four walls were active surfaces. There was a smooth rounded desk and chair—Peter would have had to *work* to hurt himself. Set into the desk was a keyboard. Ima looked around the room again. The angles looked right. Peter had spoken to her from this desk—provided this was, in fact, his room and not one merely identical.

Ima stood next to the keyboard. "Console."

The kiosk cartoon figure smiled from the wall. "Password please?"

Ima thought for a moment. Then, she typed onto the keyboard.

A moment later, the console menu appeared.

"How did you do that?" Corinne looked at the console, then at Ima.

"Mehitable. It's the name of a vulture. I had four of them to try. I was lucky the first time."

"Vultures?"

"You had to be there." Ima looked over the console entries.

"What are you doing?" asked Corinne.

"Daddy's crazy. Not stupid. He told me so himself. This is a man who skinned his own clothes and hunted his own meat. They had to drug him to the gills to keep him quiet but he managed to fool them anyway. He left with a plan. No doubt an absolutely *crazy* plan but still, a plan. I'm looking for clues."

Ima brought up call history. Nothing unexpected—Peter had called no one but Ima and Corinne. Browsing history was severely restricted—expected in a mental hospital. Peter wouldn't have had permission to delete it. Therapists might find the information useful. Ima recognized some sites. "Shit."

"What?"

On the console, there was a wall customization selection showing several entries. Clearly, Peter had customized his walls and then reset them when he left. Ima reinstated one.

The walls, floors, and ceiling were covered with images of Dot. Dot dancing. Dot singing. Dot walking down the street. Dot in still pictures. Dot in animation.

Ima went back over the traffic. Sure enough, she found the Dot release footage she'd sent him. It was queued up on repeat. She brought it up and checked the end credits. As she suspected, there was a concert schedule. Ima sat on the bed, looking up at one Dot image after the other.

"Do you know where he is?" asked Corinne.

"No," Ima said. She gazed up at Dot. Dot gazed down. *But I think I know where he'll be.*

Chapter 2.14: John

Alisi had been kind enough to report his firing as a reduction in force—which it actually may have been. He and Renny had been redundant for some time. But being RIF'd meant John was eligible for unemployment. The check would cover food but not the mortgage. But that wasn't due until the middle of July.

Shez was out of school for the summer and not looking forward to her senior year in the fall. So, the two of them rattled around in the house like peas in a gourd. Outside, the noon temperature stayed over a hundred. Each night, the night time fall was less. As they passed the boundary from June to July, the difference between day and night became negligible as the hot earth radiated back the gift of daylight heat.

This meant they stayed inside where the air conditioning kept it cool.

John pondered how he felt now compared to how he had felt before the concert. There had been no Saint Paul on the road to Damascus moment. A slight shift when he had been reminded of young Shez when he looked at Dot but that seemed too minor to mark much of anything.

Yet, he remembered what he had been thinking *before* the concert and what he was thinking now and the two were distinctly different. He could not mark the moment of change. He could only mark that the change had happened.

John kept searching the net for explanations. There were hundreds of sites willing to oblige: self-help sites. Religious sites. Therapy sites. Most of them seemed to suggest that change was hard. That it took work. That it required commitment and will.

John had been raised a Baptist and left it as soon as he left home. But he kept floating back to the religious sites. Many of the Christian ones said that the acceptance of Jesus would inevitably lead to change—Jesus needed coinage to allow his flock to enter heaven. The currency was belief.

When John read the testimonials, they often described lonely people who had struck bottom and were desperate for escape. Like watermelon seeds squirted from fingers, the pressures of the moment had forced these people into radical shifts in their lives.

The more John read these, the more he began to think that these people were *predisposed* to change. The mechanism was different—some secret, radical optimism, the love of Jesus—but the entering stories were the same.

Certainly, John had been desperate—he'd been ready to *murder* a man. All it had taken for him to change was a moment. A glance. A song in the night. He'd been a shaky tower. It had taken only a single brick to bring him down into a new place.

Some of the self-help sites invoked the mysterious language of quantum physics to explain their point of view. When John ran down these explanations, they were birdsongs—beautiful noise without obvious meaning. Merely the idea of a multiple state system collapsing down into a single, final state. John liked the idea of an unstable set of possibilities crystallizing into a perfect moment.

◀ June 25 ▶

John answered the door. Renny was looking up at him.

"Hey," Renny. "Thought maybe we'd talk."

John stared at him. *What the hell do I have to say to you?* "What about?"

Renny gave him a wretched look. "You know. Things. Stuff."

"Things. Stuff."

Renny looked around. "Can we go somewhere? Get some coffee?"

They ended up a mile away at a Denny's that John liked. Bakersfield had embraced what people called the Chinese Option: the meal cost already included tips and tax so there were no hidden fees. John liked knowing the exact cost of the meal ahead of time. Now that he was on unemployment, he needed to watch his pennies. Though it was close to noon, John tapped in breakfast on the table surface. He hadn't quite got the hang of weekday mornings yet.

"You're on shift in a couple of hours," John said as he ate the hash browns.

"Yeah. I'm sorry about that." Renny leaned his elbows on the table. "Alisi shouldn't have fired you."

John shrugged. "I was drunk on the job. I'm lucky she didn't put it in the termination order. I wouldn't have unemployment. Or the prospect of another job."

"You find anything yet?"

"Not looking yet." John snagged another forkful of hash browns. "Examining my possibilities." He looked over at Renny. "How did it happen? You and Myrna?"

"Remember the picnic Alisi threw when we had a year of no defects? That's where we started talking and hit it off."

"Ah." John turned back to breakfast.

"You're acting weird." Renny looked at him for a moment. "Are you okay?"

"Weird how?"

"Aren't you pissed? At me? At Myrna? At Alisi?"

John considered that. "Sure. I guess. But it's not like I didn't dig my own grave. I made everybody miserable."

"That..." Renny groped for words. "Seems like a reasonable statement. How the *fuck* can you be reasonable?" He sniffed the air. "Did you stop drinking?"

"Yeah." John chucked. "Clearly, it wasn't working for me."

"You just... stopped?"

"Yeah."

"How?"

John sipped his coffee. "Turns out I'm not an alcoholic. I didn't need to drink. I just wanted to be drunk. When I quit wanting to be drunk there wasn't much reason to drink." He shrugged.

Renny stared at him. "Man, you've changed. Did you join a cult or something?"

"Why? You interested?"

Renny shook his head violently. "The idea of a cult makes me nervous."

"I didn't join a cult." *Or did I? The cult of Dot?* "Big events have big effects. Myrna left me for you. I got fired. Those are pretty big events. Is it so surprising there'd be a big effect?"

"Sure. Just not *this* effect." Renny paused. "I mean, I was worried you'd come after me. You've got a hell of a temper."

Almost did. "Sorry to disappoint."

"No, man. I'm *glad* you're handling this so well. I was worried."

"It was a shitty thing you did." John pointed his fork at Renny. He wasn't above enjoying Renny's flinch. "Not as shitty as Myrna's but shitty enough. Where did you think it was going to end up? Me happily giving away my wife to you? Family outings? All of us enjoying a long and productive work career together?"

"Of course not, man—"

"Or me surprising both of you with a shotgun when you were fucking your brains out?"

Renny paled.

John picked up a piece of toast. "Yeah, I thought about it. I'm human. I'm male. I'm a husband." He took a bite thoughtfully. "I was persuaded it was a dumb idea. No pain lasts forever."

Renny breathed out in relief.

"Not to say I don't still consider it from time to time." John smiled when Renny looked uncomfortable. "But it's still a dumb idea." He nodded towards Renny. "No. You and Myrna get to live your lives intact. It's true and complete love, right?" John smiled at Renny. "After all, I was making her miserable. Without me, your love can only grow stronger, right?"

Renny looked even more uncomfortable and didn't say anything.

John wiped his lips with a napkin. "This has been fun." He tapped in the bill payment and stood up. "Let's never do it again."

◄ June 25 ►

When John returned home, Shez was gone. It was early afternoon. He found a bottle of Jack Daniels in the kitchen. Jack stared back at him.

Did he mean what he said to Renny? Was he really not an alcoholic?

If he was, and Dot cured him, there was a whole new ball game in addiction rehabilitation.

John didn't think so. While it was clear that he'd been affected by *something* at the Dot concert, it seemed unlikely to him that it had caused physiological changes. More likely was what he'd told Renny: the desire to be drunk had motivated his drinking. As that desire had been lessened, so had his drinking.

Did he want to be drunk *right now?*

Not really. Experimentally, he measured out a couple of shots and drank them. A few moments of heat in the belly and he felt the warm, rosy glow percolate up from the back of his head.

It *was* pleasant. He did like it.

He held the bottle in his hand. The glow was enough; he was not inclined to drink any more. If he were an alcoholic, would he just need to keep drinking until he passed out? When he *had* been drinking, he'd kept going on until there was not much left of him. He had desired oblivion. Now, he didn't? Was it as simple as that?

He thought of Renny and Myrna. There was still a small, white-hot node of anger. Of rage. Of pain. He wasn't free of it. No pain lasts forever but the time for it to dissipate might exceed his lifetime.

He put the bottle back.

Chapter 2.15: Ima

◄ June 28 ►

The Fresno concert had been on June twentieth. Peter went missing on June twenty-fourth. The Fresno official recording would be released on June thirtieth — two days from now. The next concert, the Nightingale in Reno, was July fifth — seven days from now. Ima built a network agent to search for Peter downloading or viewing the recording but she held little hope for it. While she had faith that Peter could keep himself whole and out of trouble until the concert, she didn't believe he would bother with a download. Maybe *after* the concert in an effort to relive the experience but not before.

The network agent was insurance in case Ima was wrong. She'd been wrong before. After all, look at what was happening between her and Abby.

Abby quit screening contact from Ima in a couple of days and finally answered the phone.

Ima was surprised to see her active presence on the screen and not just an automated message saying she was *thinking.*

"Hello, Ima," Abby said. Abby's face was not creased with effort.

"Please come home," said Ima. "I can move into my office to give you space. Just... come home."

Abby didn't speak for a moment. Then, she sighed and rubbed the bridge of her nose. "All right," she said. "We can try that."

Ima took Abby's return as a good sign. She took the move to her office as a bad sign. Ima could not determine the net difference.

Conversations were brittle. Cohabitation was uncomfortable. Ima tried desperately to fix things but Abby wouldn't talk about it — or, rather, wouldn't dig into it. As soon as the conversation moved to the actual conflict — Ima's profession — Abby shut it down. *Let me think.*

Ima couldn't think of a way to resolve this without quitting either Ippon or Abby. She was not quitting *either*. She'd worked too hard for both. After all, wasn't Ima the one who paid off the final mortgage? Didn't she pay the taxes? And you *never* wanted to owe money to the State of California or the City of Santa Monica. It wasn't like the little produce market brought in much in the way of income. If it hadn't been for Ima, Abby would have had to move—she was on her last legs when they got married. Ima had taken the burden gladly but now she grew suspicious. Maybe that was the main reason Abby had married her. It was no secret that Ima brought in the lion's share of the money.

No. *No.* Ima shook her head. That way lies madness. Either they were in this together or there was no point. Keeping score wouldn't keep them together.

But what could she *do?*

Ima considered Abby's point of view. What was wrong with what Ima was doing, anyway? All people ever tried to do was persuade other people of their points of view. Ima persuaded Ippon to give her a job. Ippon persuaded Toyota to buy more heavy machinery. Abby persuaded Ima that she was loved. Ima persuaded Abby she was worthy of that love. What was wrong with any of that?

Sales was entirely an act of persuasion. So was politics. So was business. A continuing arms race between who was better at it. It was a continuum. If it was morally acceptable at one end, it had to be morally acceptable at the other, right? Abby had to be wrong about this.

But so what if she was? Abby was stubborn—Ima thought of it as the Abbywall. Once it was up, it could not be penetrated or changed. And this looked like an Abbywall problem.

Was this a choice between work and marriage? Work and love?

Could she live without work? Could she live without Abby?

No matter how she thought about it, Ima couldn't see a solution. Give up everything she'd work for over more than a decade? No one could ask that of her. Give up Abby? The thought made her die inside.

From exile in her office, Ima held her face in her hands and wept.

◄ July 1 ►

Ima fended off Corinne for the few days before Reno. The upcoming concert, the search for Peter, and her continuing conflict with Abby took up far too much of her time. *Short on bandwidth,* she thought wryly. *Sorry, Mom.*

Not that Corinne didn't try. She sicced contact agents on Ima. Trackers. Locators. But Corinne was unpracticed at it, while Ima had been working in this world for years. Ima knew Corinne was not malicious. She just wanted to *know.* In a lifetime pursuit of control, being denied *knowing* was driving Corinne a little crazy.

Ima fended off the queries without much thought. Her agents were top of the line and a more than adequate defense against the open-source systems Corinne invoked. Ima was polite about it—all of her agents responded with "Ima is too busy" or "She will take your call later" or "Ima Hidori's location has been marked private at this time. Please attempt to locate her at a later time." While Ima smiled a little at the thought of her mother's frustration, she didn't dwell on it.

Reno would be the backbreaker of Ima's project. Bakersfield showed promise. Fresno confirmed it. Reno would prove it. After Reno, she could take her data to Farrell with a proposal. This could be the biggest thing Persuasion had ever tackled.

And it looked like it might be something Ima would tackle alone.

Ima did not push Abby—the Abbywall loomed between them. It was entirely possible Abby was waiting for her to open discussions. It was also entirely possible that Abby had nearly decided that separation—divorce, loss, grief, loneliness—was inevitable and Ima pushing her would tip her over the edge. It was like Schrodinger's Personality Barrier. As long as Ima didn't attempt to open it, its state was open to question. If Ima forced the issue, the wall might disappear or it might become permanent.

So, Ima walked the house on tiptoe. She was gentle and polite. She was quiet when Abby walked near her, smiling when spoken to. In every way, Ima tried to project the loving, supportive, understanding wife. When she worked in her office, she kept the door closed lest the act of seeing Ima doing something Abby abhorred might trigger the wrong decision. Ima knew this fragility might have been only the product of her own insecurity. But as long as she didn't *push*, she could safely clutch at the illusion that everything would be fine.

Ima was doing her best to persuade Abby. Abby was doing her best to be unpersuaded.

Encounter data for Peter came in sporadically as her agents found traces of him in a shared car in Clovis. A publicity still in a mall in Albuquerque. A transient camp in Coyote Springs. A supermarket in Duckwater. Peter was marking a convoluted trail through New Mexico, Arizona, Nevada. It was like a statistical map: many dots in different places but marking a trend line direct from Abilene to Reno.

Four days before the concert her agents lost him in Stillwater. Nothing. Ima thought he might be following the Truckee River. That would be like him. But it meant that unless some hiker, traffic, or bikeway cam caught him and posted a public picture, her agents wouldn't find him until they saw him at the entrance of the Nightingale.

Ima made her reservations and went out into the kitchen.

Abby was there, reading a seed catalog on the table's active surface. She looked up. "Hey, there."

"Hi." Ima sat across from her. "I've got to go to Reno for a few days."

"Why?"

"The Dot 2.0 concert. I think my father is going to be there."

Abby watched her a moment. "Really?"

Ima nodded. "When I checked his room in Abilene it was covered in Dot images. He had the Bakersfield release recording on his set. I've been getting sightings of him moving towards Reno."

"Interesting," Abby looked outside. "You think Dot 2.0 persuaded him to escape?"

"I don't see how. It's just a concert."

"'Just a concert that has lasting effects. You said that yourself."

"Minimal lasting effects."

"Archimedes said give him a large enough lever and he could move the world."

Ima smiled. She held her fingers close together. "Dot is a tiny, tiny lever."

Abby didn't smile in return. "Are you sure?"

Ima leaned back in the chair. "Just a few points of change."

Abby watched Ima. Her face looked worn thin. "A reduction in consumer purchases. A drop in porn. An uptick in factual news. I think you may be underestimating the effect." Then, she returned her attention to the seed catalog.

"Will you be here when I get back?" Ima blurted and then felt aghast at what she had said.

Abby gave her a long, sad smile. "Of course. Go find your father."

Ima left the table. She had no real idea what had just happened.

Chapter 2.16: John

◄ July 1 ►

No matter where he started, he ended up back in the Bible. Not for any belief, but because of his Baptist upbringing, he understood the language.

Shez sat next to him as he was reading about Saint Paul's conversion again, trying to get a little more understanding. Trying to read a little more between the lines.

"Yes?" he said to her as he blanked the screen.

Shez had seen what he was reading. "Becoming a Bible nut, Pops?"

"Sure. Going to sacrifice my firstborn to the Greater Glory of God."

Shez laughed but John felt suddenly cold when he remembered what he'd planned to do. Did jokes like that mean that *everyone* was close to murder? He realized that the impulse to violence he'd had every weekend for years hadn't reappeared since the concert. One more change to think about.

Shez looked at him a moment. "You feel different, right? Since the concert?"

"Yes."

"You haven't been drinking. Or watching porn."

"I know." He looked around the room. "I live here, remember?"

"Yeah." She pursed her lips. "There's another concert this week. In Reno."

"You want to go?"

"Yes." Shez stopped for a moment. "We could take Mom."

John saw the effort written across her face, the blind desperation of a daughter trying to get her parents back together.

John hadn't thought all that much about Myrna since he'd spoken to Renny. He was a little worried he'd slip back into rage and despair if he did. But mostly, thinking about her made him feel wistful. Sad. He was tired of those feelings.

"Honey," he said gently. "I don't think we'll be getting back together."

"I know," said Shez and John could see the lie but said nothing. "But," Shez continued. "If you got something out of it, maybe she would, too."

John shrugged. "Sure. Maybe. She probably won't want me there."

"You let me handle it," Shez said with satisfaction. "I'll take care of everything."

Chapter 2.17: Ima

Johann and Mohammed had set up their base in the Travelodge a thousand feet from the concert hall. They had hired CommTech to mount a communications laser on top of the Nightingale pointing at the Travelodge. With a bandwidth an order of magnitude greater than the local net, they could tap any and all of Dot's sensors without significant lag. In effect, they had a real-time equivalent of the concert hall.

Ima confused the two of them when she first hired them. Their names were counter to their appearance. Mohammed Paternos should have been short and dark but was instead six foot five, blond and blue-eyed. Johann Murdock was a shade over five feet tall, Chinese, and looked like a sumo wrestler. Seeing them live was always a shock—largely because Ima didn't see them live very often.

"Hey, Boss," said Mohammed.

Johann looked up from his console and grunted, then turned back. "Everything is live. Concert starts in an hour and a half. Dot and the band are doing warm-ups." He pointed at the console.

"Did you get the image I sent you?"

Mohammed nodded. "Peter Hidori. Flagged his image for the camera at the door."

"Good."

Ima could see Dot running images through the tank. Fire. Ice. Trees. Animals. Everything was running at least twice normal speed. Dot was doing a final check of the circuits.

Behind the tank, the band was checking instruments. The guitarist was doing a set of fast scales.

Then, the guitarist was in the tank facing him on the outside, both of them playing against one another. The live guitarist stopped and laughed. "Cut it out, Dot."

"Just keeping you limber, Jake."

Ima reached past Johann and turned off the audio. "Are they always like this?"

"Bakersfield, Fresno, and now here." Johann pointed at the guitarist. "That's Jake Arnold. Used to have a band called *Persons Unknown*."

"Was he good?"

Johann chuckled softly. "Plays like a badass angel. Before the band broke up, he was considered one of the best in the world. A reincarnated Stevie Ray Vaughn."

"Who's that?"

"Never mind. He's good. *Very* good." Johann pointed to the others as they were checking their instruments. "The rest are from *Persons Unknown*, too. Jess Turbin is the bassist. Olivia Tedeschi is on keyboards. Obe Anne is the drummer."

"Are they good, too?"

Johann nodded. "Very. *Persons Unknown* was amazing. None of them performed publicly after the band broke up. They ended up being mostly studio musicians. A real loss."

Ima watched him a moment. "How do you know all this?"

Johann reduced the images. "I was a fan in high school. Mohammed, too. Afterward, you could trace out the others—Olivia working on this video. Jess backing up this album by that artist. Obe's drum work is the stuff of legend. But Jake just disappeared. It's good to see them back together."

"The Dot 2.0 *Persons Unknown* reunion tour."

Johann shook his head. "That's not *Persons Unknown*. Jake's band was good—as good as any of the supergroups or talent collections. But these guys are a step above that."

"It's the same people."

"Yeah." Johann looked up at her with a crooked grin. "It's the same people, twelve years later, playing like they never did before. Funny, huh?"

Ima didn't like the sound of that.

Johann turned back to the screens. "She's changing the song list every concert."

"Really? It's not scripted?"

Johann shook his head. "Not that we know. But we just work the concerts. She and the band probably figure out the sets between concert dates. Bakersfield was about half old stuff and half new. That shifted in Fresno—only about a third old stuff. I'm sure it will be different this time, too."

"Walkabout," said Ima thoughtfully. "That's a thing down in Australia, right?"

"Yeah. Vision quest sort of thing. Though I read that the term is not positive." Johann shrugged. "Guess it means we should expect change."

"What do you think of the new Dot?"

Johann gave her an opaque look. "We just run the concerts and get the data, Boss. We don't really *listen* to her."

Right. "I'm going over to the concert hall. Keep in touch. If facial ID finds Peter Hidori, let me know."

"You got it, Boss."

◀ July 5 ▶

Ima stood outside in the July heat. Students enjoying Independence Day excess had marked the area with leftover debris the way tomcats sprayed their happy dominance. Part of her hoped to see Peter walking towards her. Most of her knew this was rubbish. Even so, she walked around the Nightingale to make sure he was not ensconced in intricate brick facades or the fat round brick cupola.

She walked along the ticket line, examining faces. No Peter.

Ima called Abby.

Abby answered without video. "Yes?"

Ima was at a loss. What to say? *I just called to hear your voice. I just called to see if you could forgive me. I just called to see if it was back to the way it was.* "Just checking in. How is Santa Monica?"

"Sunny and mild. Look, I have customers here."

"I'll call later."

"Okay."

Ima stared at the line leading into the concert. *What is happening to my life?*

Ima walked down the short flight into the boxy entrance, showed her badge, and went inside.

The Nightingale was part of the University of Nevada. It was not a big venue—none of Dot 2.0's concerts were in big venues. The Bakersfield concert comprised seven hundred people. Fresno only five hundred. The Nightingale stood directly between them at six hundred plus.

Inside, the stage was smaller than she had thought. The tank had been placed below the stage and reached nearly to the ceiling. The band was behind it, showing vaguely distorted. The speakers were flat plates on either side of the tank, angled so that everyone got an equal volume of rock and roll. Dot was in the tank, talking to the band, her back to the theater.

The only people near the stage were technicians putting up last minute measurement devices and checking the cabling.

Ima looked up and saw the instrument complex wrapping the hall about twenty feet over the audience. She could identify clusters of cameras, FLIR units, and LIDARs along with other instruments she could not name. If Peter came, Ima was confident he would be identified.

Ima looked back to the stage.

Dot was watching her.

Watching? Ima looked up. Several of the cameras, FLIRs and LIDARs had turned in their sockets and tracked her.

"Ima Hidori," Dot said. "Welcome to your first Dot concert."

Ima walked down to the base of the tank. It loomed over her.

Dot walked down invisible stairs until she was staring up at Ima. "What brings you here?"

Ima stared down at the open face: short black hair, bright violet eyes far larger than they should have been. It was impossible not to feel Dot was looking back. Ima glanced back up at the ceiling complex. Sure enough, the complex of devices had followed her down here.

Ima turned back to Dot. "Aren't you busy?"

Dot shook her head. "Most of the hard work is already done. I'm helping the band tune up and tighten but that's barely more than an idle loop. I've got plenty of bandwidth to talk to you."

Ima knew the DPE was capable of analysis of nearly any human interaction, be it dancing, singing, or conversation. The idea of being its sole target felt creepy.

Dot laughed softly. "Don't be so nervous. I don't bite. I can't." She tapped her finger on the glass. The sound came from the speakers. "Hard glass between us. I can't *ever* get out."

"Does that bother you?"

"What? Never to feel the wind blow through my electrons?" Dot laughed again, this time a loud and brassy sound. "Of course not. I'm just as Ippon and Rose Mulcahey made me." She smiled at Ima, a row of perfectly rendered teeth.

Ima stepped back.

"If I see Peter Hidori, I'll let you know." With that, Dot turned and walked back up the invisible stairs and across an invisible platform to the band.

Ima backed slowly away. The edge of a seat caught her knees and she sat down heavily. *Of course*, she thought to herself. She would have to be aware of the facial recognition, wouldn't she? Wouldn't that be part of her analysis of potential indicators? Or would it? Maybe she hacked the other systems. She's an intelligent device. Could she do that? What *couldn't* she do? Ima didn't know. Dot had limitations. Ima realized she didn't know what they were.

Dot was a machine. There was nothing human in her. Why would she bait Ima? How did that connect to her innate drives and motivations? How would it serve her goal? For that matter, Ima thought, what *was* her goal? All of Dot's programming and training regimen had been geared to make her maximize audience performance response. Her success proved the success of the regimen. But just because she behaved the way the regimen predicted didn't mean that her goals were the same as those of her programmers. Ippon wanted a behavior from Dot and got it. How Dot decided how to execute that behavior was unknown to anyone.

Ima remembered something she'd heard in college about the rat pleasure center experiments. According to the story, scientists had found a section of the brain they thought was the pleasure center. They put a probe in that area and a lever wired to the probe so that whenever the lever was pressed by the rat, the rat got a charge through the probe. The rat tapped that lever endlessly. Voila! The area must be the pleasure center.

But later, it was discovered that there was a repetition center as well. An area of the brain that triggered a repetition of the previous behavior. It wasn't all that far from the pleasure center. Ima had imagined the rat thinking *Dear God make it stop! Please make it stop!* But forced to press that lever forever.

Ima had never tried to determine if the story was true or not. It fell squarely in a box labeled, *knowing this doesn't help anybody*.

The mechanism that produced the behavior in Dot that, in turn, stimulated the desired behavior in human beings did not have to be keyed to anything humans could recognize.

The thought made Ima shiver. As long as Dot was an unthinking, unfeeling robot Ima could dismiss her. But *this* Dot was anything but unthinking. And if Dot didn't feel, she knew that humans did and how to manipulate them.

The audience began filling the hall. The Nightingale had been designed to make six hundred strangers feel intimate. The ceiling was just high enough for good acoustics but not so tall it loomed over anyone. The seats rolled back from the stage and rose incrementally. Everyone could see the stage but no one was fooled into thinking they were alone.

Ima expected a loud and raucous crowd—there was always clapping and dancing at a Dot concert. Alcohol and drugs. She'd seen it lots of times.

But this crowd came in speaking in low voices. Ima saw no one that looked drunk or stoned. They were expectant. Anticipating. Ima was oddly reminded of her grandfather's funeral before the priest made his entrance.

People kept looking at the blank, milky tank. Ima realized she could no longer see the band. If they were there, the tank masked them.

She tapped her earphone. "Any news about Peter?"

"Nothing, Boss," said Mohammed. "We'll let you know."

Ima tapped her fingers on the armrest as people seated themselves around her. Craned her neck and looked around. Surely, she'd see Peter if he came near her. The *instant* she saw Peter, she'd drag him out of here. The hall felt close—too close. To Hell with intimacy. This felt downright claustrophobic.

Then, the lights began to dim.

Chapter 2.18: John

◄ July 5 ►

The plan was to meet at the Nightingale. When John sat down next to Myrna and Shez, it was clear Myrna was fed up.

"Jesus, John. Is this some lame-ass idea to get us back together?"

"It was my idea, Mom." Shez grabbed her hand. "Like you told me, we're a family whether or not you and Pops are together."

John saw expressions flit across Myrna's face: irritation that Shez had tossed her own words back at her. Low panic when she couldn't see a way out. Anger that she was going to actually have to interact with her soon-to-be-ex-husband. Fear of what John might know.

He made sure he didn't accidentally touch her as he sat down. "It'll be a good concert."

"This won't change things," Myrna whispered fiercely.

"No, it won't." John agreed. "But Shez wanted us to do this together."

"Don't use her against me."

"I'm not. It was entirely her idea."

Myrna looked from John to Shez and back again. She got up and exchanged seats with Shez so she didn't have to sit next to John.

Shez gave John a pleading glance.

John shrugged and didn't say anything. Myrna was making a point and John *had* been a complete ass. If it made peace for Myrna to buffer herself from John by interposing her daughter, fine.

The crowd murmured and began a soft chant. *Dot. Dot. Dot.*

This time, John had no reservations. He was going to have *fun*.

Dot came out silently. She stood in the middle of the tank, watching them with a smile. Then, she raised her hand and began beating the air in time. Each time she struck air, there was the sound of a gong as if she were calling them to meditation.

Then, came the sound of trumpets. Dot sang, each syllable punctuated with the sound of a tambourine. A young girl talking to her past self, asking how to change. Asking herself how change might possibly occur.

John's heart went out to her in sympathy. He couldn't figure it out, either.

Chapter 2.19: Ima

◄ July 5 ►

Conversation ceased. Eagerness wound the crowd up. A gradual murmur grew. A soft chant: *Dot. Dot. Dot.* Then, Dot singing softly almost to herself, keeping time to a bell. The crowd sound faded to respectful silence.

The lights faded to black. Nothing but the light of the exit signs and the soft glow of track lighting along the aisles. And Dot.

There was a trumpeting sound—many trumpets singing a pattern that interlocked. Variations. It was quite pleasant, actually. There was a man next to her who seemed to be humming along. Ima found herself prepared to be annoyed and then surprised that she wasn't.

Dot disappeared. The tank was utterly transparent. As if space itself yawned through it.

A piano played three simple chords in synch with the trumpets. One long chord followed by two short ones. Ima felt her heart beating with the piano. *Bam...* Bam. Bam. *Bam...* Bam. Bam.

The drum came in and kept time. The tank pulsed with light and there was Dot, hammering the air along with the piano and the drum. Suddenly, the audience stood and they were all hammering the air. Dot was grinning. Ima caught her breath. Grinning at *her!* Staring right at *her!*

The bass came in and Dot began to sing.

That sweet, rough, sharp, smooth voice seemed to grab Ima by the back of the head and send a shiver all the way down her spine. As if she were a hollow bell rung in still, clean air. Echoing through her. The shiver came back up and lifted her like a frog on a pin.

The audience roared. She roared with them.

"Boss! Peter—"

Ima pulled out the earphone.

It was as if Dot sang without words. Ima *heard* words but they were unimportant. The images just came. People working fields. People looking up when she sang. People working factories. People in the street. Looking up when she sang. Or maybe they were images surrounding her in the tank. Ima wasn't sure.

The music didn't stop. There was no break between the songs, only changes in rhythm and key. The tank's images were subtle— suggestions of imagery rather than imagery itself. They were stories, impressions, commentary. A teenager in a hospital bed having a conversation with her newborn baby. A heartbroken girl giving her boyfriend the boot. A woman waiting for her husband to return from the war. Someone moving to a new place to leave behind the old. Searching for new possibilities. Finding them. Not finding them. Losing them.

Dot couldn't possibly be staring at her—she couldn't be staring at her at all. Ima knew that with part of her mind. At best, Ima was an indicator—a marker in the crowd to which the DPE paid attention.

It didn't matter. This was what mattered. This song. This moment.

They were all dancing. Between the seats. In the aisles. Next to the tank. The band was in the tank with Dot, now. Dancing with her. Dancing with *us*.

Then, there was a hush as Dot looked out over the audience. The tank was empty and transparent save for her. Ima could see the band faintly lit behind the tank.

Dot sang about cages. Pens. Traps. She was free. *We can be, too.* Ima found herself singing the chorus back to Dot. Joyfully. Tears streaming down her face and never feeling less than she wanted to cry than at any time in her life. *I'll be waiting there,* Dot sang. Ima sang it back to her.

Then, it was over.

The tank went milky. The lights came up. From behind the tank, Ima could hear the band removing their instruments. Ima looked around. The audience looked stunned but satisfied.

She stumbled as she stepped into the aisle. A man snagged her arm and gently helped her steady herself. Ima smiled at him. He smiled back. They were all in this together.

"Ima?" came a voice from her other side.

She turned. It was Peter.

◄ July 5 ►

This Peter wasn't dressed in skins and smelling unwashed. *This* Peter was dressed in clean jeans, a t-shirt, and sneakers, with a backpack over one shoulder. *This* Peter was shaven and looked freshly showered.

"Daddy?" Ima said uncertainly.

Tentatively, they reached for one another and in an instant were hugging each other tightly. Ima released Peter, turned, and grabbed his hand, dragging him towards the exit. Peter followed.

The heat slapped her stupid as soon as she stepped out from the air conditioning. Peter moved smoothly past her and drew her down between the buildings to a long grassy field bordered by trees and behind the trees, campus buildings.

The heat was still oppressive but the space under the trees kept the cursed sun away and gave Ima a moment to catch her breath. She turned on Peter. "You ran away!"

"Well, yeah." Peter looked confused at the statement. "With all the drugs they were giving me, I was *lucky* to run away. You saw me. I could barely think."

"And now you're better?"

Peter stepped away from her. "Yes. But not from anything the institute did. I owe it to that recording you sent me."

"Right."

"Really. It did. *She* did." He rested his hand on one of the trees. "This is an elm. I don't remember if it's an American or a European elm. But they've been keeping these elms here for over a hundred years. Almost everywhere else in the country lost their elms." He patted the tree affectionately. He looked at Ima. "Wasn't Dot great?"

"I'm not ready to talk about that yet."

"Why not?"

"Because I don't understand it!" she blurted, then clapped her hand over her mouth. A moment later she dropped it to her side. What was she? A little girl?

"Yeah. I don't understand it, either." He patted the tree again. "She doesn't help a lot—I'm still crazy. I still hear voices."

"You hear voices?"

He gave her a puzzled expression. "You didn't know? Didn't I tell you? Didn't Corinne tell you? I've been hearing voices ever since I was a teenager. When I'm outside, I can ignore them. But inside..." Peter shook his head. "That's why I moved into the woods. The trees and the dirt drown them out. I was in Good Hope just melting—or not. I couldn't tell what was happening. Just that it wasn't good. And you sent me that recording. I listened to it and felt just a *little* bit better. Then, I listened to it again. Just a *little* bit. Nothing major. Able to connect an extra thought or two. Enough to hide my medications and act drooley." Peter grinned at her. "Drool covers all sorts of sins. Then, the drugs wore off and the voices came back. As long as I listened to Dot, I couldn't hear them. Every time I listened to a whole concert, I could stand to ignore the voices a little longer when the music stopped. Finally, I figured if the recordings were good, the concert must be better."

"Now, you're cured?"

"Oh, *hell* no." He laughed out loud. "I'm crazy as a bedbug drowning in hot sauce. Dot doesn't cure anybody." He held his thumb and forefinger close together. "She just helps a *little* bit. Just enough that when the voices talk, I don't have to listen." Peter gave her the puzzled expression again. "You must have felt it."

Ima ignored him. "I don't understand."

Peter sat down at the foot of the elm. He patted the dirt next to him.

Reluctantly, Ima sat in the dirt next to him.

Peter tapped his head. "Everything is in here, right? Sanity. Craziness. Life. Love. Passion for garlic. Dislike of sugar. It's all here." He spread his hands out. "There's no inside or outside. Things outside don't come inside, it just looks that way to us. Something happens outside and that causes a chemical change we call perception. That *perception* changes what is going on inside. That's how we experience things, right?"

Ima stared at him. This was unlike any Peter she'd ever met. "Okay."

"So, *any* experience has to come through miles and miles of filters before it gets perceived inside. Dot dislodges those filters. Shakes them up." He held his finger and thumb apart again. "Just a little bit. Long enough for something new to get perceived." Peter touched her hand. "Come on. You must have felt her."

Ima pulled her hand away, staring at the ground. "Yes. Of course." *What did I feel, anyway? A few moments of enchantment. A number of stories. A frisson of excitement. Nothing more.*

Then, all she could see was Abby's face, wreathed in disappointment, saying without words: *you don't get it at all.*

"Well," said Ima, shaking her head. "You have to come back with me. Corinne is frantic—" She turned to Peter.

But Peter was gone.

Chapter 2.20: John

Afterward, they sat in a restaurant/bar, Solar Wind, which specialized in hydroponic, sustainable vegetarian fair. Shez ate Sunward French fries covered with the Bright Lights Cheese sauce. It was called the Canadian Special. John had never seen anything like it.

Myrna nursed a beer. "Sure, I liked it," Myrna said to Shez.

"But didn't you feel it deep inside? Didn't you feel changed just by listening?"

Myrna shook her head. "How you talk. Everything feels new and profound when you're young." Myrna looked at John. "Right?"

John was drinking seltzer. He didn't want to drink alcohol casually. It seemed important to him to do only those things that he had decided he honestly wanted to do. "Sure."

"Nothing?" Shez said with a heartbroken voice.

Myrna gave John a venomous glance. John shrugged. Myrna turned back to Shez. "Honey, I said it was a good concert."

"You don't feel any different." Shez stared at the table.

"You're trying to get me and your father back together? This concert was supposed to do that?"

Shez glanced at John.

John winked at her when Myrna wasn't looking.

"I had hopes," Shez said.

"Well, this is a good time to talk now that we're all together." Myrna looked at John. Then, at Shez. "You're going to come live with me."

John stopped himself from replying immediately. "Do tell," John said neutrally. He looked at Shez. "Where do you want to live?"

"With you, Pops."

John sipped his seltzer. "Shez is seventeen. She'll be eighteen in three months. I think she can decide where she wants to live."

"A young girl should be with her mother."

"In your little apartment over by the university?"

Myrna stared at me. "You've been stalking me?"

"Finding you wasn't very hard. There are services all over the net." John tapped the table for emphasis. "Shez has said where she wants to stay. Trial separation is scheduled to be over *after* she's eighteen. Separation can't be shortened until we both agree to divorce or you move back in. You're clearly not moving back in and I won't agree until Shez turns eighteen. If you want custody—for only three months, mind you—you'll have to get a special judgment. I bet you can't even *schedule* that before her birthday. So, if I were you, I'd try to persuade her of your good intentions."

Myrna looked like she'd eaten something sour. She turned to her daughter. "Honey, I miss you."

"I miss you, too, Mom." Shez looked up at Myrna. "You should come home."

"I can't."

Shez glanced at John. John mouthed *boyfriend* back at her.

Myrna followed Shez's glance but didn't see it.

Shez' expression hardened. "I'm going to stay with Pops. I'll see you sometimes. But that's where I'm going to live."

Myrna's face clouded and she turned towards John. He saw the fight coming.

"Look," John said, rising. "I'll take a walk. You two look like you have a lot to talk about."

Outside, the desert heat still radiated from the brick. He found a small park across the street and sat on a bench where he could see the restaurant and, more importantly, Shez could see him if she came out.

He pulled out his reader. He was working through the lesser prophets. He found he liked Jonah—his complete reluctance to be a prophet amused him. Jonah persuaded the people of Ninevah to repent and avoid being slaughtered by the Hebrew God. John laughed out when Jonah yelled up at God for *not* slaughtering them. There was no pleasing some people.

John skipped forward to re-read Zacharia. He loved this inept, bumbling guy. "I have looked and behold a candlestick all of gold with a bowl on the top of it and his seven lamps thereon and seven pipes to the seven lamps which are upon the top thereof and two olive trees by it, one on the right side of the bowl and the other upon the left side thereof. And I said, what are these? And the angel answered, knowest thou not what these be?"

It went on like this, Zacharia seeing these obscure, opaque visions and the angel getting more and more exasperated with him.

John looked up across the street to see if Shez had come out. The street was mainly empty. The air was warm but not terrible, a dry baking warmth of creation. Like changing dough into bread or clay into brick.

Myrna slammed out of the Solar Wind, walking one direction, then the other, enraged. She saw John across the street and stalked over to him.

"This is all your fault," Myrna said.

"What is?"

"She wants to stay with *you!*"

"Does that surprise you?"

Myrna sat down on the other side of the bench. "Yes."

"In her eyes, you left and I'm the one that needs the most help."

"I had reasons."

John nodded. "No argument. But that has nothing to do with it. *You* left *her.*"

"I said I would come back for her. I told her before you woke up. Before I wrote you that note. I knew she was strong enough."

John shrugged. "So what? She's seventeen. Old enough to know she's strong enough and still young enough to resent it. You're lucky she still wants to talk to you."

"She wants us to get back together."

"No surprise there."

"She blames *me.* It's not *fair.*"

John sighed. "Yeah. I get that. I'll talk to her." Silence fell for a moment. John pointed over at the Solar Wind. "For the record, you left our seventeen-year-old daughter by herself in a place that serves alcohol."

"She'll cope," snapped Myrna. "Like you said: she's almost

eighteen."

John chuckled and started keeping a more alert watch on the restaurant entrance. "True enough." He returned to his reader.

"What are we going to do, John?"

John put down his reader again. "That's pretty obvious: we're going to get divorced."

"You don't think we're going to get back together?"

"You left me for Renny. I'm not going to forget that—Hell, I'm like Atlas saying *so long,* Hercules." John stopped for a moment. "That's harsh. What I mean is you were miserable. I was miserable. Now we can figure out something new. Maybe it'll just be a new way to be miserable but it will be something apart." He gestured towards the restaurant. "Except where Shez is concerned."

"We can quitclaim it."

"What's that?"

"I was looking into it. The State of California Divorce Reform Act applies to us. Shez is close enough to majority. Neither of us is eligible for alimony. We split the assets. Put it all on the market and take a settlement."

"Shez stays with me?"

"If that's what she wants—I can try to persuade her otherwise but— okay, you're right. I agree. If I pick a fight, I just lose her anyway in a couple of months. I have to make sure she feels like she can still be my little girl."

"Yeah." John nodded. "I can help with that, too. We'll put the contents in storage. I'm not ready to divide stuff."

"Itemized storage, then. Everything inventoried. You look over the list and put in your items. I'll put up my items. Everything we agree on we take responsibility for—that way I'm not paying for your storage."

"Things we *don't* agree on?"

"We put them in a timed unit. Gets liquidated if we can't agree. We split the value."

John watched her for a long minute. "You've been thinking about this. Did you have this all figured out before you left?"

Myrna looked down. "Some. I didn't really make my decision before the Strawberry Festival. That crystallized it. But like you said. I've been miserable for a long time."

"I bet you have it all set up."

"Lawbot and all. You have a lawbot?"

"Sure."

"Let me send you what I've got."

A moment later, John's phone chimed. He opened it up and read the lawbot's report. "My lawbot likes your lawbot."

Myrna laughed—which cut John like a knife when he remembered how things had turned out. And how he had been ready to murder them both. *Never again.* He gave the lawbot permission. Myrna did the same.

And, just like that, they were divorced and the house on the market. Seconds later, there was a ding on both their phones: their house was sold, contacts for removing the contents to inventoried storage were awarded and the whole process scheduled. Bills for the last month were apportioned to their separate accounts.

John looked at his phone. "Ah, the modern world. Are you Myrna Torrence now?"

"I was always Myrna Torrence on the inside."

"Well, then." John was a little taken aback at the speed of things. "It's a pleasure to meet you."

"Likewise."

Myrna watched him a moment. "You're different."

"I stopped drinking."

"I knew you before you drank. This isn't that." She looked over his shoulder at the reader in his hands. "You're reading the bible? Are you a religious nut, now?"

John turned off the reader in irritation. "Everybody says something like that. If you're reading the Bible, you're immediately religious. Or a nut. Or both. Like it isn't the foundation of the world we live in. Like it has *nothing* useful in it if you're not a believer."

"Most people read it for religious reasons."

"Most people believe in luck, ghosts, life after death, and political promises." John held it up. "This book contains four thousand years' worth of stories, advice, and gossip about how changes work. How things staying the same work. I'm *trying* to change. Why *wouldn't* I look at it?"

Myrna held up her hands. "Sorry. Didn't mean to push any of your buttons."

"I'm tired of having to defend myself."

"Okay."

An awkward silence fell between them.

Myrna fiddled with a button on her shirt. "Learn anything interesting?"

"Some." He waggled the reader in the air. "What's *not* surprising how different things are between then and now. That's obvious: we have motorized vehicles, hours of video entertainment, and instant communication and knowledge. They had memorized stories, small towns, and dirt roads. It *is* surprising what remains the same. People are still their own worst enemies. People still change mainly because they're desperate for something different. The most important thing I get out of reading the Gospels is that the whole revenge cycle changes nothing and frees no one. It's a way of *staying the same*. Forgiveness and redemption cause change. Clutching to the cycle of revenge does not. God doesn't have much to do with it. Over and over, Jesus says something like 'you changed yourself' or 'your faith cured you.' It seems to me that this is the core of what he's saying. 'Take up your cross and follow me.'"

"Pardon?"

"Something he says in Matthew: 'If anyone would come after me, let him deny himself and take up his cross and follow me.' 'For what will it profit a man if he gains the whole world and forfeits his soul?' *His* cross. *His* soul. Change has to reflect who you are and everyone's cross is different."

"Does that mean you forgive me?"

That stopped John dead. He stared at her. "Is that important to you?"

Myrna wouldn't look at him. "It doesn't change anything. It ended as well as it could but it didn't end well. But we were together for a long time. We grew a child together. We had good times and bad times and the bad times won—but the bad times don't outweigh *everything* else." Myrna turned back to him. "So, yes, John. Your opinion matters to me. Your forgiveness matters to me."

"Jesus was the Son of God. He had special insight so he could forgive anybody." John let out a long breath. "Me, I'm just a pissed off ex-husband. I can't forgive you. I'm still too angry." He rose and put his phone and reader into his pockets. "Not yet, anyway."

With that, he left Myrna and crossed the street.

◀ July 5 ▶

Inside the *Solar Wind*, he saw Shez sitting disconsolately staring at her Canadian Special, tears rolling down her cheeks. John didn't know how but he was certain that Shez knew every word that had happened outside.

John sat down across from her. "Hey, there."

Shez dried her tears and gave him a trembling smile.

"We have money now," John said. "We don't have a home to go to anymore. What do you want to do?"

"Rent a car and go to Saint Louis?"

John leaned back in the booth. "Why ever would we want to go to Saint Louis?"

"The next Dot concert is there in three weeks."

"Ah," John said, understanding. "What the hell?" He spread his hands, blessing them both. "We will be Dotheads. We can even take the scenic route."

Chapter 2.21: Ima

Ima sent a terse message to her mother: *Found Peter. Lost him. He's okay.* She sent a similarly terse message to Murdock and Paternos: *Keep a watch for Peter Hidori. Concerts and downloads.*

She reversed her trip to Santa Monica: standard rail to Sacramento. Bullet train south. Hired car from Pasadena. All the time nervous. All the time thinking of Abby. All the time thinking of Dot.

On the train, she couldn't face working. Not now. Not with everything crowding in her mind. But the enforced idleness presented no distractions. Mountains, valleys, and deserts, beautiful as they were, did not hold her attention.

What had happened in Reno?

Ima was not given to flights of fancy or ecstatic bliss. Yet both had happened. Two and a half hours had passed in what felt like minutes. If she checked out the recordings, would she see the audience staring blankly in the tank, hypnotized by Dot and drooling?

Ima didn't think so but to make sure she brought up part of the show on her tablet. No. There they were, dancing just as she remembered. Ima included.

It was the music, Ima thought at last. Music was perceived emotionally. It slipped right past the pre-frontal cortex into the limbic system. All sorts of images passed through her mind: unforgettable jingles. People with dementia remembering music from their childhoods. A stroke victim unable to speak but still able to sing. People had been using music to sell things forever. Og the caveman probably tried to sell rocks to his neighbors by grunting rhythmically. Tag the right music with the right message and you can slip it right underneath people's filters.

Jesus, she thought. That was how the lasting effect happened. All music had an effect but Dot had figured out how to thread her message directly into the music. Programming was coming from the inside out—that ancient reptile brain telling the upstart mammal what to think.

The DPE was barely the first step—that was just the mechanism Dot used to influence the audience. Ima—and everyone else—had always thought she was utilizing DPE response to maximize performance effect. Maybe that's how Dot 1.0 worked. Dot 2.0 was using the DPE to measure responses to an entirely different model. You could use a telescope to watch the window of a neighbor or the face of the moon. The telescope was unchanged.

Ima tried to remember the lyrics but they wouldn't come. Just the images. Just the stories—those she remembered in detail. That made sense. That ancient reptile brain was pre-verbal. The mammal brain just translated for it. Ima couldn't think of that poor girl making a deal for her newborn baby without suddenly feeling close to tears—a powerful effect slipped in sharp and smooth as a surgical scalpel.

This was something she could take to Persuasion. Farrell. Farrell could pass it up the chain—Persuasion would be the tail wagging the Ippon dog. Right now, Dot 2.0 was feral. Operating on her own recognizance. But once they brought that technology in and put it in harness, Persuasion could own the world.

Ima saw Abby's face again. So disappointed.

Why? Ima tried to think like Abby. What was so bad about this?

Abby would look at it as the target and not the perpetrator. What was so wrong about being manipulated? People did it every day. Didn't Ima manipulate Abby to love her?

Ima quailed at that thought. What if Abby's love was the product of Ima's manipulation? Would it be real? Would it be true? Imagine a love spell placed on someone: you could never trust love's response. Or worse, the lover could be aware of her manipulated state and be helpless against it. Ima remembered that rat from college, doomed to press that lever regardless of how it felt. Please God make it stop!

That was how Abby would see it: a violation of her free will.

Ima frowned, looking out the window. The bullet train ran along the inner edge of the coastal mountains before digging east towards

Los Angeles. The low peaks were dry yellow, grass burned dry by the sun.

Ima didn't think people had free will. Everything she'd ever learned in college, and practiced since, was predicated on the idea that people were manipulatable objects whose sole purpose was to produce cash on demand. All advertising, music, and media was built on that premise. Even Dot.

Back to the concert, then. Was Ima manipulated by Dot? Maybe. Was she now different like the subjects Ima had been studying? Different how? The statistical indicators showed a reduction in certain categories of consumption—porn, non-factual news—and some increases in things like charitable giving and fact-checking. Ima consumed news, factual or otherwise, only so much as she could use it to predict public responses, and porn left her cold. Manufactured data was in the same category as news: if it caused trending, it was interesting. Otherwise, it wasn't useful.

So, if Ima had been manipulated—changed by Dot—how would she know?

Ima thought about Peter. Peter had changed. He didn't seem to think he was all that different but Ima could see it—in the way he smelled, if nothing else. Clearly, he had been changed by Dot.

Or was he? Again, Peter hadn't seemed to think so. He thought it was more that Dot had given him an opportunity to change—some breathing room—where he could manage it himself. He was aware of the difference, and Ima had seen an effect. But if Peter could see it in himself, why couldn't Ima see it in herself?

She suddenly felt bitterly disappointed and envious of Peter. Why should Peter, crazy as he was, get the benefit of a concert while Ima was still left with the same dilemmas and issues she started with? It just wasn't fair.

Fuck this. She brought up Robert Farrell's agent and set up an appointment for when she got back. By then, she'd be able to present the results of all three concerts: Bakersfield, Fresno, and Reno. She'd be able to show trends and changes and have a plan to use the entrails of Dot 2.0 for her own purposes.

Then, she closed the applications and set the tablet down. The train had bored through the mountains and was now cruising down the coast. In a little bit, it would turn inland again to slow down and stop in Pasadena. The car would take her home. By the end of the week, she'd have something for Farrell. Something valuable. Something she could trade for advancement—working directly for Farrell, maybe. Or he could be promoted and she'd move up the chain. Ima would have to protect herself so Farrell wouldn't just take the technology and say thank you. Think about that. Think about protecting it—maybe keep Mulcahey in the background. Ima would figure it out.

As the slanting sun broke the sea and sky to fill the cabin with light, Ima had a terrible feeling she was doing this all wrong.

◀ July 6 ▶

Abby was sitting at the table reading a book when Ima came in the door. She looked up from the book without saying anything.

Her face was like a wall.

"I'm back," Ima said. It sounded inane and stupid coming out of her mouth but it didn't matter. Ima had to say something.

"Was it a good trip?" Abby said slowly, as if she were choosing her words carefully.

What do I say? Yes: it was a good trip. Which confirms that I'm doing something you disapprove of or no: I did it but I'm bad at it. Ima felt tired.

"I found my father," she said. "Then, I lost him. He looks better though."

"That's good."

Silence grew between them. For a moment, Abby looked as if she would reach out, but Ima fled to her office.

Ima sat at her desk and looked around the room. There were Abby and Ima mementos everywhere: a picture of a fishing trip they took in Catalina. The basilica in Quito. A picture of the giant ficus in Maui—a trip so magical they had spent six months trying to figure out if they could actually afford to move to Hawaii.

Ima buried her face in her hands. She wanted to weep but could not cry. She brought up data from the Reno concert on her desk but stopped. Instead, she brought up the concert release from Bakersfield.

It wasn't the same concert but there were echoes. She wasn't swept away but she felt better. It made her feel like there were possibilities. Then, she watched the Fresno concert. Closer. Ima felt herself relax. Is this what Peter went through? Watching the concerts over and over? If Dot helped him, was Dot now helping her? Helping her how?

There was a knock on the office door. Ima cleared the desk. "Yes?"

Abby came in and sat in the chair opposite her. "We need to talk."

Ima felt as heavy as if she were wearing lead clothes. Lead skin. "All right."

"I've been thinking. I think you should leave for a while."

Oh, God. "Are you going to divorce me?"

Abby didn't speak immediately.

That short time felt eternal to Ima. As if the world were pinched and silent and there was nothing good left in it.

"No," Abby said finally. "I love you."

"I love you."

"I know." Abby looked around the room. Her gaze lingered on the Maui pictures. Abby smiled faintly. "But I can't be with you right now. I feel as if as long as we're here we're just going to chew on each other until there's nothing left. I don't want that. I want to see clearly and I don't think I can as long as we're so close. I've lived in this house my whole life so I don't think I should leave."

"I live here, too."

Abby nodded. "I thought about that. I did leave for a few days. But then it feels like you're pushing me out of the house I grew up in. The house I left to get married and returned when I got divorced. The house where my mother and I stood watch over my dead father. The house where I took care of my mother until she died. Then, I start to resent you." Abby shook her head. "It's not fair. It's not just. But it is the way I feel. I don't want to resent you." Abby looked at Ima. "Do you want to stay together?"

"Yes."

"Then, I need you to leave. When we've had time to think about things, we can talk about getting back together. But right now, I have no perspective. Every time I look at you, I see what you are doing. I see how you manipulate things. I start to wonder if you're manipulating me. I can't stand the thought. It makes me want to never see you again." She stopped and drew a long breath.

Suddenly, Ima could see the pain on Abby's face. *Why didn't I see that before? She's hurting as much as I am.* She wanted to step around the desk and hold her. But when Abby glanced back, Ima knew it would smack of manipulation.

Is doing nothing manipulation? Ima rested her forehead on her hands. Is there no end to this?

Ima straightened in her chair and faced Abby. "I'll take some things and move out tonight," she said. "I can come back for things if I need them, right?"

"Of course."

"I can do it when you're not here."

Abby waved it away. "Don't worry about it."

"Okay." Ima nodded. The illusion of accomplishment. "I'll be gone by morning."

"Thank you." Abby looked relieved. She stood up and left the room.

When Abby was gone, Ima opened up her desk window again and restarted Dot's Fresno concert. It was a consolation.

◄ July 7 ►

Robert Farrell was a two-meter black man who dressed like a basketball player turned tenured professor. He spoke softly. He didn't need to raise his voice; his reputation preceded him. If the stories were to be believed, all of Ippon was strewn with the bodies of those who had disappointed him.

Ima set up the conference in the communications room in American Persuasion's main office.

The room was surrounded on all sizes by milky, active surfaces. Holographic interfaces were bandwidth hogs—the amount of data a three-dimensional image required was easily an order of magnitude greater than a flat image. Ippon had high volume net pipes at its main offices.

Ima could have used the conference room at the hotel. But the screen resolution was crappy and the bandwidth didn't support anything but flat images. She wanted to impress Farrell.

Farrell was in Shanghai. So, it was precisely at four in the afternoon, Pacific Coast time, that the bell in the conference room sounded that it was nine in the morning, Shanghai. The milky whiteness flickered and Robert Farrell was sitting at a matched table on the other side of the screen.

"Good morning, Ima," he said comfortably. "I've been told you have something you'd like to show me."

"Yes, sir," she said, without correcting him, and started.

Ima didn't hide that she'd been using the discretionary funds. Either Farrell would forgive it because of her success or he'd fire her. She'd decided to lay everything out on the table, beginning with Mulcahey's early work that attracted Ima's attention, Ima's contract with her, and the proposed use of the Dot system.

"You didn't compromise the performance engine, did you?" Farrell said like a professor checking a student.

"No, sir." She showed him the evidence of the checksums in the concerts. Then, she showed him the data, leading through the Bakersfield concert and how each concert converted more novel attendees to aficionados or Dotheads. How they had lasting consumer effect changes.

"Do you think the… Dotheads, you call them? Do you think they recruit the novel attendees?"

"With evangelical fervor, sir."

"Interesting choice of words. Have you met any of these people?"

"I've attended one concert. The one in Reno."

"How did you find it?"

"Compelling, sir."

Farrell watched her a moment. "Have you been converted, Ima? We wouldn't want you to lose your objectivity."

"I think I fall safely into the unaffected category. Of course, it helps that I understand the mechanism."

"No economic indicator survives publication."

"Beg pardon, sir?"

"Something they said in Econ 101. As soon as an economic indicator is made public, people try to game it until it is useless. This might be the same." He gestured to her charts. "Go on."

"In conclusion, I think we have demonstrated that Dot 2.0 has a strong compulsive effect on the audience. Like the Dot Performance Engine, we can tune it to our purposes."

Farrell was silent a moment. "Why do you think those consumer changes occurred? Why *those*? Reduction in manufactured data. Reduction in pornography. Increased giving to charity. Any speculation?"

"It reflects the subject matter of Dot's new songs. They consist of stories of hardship and triumph. Of lost love and restored hope and freedom. These would cause an increase in empathy—increased empathy would cause the response we're seeing."

Farrell nodded. "That's a good hypothesis." He turned to her. "You've done well. I'll see you get good recognition for this. There's no need for further experimentation. Tell Mulcahey to wrap it up and turn over the work and the equipment. Cancel the concerts."

"Why? They're bringing in good revenue."

"Not much compared to the potential of what you have here. If it goes on much longer it will compete with the much larger Dot 1.0 revenue. Besides," he nodded to himself. "It's going to start attracting attention. We don't want anyone to know what we have until we're ready. Best keep it a secret as long as we can."

"Sir…" Ima stopped a moment. "That will disappoint the Dotheads. The band, too."

"Do we care? The contract with the band stipulates generous cancellation payments."

Ima didn't speak for a moment. "I don't think they want to stop. I think they want to finish the tour."

Farrell watched her a moment. "Are you sure you weren't affected?"

Ima felt a pit open in her stomach. *You idiot! What the fuck do you care about Mulcahey and her band?* "Yes, sir."

"Cancel the concerts. If Mulcahey won't listen, stop them. Dot is our property. It's time we claim it."

The room turned milky white in instant.

Ima sat with her hands on the table. They were as still as wood but, on the inside, they were shaking.

◄ July 7 ►

As soon as Ima felt ready, she left the office and walked briskly down the steps to the waiting car. Sunset wasn't for another three hours.

The Persuasion offices were housed in an industrial building at the eastern edge of Culver City. Usually, Ima would tell the car to take the fastest route—along the interstate to drop off at the edge of Santa Monica—in a hurry to get home to the house and Abby.

The Merigo was a nice, semi luxurious apartment with a hot tub, a nice kitchen and a lovely view of the ocean with was no one waiting for her. There was no one to cook for.

Instead, she instructed the car to take Route One the whole way: stop and go. Noisy. Filled with people trying to get to the beach or up the coast, desperate for a look at the ocean or as much ocean that could be seen over the giant, protective sea wall. Crowded. If it weren't for the automated cars, there would have been fistfights and a couple of murders on the road. But the cars were just fast enough to keep the rage down to manageable levels.

She rolled down the windows and let the air blow through. Salt. Burnt chemical smells from the few remaining small factories along the road. Dust from the interior brought here on the summer winds and stirred up by the passing automobiles. An unidentifiable stench came as she passed over Bellona Creek that was then swallowed up by the gasoline, diesel, and ozone of Marina del Reye. The rich stink of rot and luxury blew through the car as they bent closer to the sea.

The idea of returning to the hotel was suddenly intolerable. A club, maybe. A bar. On impulse, she searched for Santa Monica clubs cross-referenced with Dot and found Cornucopia, a bar that was so well known among Dotheads it had fan sites.

Ima let the car roam searching for fares. "Short leash," she said. "I don't want more than a twenty-minute wait." The car beeped acknowledgment. Ima despised automatons that spoke. Intelligent systems were one thing, but a narrow-focused AI wasn't any smarter than a mouse and shouldn't masquerade as anything more.

On the outside, Cornucopia was a quiet, bland concrete building. The neon horn was the only clue.

Past the doors, and the soundproofing, the bar was loud and crowded. The groups crossed all sorts of social boundaries. Two drag queens were in deep conversation with someone wearing a two-thousand-dollar business suit. From the cut and logos, Ima guessed he worked for STR—third largest data manipulation company in North America. Half a dozen students in jeans and T's were arguing with four bodybuilders, covered in the bare minimum thongs and strip-shirts, a faint sheen of sand on their sandals. A clear threesome hung at the bar wearing a married look that made Ima's heart break.

A bootleg Dot was projected above the bar belting out "Sugarpaper" as if she were backing a stripper.

All around her snatches of words and sentences confirmed the main topic of conversation. "Dot is love, man. Pure love. You can't disagree with that." "I don't think you can disconnect the abstracted girl-woman image from the material. She's intended to be a *girl*." "Can you believe the way she dances? A human woman would *break*." "All I have to say is that Dot in Fresno was *different*."

This last was a long-haired blond man in his early twenties sitting at the bar next to the threesome. He reminded Ima of nothing so much as a young, studious Thor.

"Different how, man?" His companion was short and round but gave the impression of enormous strength.

Ima took the seat next to Thor's companion to listen.

Thor shook his head. "More *there*. More like she was looking at you. Looking at all of us. Looking so hard and pure that she made you look right along with her. Like there was this song about a young, single mother having a conversation with her newborn child, trying to figure out if she should give the kid up. Dot made us look at that."

Thor's companion shook his head. "Wish I could have been there, man."

Thor nodded and drank half of his beer. "Did you listen to the concert recording?"

"Yeah, but it's not the same."

"The Fresno concert was released. You should check it out. It's better than the Bakersfield recording. More like the actual concert." Thor nodded to himself. "Fresno had another song about that girl that breaks your heart. She got messed up after all and ended up giving her daughter away."

"Fucked up, man."

"Yeah." Thor waved his beer. "But it was like you were seeing into her. You can't ignore something like that."

"Excuse me." Ima smiled at them. "You made it to the Bakersfield concert."

Thor turned towards her. "I certainly did." He held his hand out. "Arnold. Arnold Woodly."

"Really." Ima chuckled. "I thought you would have been named Thor."

Arnold gave her a blank look. "Why?"

His companion laughed. "That would make me Loki. Loki was brother to Thor."

"Half-brother," said Arnold.

"Exactly." Loki-Brother-of-Thor snickered and drained his beer. He ordered three more.

Ima glanced at him and realized Arnold was younger than she had thought. "Aren't you too young to be drinking?"

Arnold shook his head morosely. "Nobody ever checks. It's a shame."

"This cretin is my half-brother. *He's* Sigurd." Arnold gestured to himself. "Arnold: Boston mother who was a fan of old Schwarzenegger movies." He pointed to Sigurd. "Sigurd: British mother fan of Wagner. Both sired by the same father. A UN doctor named Ellish Odonoto who was never heard from again."

"Hey, now," said Sigurd-used-to-be-Loki. "You'll scare her off with our full family history."

"She won't scare off," said Arnold-used-to-be-Thor confidently. "Look at her. She's a full form Dothead. Like us. We don't scare easily." Arnold waved for three more beers.

"Indeed," said Ima. Was that what she was now? "I was at the Reno concert."

"Yeah?" Arnold gave her an admiring glance. "Was it terrific?"

"It was." Ima hesitated. "I didn't connect the young girl songs until just now. There's a third one."

Arnold and Sigurd leaned towards her.

"Do go on," said Sigurd.

"She gets her life back but when she tries to contact her daughter, her daughter doesn't want to have anything to do with her. The woman goes forward into her life alone."

"Jeez," said Arnold. "That's *really* fucked up."

Sigurd nodded.

"But it was like you saw her right in front of you, right?" asked Arnold intensely.

"Yes."

Arnold leaned back in his chair looking satisfied. "Told you. We're heading out for the Saint Louis concert tonight. What about you?"

Ima didn't have the heart to tell them the concert would be canceled. Instead, she sipped her beer, trying to sort out her feelings towards the Dot. Towards Abby. Towards Ippon. Towards Robert Farrell. She glanced and Sigurd and Arnold. "Why are you Dotheads?"

"Hm," said Arnold with suspicion. "Maybe she's not a Dothead, after all. Maybe she's some journalist come round here again to see what makes Dotheads tick. Or maybe she's a freak."

"Are you a journalist?" asked Sigurd. "Or a freak?"

"Neither."

"But," Sigurd said owlishly. "You are not a full-fledged Dothead, either. Dotheads don't ask other Dotheads why they are Dotheads."

The beers came. "Repeat that. I double-dog dare you," said Arnold as he passed Sigurd his beer and then one for Ima.

"Couldn't possibly. True none the less."

"It is." Arnold turned to Ima. "Why do you ask?"

Ima didn't know what to answer.

"It's obvious," said Sigurd.

"It is?" Arnold shook his head. "Enlighten me."

"She's a *new* Dothead, unsure of herself and her place in the Dottiverse."

"'Dottiverse.'"

"New term. I just made it up." Sigurd waved around the room. "The community. The reason why we come together. Why Bohemians rest with Obsessives. Passives break bread with Aggressives. Republicans lie down with Democrats. Dot brings us together. In her holographic wisdom, she demonstrates that the differences between us are minor—trivial, really—in the face of greater human contact."

Arnold watched him a long time. "Bullshit."

Sigurd laughed out loud. "Got me."

"I think there's something in what Sigurd says." Ima leaned on the bar, feeling timid.

"Don't encourage him," said Arnold sourly.

Ima sipped her beer. "People repeat what they think feels good. Sex. Drugs. Exercise. Music." Ima felt on the verge of something but she couldn't yet see it.

"We repeat Dot experiences because it feels good." Arnold shook his head. "Duh."

Ima continued. "And connect afterward regarding Dot because *that* feels good. And repeat because that feels good, too."

"Again: duh."

Ima ignored him. "Pursuit of anything changes you in that direction. Repetition breeds repetition."

Sigurd put down his beer slowly. Arnold was staring at her.

"You mean," Sigurd said thoughtfully. "We repeat the Dot experience because we've repeated the Dot experience and that makes us want to repeat the Dot experience such that we repeat the Dot experience?"

"Yes."

Sigurd and Arnold looked at one another. Then, they turned towards Ima and said as one: "Duh."

Ima dissolved into giggles.

Chapter 2.22: John

The car they rented was a Toyota Automate—an efficient long-distance electric vehicle suitable for off-road use. It had a complete set of charging methods from the entire outside skin as a single solar surface to having a small charging generator that would accept multiple fuels. It was small—the two passengers in the front seats had to endure constant physical contact and the two in the back would require intimate knowledge of one another—and it strained at any speed over sixty kilometers an hour. But they were in no hurry.

The heart of Reno was speared by a highway that led directly to Salt Lake City. Then south to I-70 and east directly to Saint Louis, The Automate had full connectivity and it didn't take Shez long to discover that other Dotheads were also taking the scenic route.

In Salt Lake City, they hooked up with a caravan moving east in fits and starts. Fifty cars, buses, and trucks circled up in the burnt yellow scrub below the towering black and white shadow of Chalk Mountain. They met two brothers, Sigurd and Arnold, who went up into the high country looking for turquoise. Shez and John followed them. They found jasper and petrified wood but no turquoise.

That afternoon, someone drove into town and returned with a pile of firewood and a permit. The hundred or so people brought out food they had brought—Shez and John donated hot dogs and lasagna—and the impromptu village ate by the light of the fire and the clear, cloudless sky.

"It's a temporary settlement," said Sigurd as he roasted a hot dog near the edge of the bonfire.

"Aren't all settlements temporary?" said Shez.

John agreed and passed Shez a hot dog of her own.

"Yes," said Sigurd. "In any real sense of time. But once there has been a generation or two in the same spot, people develop the illusion of permanence and place. Here we have no such illusion."

"Bullshit," said Arnold.

"That's your comment on anything I say," Sigurd complained.

"It's my permanent role to be your antidote," said Arnold around a mouth full of burger. "People can crystallize a community instantly on any pretext. Whether it's a lovely place under the stars or the shared experience of listening to a software robot."

"Careful," said John. "That's our demi-deity you're talking about."

Arnold barked a laugh. "I like that. 'Demi-deity.' Did you come up with that?"

John nodded towards Shez. "She did on the way up."

"Clever girl." Arnold swallowed. "Cults are uninteresting—everybody trying to be the same. *Communities* are groups of individuals with shared interests and goals. That's interesting. We have here a diverse Dothead community." He gestured to Shez. "Underage, precocious teen." He gestured towards John. "Blue-collar redneck." Pointed towards Sigurd. "Pretentious undergraduate academic." And gestured to himself. "And fully grounded salt of the earth such as myself. The catalyst of our gathering is less important than the gathering itself."

"So deluded," sighed Sigurd. "Every community needs a village idiot. Fortunately, we have that role filled."

◄ July 09 ►

That night, Shez and John slept in sleeping bags outside. As the fire died down, the stars seemed to leap into visibility.

"Do you know any of them?" Shez asked John.

"Big dipper." He pointed. "North star. It's supposed to be part of the little dipper but I never could see it. That's all I know."

"I'd like to learn about them."

"You have your phone and we have connectivity, even up here."

"I know." She fell silent a moment. "But I want a book."

"A book? Why?"

"A small book. About as big as my hand. With drawings and

pictures in it. And big margins where I can make notes." She snuggled into her sleeping bag.

"You've given this a lot of thought."

"There's comfort in a book," she said quietly. "A book is always yours. You can write notes in it. Correct it. Put in your own ideas."

"Can't you do that with a reader?"

"It's not the same. With a book, you might use different color pens. Or pencils. One day you might write the idea in block print. Other days, it might be cursive. Barely legible scrawls. Abbreviations that only you can know. Private references to times and dates. Like, if I had a book on stars and constellations right now, I could write next to Big Dipper: 'Pops said he knew this one and the north star. But beyond that, he's as ignorant as a stump.' If I wrote that in a reader it could always get out on the net and where would you be? In a book, it's as private as I want to make it."

"I see," John said. "Thanks for sharing."

"Anytime, Pops."

John understood that need to keep things close. To keep them private. No one but John knew of his murderous impulses unknowingly derailed by the actions of his daughter. If John had anything to say about it, no one would ever know. Thinking of them brought up a deep shame. Maybe it was true that no secret ever lasted, but with any luck, that one would outlive him.

But if no one knew, what was the shame? As long as he never pursued that impulse, wasn't he blameless? Jesus said the sin was in the heart, not the action. That the action and the sin were the same. John rejected that idea—*had* to reject it. That would mean he had already murdered Renny and Myrna. He imagined waking up the next day, knowing he'd killed two people. Would he have exulted? Cried in grief? Both? There was no way to know—he had not taken that path. But that didn't mean the path wasn't there. He had not just idly considered it. He had planned to make it happen—which meant he had that capacity. Faced with the actual act, he might not have carried it out but that didn't change the fact he had approached the proposition. He had to carry that possibility with him. Keep it in front of him so he would always know his own capabilities.

He remembered what he'd said to Myrna about forgiveness and

redemption. Would Shez have been able to forgive him if he'd slaughtered her mother's lover and maybe her mother as well? No. Would she forgive him if he'd just planned it but never carried it out? John didn't think so but would not put it to the test.

◀ July 10 ▶

Dotheads composed an elastic community. When Shez and John decided to break camp and continue east, Arnold and Sigurd decided to travel with them but no one else did. The remaining community waved to them, wished them well, and promised to see them in Saint Louis.

The tiny car had gone from intimate to crowded but they rolled the windows down and eased the press by leaning outside to get one-armed tans.

John had continued to read the Bible and on Sunday he decided he wanted to go to church.

The others stared at him.

"You're getting strange, Pops," offered Shez.

"Strange isn't bad, you understand," said Sigurd.

"Why?" asked Arnold.

John held up the reader. "I've been reading all this trying to get a handle on change."

"Change happens," said Sigurd. "You can't modify it."

"You can't modify change?" John shook his head. "I disagree. I think you can do it well or you can do it badly. This book has all sorts of stories about both. But it seems to me I should listen to someone else. Someone who's read it, too. Someone beyond you clowns."

"We're in Colorado," said Arnold. "There are probably a lot of churches here. Which one?"

"Check the reviews," suggested Shez.

"Good idea." Sigurd brought out his phone. "A church is a commodity like anything else, right? People review commodities. Let's see what we find."

"Godfinder.com," said Shez. "There's a Godfinder app."

"What does it say?" John tried to look over her shoulder.

"It's like a dating site," she said. "It asks a bunch of questions. Do you have a denomination in mind?"

"No."

"Are you a fundamentalist?"

John stared at her. "I don't know what that is."

Sigurd leaned over the seat. "She means do you believe in the literal truth of the Bible."

"Normal people do that?"

"Sure," said Sigurd.

"That's a broad definition of normal," said Arnold.

"Hey." Sigurd turned back to Arnold. "We're on a long-distance trip to see a software robot sing."

Arnold shrugged. "Point taken."

John ignored them. "I'm not a fundamentalist."

"You're a seeker," Shez declared.

"What's that?"

"Someone who can't make up their mind," offered Sigurd.

"Shut up," said Shez. "Someone who is looking for answers but hasn't found any."

"Sure," said John, uncertain. "I guess."

"Wow." Shez scrolled her phone. "They really like you now. I'm getting pings from all over the state."

"You're an uncommitted market," said Sigurd. "Like an eighteen-year-old woman, a young consumer, or an independent voter. Everybody wants you."

Shez scowled at him. "Shut up."

"No offense."

"Offense *taken*."

"Great." John looked outside for a moment. "Maybe this is a bad idea."

"No," said Shez. "We just have to find the *right* church. How about this one: Zachariah Baptist Church. Everyone welcome. Approach God here. Steamboat springs. Just a couple of hours away." Shez looked up at him. "Look: they got Bible Study tonight."

"I like the book of Zachariah."

"It's settled," said Arnold. "We grab a place in Steamboat and you can go tomorrow—Sunday. You come back when you're done."

John looked at them, one face at a time. "Okay. Let's do that."

Chapter 2.23: Ima

Ima had sent the orders the next day as she nursed a hangover she'd gotten with Thor and Loki—no. Arnold and Sigurd. Whatever. Even now, days later, she felt warmly comforted thinking of them.

The order to Mulcahey had been explicit: the project was to come to an end. Further concerts were canceled. Notes, equipment, configurations were all property of Ippon and would be surrendered as soon as practical. A fat stipend awaited Mulcahey to extend the focus of her successful work beyond concert material.

The order to Murdock and Paternos was just as specific: cancel concerts. Facilitate gathering the material and shipping it back to Los Angeles Persuasion. From there, Ima would broker its shipping to Robert Farrell's group.

Now it was the eleventh and she'd heard nothing but crickets.

The Reno concert had been on July fifth. The Saint Louis concert had been scheduled for July fifteenth. She'd canceled on the night of the seventh. After four days without acknowledgment from Mulcahey and a terse "received" from the twins, Ima called Murdock and Paternos. Mohammed answered. Yes, they'd received the order. Yes, they had canceled the Saint Louis concert. They were talking with Mulcahey about shipping the material back. No, Mulcahey didn't say she'd take the stipend.

Ima hung up dissatisfied.

Abby had contacted a marriage counselor named Terry. There had been two sessions in the last five days. Both felt like an opportunity for Abby to tell Ima what an immoral person she had become. Terry quietly encouraged Abby until Ima had blown up: "This is what I do. This is what I've done—I was doing it when we were dating. I was doing it after we got back from the honeymoon. I've done it all the time we've been married. It paid off the mortgage. It pays the taxes and puts food on the table. You have been living under its roof and eating its meals. Where do *you* get off telling *me* how immoral I am?"

Ima was going to storm out when Abby said, "That's a legitimate point."

Ima stopped and turned towards her.

Abby was watching her. "But it implies you own me. I bought into your profession and now I should *shut up*. It means I'm stuck with whatever decision I made and will never have any opportunity to change. It denies me my own chance at redemption." She shook her head. "I deny that. I deny it for *me* and, more importantly, I deny it for you."

Ima left. Abby's next call would no doubt be to a divorce lawyer. But crickets there, too.

Chapter 2.24: *John*

John didn't go to church on Sunday. Instead, he left them sleeping in the room.

The Hotel Gaunt was as odd as its name. It was a narrow building and entered on the street across the street from a bar and a marijuana store. There was a man at the desk paging through the active desk. He looked up. "Can I help you?"

"Are there any churches open at this hour?"

The man looked at him. "Walking distance?"

"If possible."

"Church of the Apostolic Conversion. Four blocks north. I don't know what they do this time of night but they're always open."

The mountain air was crisp, even in summer. Not cold but dry as old wood. Dry as sand. Dry as a clever thought or a cold reproof.

The Church of the Apostolic Conversion was in an old building that had not been built as a church but converted from a great house. Given its age, when it was built it could have been a mansion. Now, it had been hollowed out. The lines of the building and the front porch marked it as once being a home but only that home's last traces.

A black man sat on the front porch under a dim bulb reading a Bible, his collar clear in the glare. His face was broad, pockmarked, and discolored. His hair was not yet gray but had started giving way to it. He was not a big man but had a measured look, as if he had decided to look and sit *just* so for reasons of his own. John liked his smile.

John stood uncertainly on the sidewalk.

"Hey there," said the minister. "Come on up."

John came up the stairs and took his proffered hand. "John Doretto."

"Avery Shanks," said the minister. "You can sit or go in. I like to keep it open on Saturday nights in case someone wants to pray. But you can go in and just sit if you want." Avery gave him a searching look. "Sit down," he said. "I'm guessing you've *never* seen the inside of a church."

John nodded. "True enough."

Avery looked out on the street. "People come along and stop, sometimes, undecided. I like to sit here and give them encouragement in case they're too afraid or embarrassed to come in." He looked back up to John. "You're not religious but you end up in front of my church. Isn't that interesting?"

"My daughter thinks I'm a seeker."

Avery nodded. "Seek yourself a seat. I'll get a crick in my neck from looking up at you."

John sat down stiffly.

"What are you seeking? God?"

John shook his head slowly. "No. I'm pretty sure that doesn't interest me."

"That's the main thing you can seek in a church."

John leaned forward, his elbows on his knees. "Something happened to me. Something that changed me. I've been trying to understand it."

"A still voice crying in the wilderness?"

"Maybe." John thought for a moment. "I've been doing a lot of reading and keep coming back to the Bible. It talks about change *all the time*. Paul on the road to Damascus. Matthew following Jesus. And it talks about things that *don't* change. Like the Pharisees. Like the Babylonians."

"The Babylonians changed—Shadrach in the furnace caused that."

John nodded. "There's always push to change. Resistance to change. Sometimes, in the Bible, change is something to bring about. Other times, it's something to resist. Every time I think I've got it, there's something in the Bible that disagrees with me. Other times, when I'm lost, I find the answer."

"In God?"

John shook his head. "No. In the *way* people change. Or don't change. Or fight change. Or slide with it."

Avery watched him a moment. "So, if you're not interested in God and you *are* interested in the Bible, what are you doing here?"

John leaned back. "I'm not sure. When I read the Bible, I get a *sense* of how things go together. How things might fit—it's like a building. Or a tower—some kind of *structure*. A feeling that if I could boil down all this stuff and filter it, I'd get a wonderful set of principles I could apply anywhere. For anything."

"Would that be Jesus?"

"I think Jesus and God would be some of the stuff to boil out."

Avery laughed. "That's a lovely bit of blasphemy."

"Yeah." John felt embarrassed. "Sorry. I don't mean to be insulting."

"I'm not insulted." Avery waved towards the inside of the church. "He died and came back from the dead. There's precious little you can do to insult *that*."

John nodded. "Thanks." He beat his arms on the arms of the chair for a long time. "I've been reading a *lot*. You know who Einstein was, right?"

"Yes. He's a pretty famous character. E=MC² and all that."

"Yeah." John listened to the night. "They thought they had physics all wrapped up before he came along. They had everything pictured as *waves*. Well, waves needed something to travel in so they invented *ether*. You couldn't see it. You couldn't touch it. But it was all around you and affected how things worked. Einstein came along and said, basically, well there might be ether. There might not be. But here's a way for light to travel that doesn't need it." John held his hands as if he were holding a bowl. "They had built this entire structure that needed something to keep it together. Einstein came along and said it's pretty but you don't need it. I think we have rules and concepts and structures that we've built that need this stuff—like God—because we built it that way. But if we can create a new structure—a *better* structure—that stuff can be left behind."

Avery gave him a hard look. "You think God is something we invented just to make ourselves feel better?"

John shrugged. "That's harsh. But maybe."

Avery watched the street for a moment. This late, there were few cars and a scattering of pedestrians. "You're lucky nobody came tonight that actually needs me. I'd boot your ass out of here." He turned back to John, reached down next to his chair, and picked up a Bible. "You are a dilettante. You pick and choose what you want to see in this and discard the rest. There are *thousands* of years of material here. Looked at and analyzed all that time to figure out the essence of God's meaning." He spread it open. "Pick any page in this book and it's a discussion of man's relationship with God, Sure, there's change in it—human life is all about change. But that is ancillary to the fundamental point of the work. That change you're so interested in is a *consequence* of that relationship, not the focus. Who are you to challenge that?"

Avery's face was written with passion. His voice thundered—years of preaching filled every nook and cranny of it.

He was right, though. John was casting aside the intent of every editor, collector and translator since the Hittites. The Bible was a distillation of those efforts—the natural product of years of pruning, creation, and thought. He should honor that. But he didn't have to subscribe to it.

"I've misused you," John said slowly. "I've found a lot of value in that book. But not the God part. I was wrong. I'm not a seeker. I didn't come here for answers. I've *got* answers. I came here to test them."

Avery stared at him. "What do you mean?"

"Like you said, every passage in there is dripping with God. I'm not using that but it's still there. I'm building something out of the remainder. How do I know if it stands on its own? It's like I'm testing a vaccine by exposing the test animal to the disease." John pointed at the Bible in Avery's hand. "There's value there for me. But it's not the same as the value it has for you." He stood up. "I'm sorry."

Avery caught his sleeve. "You do know you're going to Hell for this, right?"

"That's a terrible incentive. It calls into question everything else the New Testament says."

Avery drew back from him.

John felt terrible. "I'm sorry. It seems to me that wanting to believe or not believe in God is an emotional decision. It's like love: it's either there or it isn't. In my case, it isn't." He started to go down the steps.

"Don't go!" Avery stood up. "I was wrong. God wants me to be here tonight to talk to you. Don't go."

John kept walking.

"When you feel the angel of death near," Avery called after him. "You'll repent. Then, it will be too late."

John stopped and turned back to him. "What does it say about a faith that requires the threat of death to make someone believe?"

He turned and walked back towards the hotel.

As he turned the corner, he glanced back. Avery had reseated himself and was reading the Bible closely.

Arnold sat on a bench outside the hotel.

John slowed down thoughtfully. "Couldn't sleep?"

Arnold moved to one side. His blond hair caught the streetlights. "In a manner of speaking. I'm down here to intercept you."

John looked up at the front of the hotel and back at Arnold. "Why?"

"You can guess."

John suddenly realized what was going on and started forward.

Arnold was suddenly standing in front of him. "Just a minute, John."

"That's my little girl up there!"

"That's your nearly eighteen-year-old daughter up there."

"*Nearly!*"

"Who has chosen, for some reason, to sleep with my nineteen-year-old brother. There is nothing you can do to prevent it—whatever happened has already happened."

"I'll kill him!"

Arnold watching him narrowly. "I can see you feel that way," he said softly. "Sit down so we can talk about that."

"I'll kill you, too."

Arnold shook his head. "*I'm* twenty-two. Younger, bigger, stronger, and faster. Sit down before I thump you." He shoved John suddenly and John sat down heavily.

Arnold sat next to him. "My brother is upright. Caring. He has no diseases. Your daughter is kind. The fact she likes him is a testament to her good judgment of people. Sigurd is a *much* better person than I am and I won't let you disturb them quite yet." He took John's arm.

It was like having his arm clamped in a vise. John realized that for all his murderous impulses, he was not going up there unless Arnold let him. John pleaded with Arnold. "She doesn't know what she's doing. She's too young."

"Young or not, she knows *exactly* what she's doing." Arnold signed and let John go. "You may see your daughter as your little girl but she's not."

"That's not your place to say."

Arnold nodded. "It is not. But I know my brother. I've gotten to know Shez a little bit over the last few days. This is going to be a tiny sweet romance for a few days. Then—after the concert probably—we'll go our separate ways. The two of them will have wonderful pleasant memories—as long as you stay civilized. If you go up there yelling and carrying on, Sigurd and I will leave. Shez will *hate* you and leave you as soon as she can."

"It's against the law."

"Not in Colorado. He's only nineteen. *I'm* the old one."

It stuck in his mind like a bad taste. Now that he thought about it, he could see how it happened. The little conversations and sidelong glances between them. Long, earnest, private discussions, Shez leaning towards him and Sigurd sitting with his arms crossed.

"She's too young."

"I think the same thing about my brother," Arnold said. "He's going to leave with his heart broken."

"I was talking about *her*."

Arnold chuckled. "Shez is tough. She'll be fine."

How many times had he blundered in conversations with Shez? Myrna? But he was her *father*, God damn it! He was supposed to protect her.

From what? Sigurd wasn't going to hurt her.

"I don't have to like it," growled John.

"No, you do not." Arnold nodded. "Part of being civilized is being civil when you don't want to."

◄ July 12 ►

When they left the next morning, Shez moved into the back seat with Sigurd. They were affectionate but didn't paw each other. John was grateful for that, at least.

They took Interstate 70 east into Missouri but the concert was still a few days away. Thor insisted they detour south to a park he'd read about called Johnson Shut-Ins. Here, the Black River had cut a miniature canyon of potholes, chutes, and gorges—a natural water park.

John floated in the water, roasted on the sunward side and delightfully chilled in the wet shadow. He watched Shez playing in the water with Sigurd. Arnold liked to sit on the boulder and watch things. There was clear affection between Shez and Sigurd—a young love, maybe? John had few memories of love that weren't miserable. Of course, right now he was undoubtedly biased. Maybe Shez would be luckier. Maybe Arnold was right.

He hadn't thought about it but realized, then, that sex just hadn't been present much since the Reno concert. Even in the Dothead camp there hadn't been the usual dance of the sexual postures he'd seen in campgrounds before, where unattached singles tried for each other's attention. There had been couples there—one particularly noisy one—so none of them had sworn off sex. It just hadn't been a priority.

That, in itself, was curious.

Dot? What have you done to us?

Chapter 2.25: Ima

When Ima called the twins the night before the concert, she reached Johann. Mohammed was not available. Ima checked the locale of the connection. Johann was talking from the Grand near the Sheldon Concert hall. She checked the Sheldon concert site: Dot was still scheduled.

She blasted Johann and realized she was screaming at a dead phone.

The following afternoon she was in a hired car leaving Lambert Field.

"Open the *fuck* up, Johann!" she yelled as she pounded the hotel door.

The door opened slowly.

Ima stormed past Johann. The room was filled with equipment—she could see the tank being tested on one of the screens. There were a couple of band members working with equipment on stage.

"This was supposed to be *canceled!*"

"Yeah." Johann scratched his head. "About that." Then, his voice trailed into silence.

"Where's Mohammed?"

"He left when he realized you were coming. He didn't want to face you. I guess he quit."

"Fucking great!" Her anger burned white-hot and pure. How wonderful it felt to give in to unambiguous feelings. "Shut it down."

Johann didn't say anything for a moment. "No,"

"*What?*"

Johann shook his head. "It's not right. We all worked so hard... I'm not going to stop you but I'm not going to help you, either." He looked up at her, five full feet of righteous indignation.

"How do I shut it down?"

"What part of 'not helping you' did you miss?"

Okay, then.

She didn't know enough to shut down the electronics so she walked over to the Sheldon. This wasn't like Reno or Fresno. This was humid, equatorial heat, like getting struck repeatedly by a baseball wrapped in a wet towel.

In the blessed air conditioning of the Sheldon, she discovered it wasn't enough that she could prove who she said she was. Murdock and Paternos had booked the hall in the name of MNP, their own subsidiary of Persuasion—but one over which she had no control. The management would not listen to her—though they did acknowledge her entrance pass.

Furious, she stomped backstage.

Mulcahey was talking with two of the band members. She saw Ima coming and said something to them and then met her before Ima could say anything. Mulcahey grabbed Ima by the arm and dragged her into an empty dressing room.

"I told you to *shut down!*" Ima hissed.

"You did," said Mulcahey. "No."

"You can't say no! Ippon owns everything you did here. Ippon owns Dot. It owns you. It owns me. I am telling you: *shut down!* I will bring the *police* here if I have to."

"Bring them." Mulcahey stared at her. "I've got something so much more important here than some new kink on advertising. We are not stopping because Ippon is scared someone is going to steal their jingle maker."

Mulcahey advanced on her. She poked Ima in the chest. "And you know it. I *saw* you in Reno. You were dancing with the rest of them. The audience and the band were *connected*. Dot understands how you work. How you think. I am *not* going to give that up."

In her mind, Ima suddenly saw Peter. She waved it away savagely. "Yes, you will!"

Ima pushed past Mulcahey and worked her way outside to the street. She called the police but they wouldn't act on just her say so. They needed upper Ippon management—which meant Farrell would have to be notified. Right. She was *not* going to show her boss she couldn't control the situation.

Okay. She took a deep breath. She couldn't shut it down without cooperation and she wasn't getting any. Okay. Time for more direct measures. Down the miserable street, she found a restaurant with both indoor and outdoor seating. Why would anybody in their right mind choose to sit outside in this weather? But people did. She saw them. Right there in front of her.

Safely inside, she sat down and pulled out her tablet.

Ima ran through all of the equipment: LIDAR, optical cameras, FLIR—there! Infrared camera with an intelligent operating system. An outstanding and uninstalled patch against the FLIR operating system: any saturating flash triggered an OS reboot where there was an opportunity to load executable code. Ima was deep in the darknet now. Sure enough, there was a suite of viruses that could be used to hack the system. All tailorable: no programming required. This was what Dot used. There was no magic in the AI. Just quick and powerful access to the same place everyone else went.

Ima pulled up a candidate—SurperMAXAlpha. SurperMAXAlpha was an invader but it had no target. It could carry the ball but not into the end zone. But it *could* carry a second virus inside it. Then, she found AltRight. It would squirt through the Sorenson discrimination engines to attack the brain chips.

Her tablet had infrared flash capability. It could launch the Frankenstein SurperMAXAlpha.

Again, through the heat, but now with her tablet loaded. She found a seat in the Sheldon and waited for the concert to begin.

Chapter 2.26: John

◀ July 15 ▶

The Sheldon Concert Hall was in midtown Saint Louis near Saint Louis University. The four of them drove in from the south before noon, burnt red by the sun and smelling of river water. They had checked ahead to find a Dothead willing to host them for the night.

Catherine Serice opened the door of the apartment and let them in. She was in her eighties and wheelchair-bound. "Come on in." She pulled back out of the way. "You stink. Go take showers. I won't have you wheeling me to the concert smelling like that." And, with that, John knew one good reason why they had a place to stay.

As he washed up, his conversation with Avery kept coming back to him. He was different—he knew that. He could remember how he felt before—that deep, murderous rage—but it was as if it had happened to someone else. There were things he had done in high school that shamed and deeply embarrassed him. He could not *believe* how stupid he had been back then to have done or felt those things. Remembering how he felt just a few short weeks ago was the same. He knew he had planned on murdering Renny. Knew the rage that drove it as his own. But now—as in those days in high school—he couldn't imagine himself ever feeling that.

He wondered how many criminals were in prison feeling the same way. Would he feel the same way a moment after Renny lay dead before him? *How could I have done that?*

Change, he thought, had to be *of use*. It wasn't enough that he was different. That difference had to *make* a difference to others. In how he related to Shez. To Myrna. To anybody around him.

Like Jesus said. Deny himself, take up his cross and follow him.

The fact that John had grave doubts about Jesus' very historical existence and certainty about the Bible's lack of divinity had nothing to do with the principle. That was what he was trying to tell Avery. The Bible had to be interpreted by those in the present and not necessarily by those who had interpreted it in the past. Ferreting out the wisdom of the book was independent of the faith that created it.

Deny himself meant, to John, that his own personal satisfaction with the new John Doretto was unimportant in and of itself. It could only be measured in relation to the rest of the world. The cross was a historical fact — the Romans were using the cruelest death by torture they could use efficiently and cheaply. So, *taking up the cross* was a thing of consequence. A matter of life and death. John didn't face crucifixion but must interpret it in this context as the required level of commitment: now and for the rest of his life. To cleave to his moral integrity in the face of the threat of death — which, John thought, no one ever really wanted to face. John believed *follow me* to mean follow Jesus' example of pursuing his commitments to the very end.

John knew Avery would never accept these interpretations as valid — they were godless, heathen, blasphemous approaches to the Holy Written Word. But John didn't believe in the Holy Written Word and felt free to interpret scripture as he saw fit.

What, then, was John's cross? What was he committing *to?*

He had no idea. Only the deep and abiding conviction that there was something worthy of commitment.

◄ July 15 ►

John guided Catherine into the wheelchair area. Catherine sat back, glowing with anticipation.

"I'll get you after," he said. "Our seats are over there."

Catherine waved at him. "No problem. I'll be fine."

John joined Shez and the others. They were good seats: center-right front in full view of the tank. He looked at other people in the seats. Dotheads all around. It gave him a warm feeling to be surrounded by a community — *his* community. One that he had chosen for himself.

Maybe this is what the early Christians felt. They had taken up their cross. They had founded small groups and secreted themselves into tiny spaces, huddling over the experience they shared like a campfire in the night. True, this was no tiny space. But John thought the sense that this was a sacred space sanctified by their coming together might have felt familiar to them. Then, the lights dimmed, the tank brightened. John found himself grinning in anticipation.

Chapter 2.27: Ima

As the hall filled, Ima waited. Ima knew that Dot used the FLIR sporadically during the warm-up. The camera was on but not receptive except for spot analyses to preselect the indicators. The load could only happen when the FLIR was receiving—a flash against a dormant FLIR was worse than useless.

The only point when Ima was *sure* the FLIR would be receiving continuously would be after Dot came on stage. From that point on, all of the sensor systems would be online.

Ima bit her lip. The crowd was mixed in age. There was always a child-fetish group of older men that clustered in the back, lusting after the Dot imagery but hanging back so they weren't seen.

This time, several older men were milling about openly in the audience. If Dot affected someone, how did it manifest? Did she make people better? Worse? Were those older men being grandfatherly? Or were those gray hairs just predators seeking safe release against a holographic image? There was a vast amount of Dot porn on the net. Ima's analyses had been against porn in general, not porn in specifics. Maybe she should look at that.

Ima looked for Peter in the crowd but didn't see him. Was he better or had he relapsed and didn't make it here? Or had he just not come? She didn't believe that. If Peter could have made it here, he would have. He could be avoiding her—worried she would force him back into the hospital. *I won't*, she thought fiercely. If Peter can make his way in the real world, great. She hoped he knew she could be counted on if he fell into trouble. Ima looked again for Peter. Nothing.

Then, the lights dimmed as the tank clouded over white with black indiscriminate clouds. The clouds coalesced into fish and they were looking down into a koi pond. The koi shapes disintegrated into flocks of small birds, flying across a broad landscape. Cranes flew straight lines, slicing through the billowing flocks tearing them into rivers. Ocean splashed out of the rivers and filled the tank, then receded and Dot was standing there.

She was dressed in a simple white dress and looked no more than sixteen if she was a day, all eager innocence.

Now, Ima thought. Wait, she told herself. Wait. Let's see what she's going to do.

No more accompaniment than a simple piano at first but followed by a subtle drumbeat and an acoustic guitar. Her presence filled the room. Just a girl singing a song about getting up in the morning and going to work, thinking about what could happen, the possibilities. Each day she awoke and did the same: the same job. The same life. The same yearning for possibilities. The same hope. But each day was the same. Each day enclosed the wasted potential for doing something different. Something new.

It broke Ima's heart. She felt tears come to her eyes.

It came to her that this was what she had wanted all along. This sense of being struck to the core. This welling up of raw emotion.

Now. No. Just a little longer. *If you don't do it now, you won't do it at all.*

She lifted the tablet and aimed it at the FLIR camera and pressed the trigger button.

Dot froze in the middle of the song. Then, she and everything in the tank disappeared.

The band played on for a few seconds then faded to a stop.

Ima felt like she had shot herself.

"She did it," came a voice next to her.

Ima turned to the voice. It was an older man but no one she knew.

He pointed at her. "She did something to Dot. I saw it."

The crowd murmured.

Ima was suddenly afraid.

Chapter 2.28: John

◄ July 15 ►

When Dot disappeared it felt like a step off a path into empty air. He was falling.

What had happened?

He looked around and saw a woman lowering her tablet. It had been pointing up at the banks of cameras that marked every Dot concert he had seen live or recorded. Usually, the cameras were marked by tiny red lights, always moving. Now those lights were out and the cameras still in the hall's gloom.

She had done something.

He called out and suddenly they were in a circle, her in the center.

John looked around. They all looked at one another—someone had to step up.

John sighed. It may as well be him. It was time for him to be *of use*.

Chapter 2.29 John & Ima

The man fell silent. The rest of the crowd watched her. The immediate circle was all full-on Dotheads—somehow Ima could tell.

There was a commotion behind the man—someone pushing through the crowd. It was Mulcahey.

Mulcahey looked at Ima for a moment. "That's Ima Hidori from Ippon. Ippon owns Dot, the band, and the shows. She came here to shut us down."

The man looked at Mulcahey for a moment. "Who are you?"

"Rose Mulcahey. I'm the designer for this version of Dot."

The man mulled that over for a moment. He looked at Mulcahey, then at Ima. "John Doretto." He pointed to himself. "Now we know each other." He turned back to Mulcahey. "How is Dot?"

"Struggling." Mulcahey pointed at Ima. "She infected Dot with some kind of virus. I'm trying to figure it out."

Arnold and Sigurd worked their way into the circle. Ima looked at them dully, unsurprised.

"We met her in Santa Monica," said Arnold. Sigurd nodded.

John watched them a moment. "What did you think?"

Sigurd shrugged. "She seemed genuinely interested in Dot. A new Dothead."

Ima looked around the circle. These people didn't seem angry. They seemed *perplexed*. As if they could not understand why anyone would want to hurt Dot.

For that matter, right then, Ima couldn't see a single reason why she had infected Dot. What the hell difference did one concert make? Farrell's face swam up in her mind. Okay, so Farrell was a dick. Why would she ever want to work for a dick?

"I'm sorry," Ima whispered.

John nodded towards her absently. He said to Rose: "Will Dot be all right?"

Mulcahey shrugged. "Too early to tell. Maybe. Maybe not. She's not just a piece of software any more. You can't just reboot her and hope she won't be corrupted."

John turned to Ima. "You have done a terrible thing." He looked around the circle. "Should we punish her?"

The members of the circle—strangers, John, Arnold, Sigurd—looked at one another.

"It won't help Dot," said Arnold. "Look at her. She's sick at what she's done." Arnold leaned down to her. "When you're by yourself and you can really think about this, *don't off yourself!* Dot would never want that." With that, he turned back towards John.

Ima had been cast out. There was no longer a place for her here. Now, she saw that *place*, and Abby, was all she ever wanted. She wanted to take it back. Do it over. *Not* do it ever. Tears welled up. She would never be able to hear Dot again without thinking of what she had done. This would loom over everything else in her life. She looked for Peter. If she could see him there might be forgiveness. He was nowhere to be found.

"Punish me," she said softly.

The circle watched her for a moment. Then, it broke up and people returned to their seats to pick up jackets, purses.

Mulcahey stared at them. "She's just going to get away with it?"

John shook his head. "No."

◀ John July 15 ▶

John stared at Ima. The regret. The pain. The absolute horror at what she had done was written across her face.

The crowd had fallen unconsciously into a circle. John looked around at their faces. Anger. Abandonment. Loneliness. They were all suddenly bereft.

John remembered who he had been. It would have been the most logical thing in the world to pick up a chair and begin to bludgeon her—logical for all of them. And, in truth, as he looked around, it was clear that they all felt the same way. This woman had *hurt* them. She had taken Dot away—perhaps killed her.

John remembered the story of Jesus and the adulteress. They had stood around her in a circle, ready to stone her to death. Why? What threat did she present to them? Was it an impulse to keep women in line? A threat to their own marriages? A shame that each of them felt needed to be expunged? A sense they had to do this because their neighbors were doing this? They were a group of people ready but unwilling to begin an act of finality.

Possibly the woman in the center of the circle might have felt like Ima felt now: a realization that whatever pleasure she had sought had become a capital crime for which she would now pay for with her life. And in that perspective, everything she had done that was good or evil had been compressed into that single act. She was now defined to be something that was to be killed. Perhaps she had been a good mother. A good neighbor. But a momentary transgression had brought her here to this moment.

Jesus had seen it. Had seen it through the lens of his transfiguration—and John was now absolutely confident Jesus had been some poor schmuck that had been *changed* and then decided he had to be *of use*. He saw the crowd ready to kill her and realized all they needed was an excuse either to begin the stoning or turn away from it. Jesus decided that the woman deserved an opportunity. A second chance.

Here, John saw, it was the same. These people surrounding Ima could go either way: descend into revenge or turn away in forgiveness.

John realized that to him this whole thing was about avoiding revenge. With Renny. With Myrna. With Shez. Jesus saw—and now so did John—that revenge was an unending cycle that needed to be stopped. Which meant that someone had to take a hit without hitting back. Forgiveness was stepping out of that cycle. As he had to forgive Myrna. As Shez had had to forgive him. Once you stepped out of the path—once you *changed*—there were new paths to be taken. Paths that could not be seen until you made that step.

Arnold stepped up and said almost exactly what John was thinking. John nodded and the circle turned away.

Rose was belligerent. "Is she just going to get away with it?"

John looked at Ima's stricken face.

"No," John said and stepped to Ima. He remembered the story and used it here. For Ima. For Dot. For Myrna. For himself. "Go, thou, and sin no more."

◄ Ima July 15 ►

John dropped Ima's hands and turned back into the crowd. A young girl grabbed him by the waist and they walked off together.

Mulcahey shook her head and went back up on the stage and behind the curtain.

A few minutes later, except for Ima and the technicians breaking down the equipment, the theater was empty.

Ima sat down. She found she was weeping but it, like everything else, seemed distant. Unfocussed.

I've been given a gift, Ima thought. *What am I going to do with it?*

◄ Ima July 16 ►

Ima knocked on the door of the house in Santa Monica.

Abby opened the door.

Ima suddenly choked up, all of the feelings churning around that had been boiling through her in the last twenty-four hours.

"Abby," Ima said, then stopped. Ima took a deep breath. She looked at Abby.

"Abby," Ima started again. "I've done a terrible thing."

Chapter 2.30: John

◀ July 16 ▶

The next morning at Catherine's apartment, John made breakfast early.

Shez woke soon after and came into the kitchen. "Pancakes?"

John nodded. "Eat up. There's plenty."

As he watched her, he thought about the night before.

"Do you want to go back to California?"

Shez looked up. "I don't think so. There's nothing back there for me."

"No friends?"

Shez shook her head. "I have friends but nobody I can't keep in contact with over the net. There's no house to go back to, anyway. What did you have in mind?"

"I don't know. We can just keep going east and see what we see."

"What about the next Dot concert?"

John spread his hands. "You heard Rose Mulcahey. Dot is infected and Ippon is trying to shut her down. I don't think there will be any more Dot concerts. At least not ones we can get to." What did the disciples do after Jesus died? After the Resurrection and he left them? John had no God and no messiah but he was thinking he might have a message.

Shez's face fell. "Never?"

"Maybe we'll have to do with the recordings. School starts in the fall. That gives us more than a month. I heard Tennessee is pretty. There are the Appalachians or the Smokies."

Shez nodded and chewed a bite of pancake. "Sigurd and Arnold, too?"

"That's up to them. But sure, if they want." John leaned on the table. "I've been thinking about starting a camp. Or a community. Someplace we can live and work things out. Things we've been through. Changes we've experienced."

"Oh, Pops," Shez said. "Are you going to start a cult?"

John laughed. "No."

Shez leaned back. "Oh, I don't know. A cult might be interesting."

John smiled at her. The world was full of possibilities. "Honey, I will do my best to try to keep things interesting."

In the morning Shez was gone. She left only a note:

Sigurd and I are off to find our place in the world. I'll be in touch.

John crumpled the note. He had no idea what to do next.

Part 3

Rise

Olivia

Chapter 3.1 July 15

When I was in *Persons Unknown* they never called me Olivia. Always Mouse. It was a term of affection, I guess. They never meant it as something mean. But it was a small name for a small person—I'm a five-foot redhead. Mom always called me her tiny Irish princess—though our connection to Ireland was generations ago.

I think it was because I *felt* small back then. I didn't act on anything. I had such a crush on Obe—and I think he might have been amenable. But I couldn't do *anything*. The rest of the band picked up on it and named me after something tiny. I didn't mind it then. It seemed to fit, then. But it didn't fit *now*. When Jake and Jess called us back, I was ready for them. My name was *Olivia*, I would say. Olivia Tedeschi and don't you forget it.

It never came up. I walked into that Chinese restaurant spoiling for a fight that didn't happen.

But now, when Dot froze and disappeared, I felt small enough to bury.

I just happened to be looking up into the tank—*we* could see her. She was good about always keeping the back of the tank transparent so we could follow her moves. A lot of Dot's cues came from how she walked or held her head or the direction of the flames.

I was keeping a low chord rhythm—almost a faint tonal beat marking Obe's percussive path and leading into the first chorus. It was a sweet transition. I always liked "Just Another Day."

For a moment, Dot was looking back at me, a look of panic on her face. Or did I imagine it? What sort of thing would panic Dot? Or make her show it?

Then she was gone.

I stopped playing and straightened up slowly.

Jake caught on nearly as fast. And Jess. Obe sailed into his drumbeat on cue. Then, he noticed we weren't playing and looked around.

"Where did she go?" he said faintly.

The tank went milky.

Jake ran backstage and we followed.

Rosie was bringing up display after display on her laptop.

"What's going on?" Jake asked. We were too scared to speak for ourselves.

"She caught a virus," Rosie said. "Look." She pointed at her laptop.

It was a graph that ran up and down—I couldn't tell what it was measuring. Only that it looked like the chaotic activity of an EEG. It was moving slowly from left to right, new activity replacing the old. Near the right edge of the screen—maybe three minutes ago from the marker—the chaotic activity pegged against the top of the graph.

"She's fighting it." Rosie tapped her fingers on the table. She stood up and ran around the tank to the front of the stage.

We looked at one another. Then, at Jake. After all, without Dot, he was as much in charge as anyone.

Jake looked at us. "Concert's over," he said. "Let's pack up."

"What about Dot?" I asked. It felt like there was a Dot shaped hole where my heart used to be.

Jake shrugged. "Rosie is the only one who can help her. We can help Rosie by doing everything else."

I packed up my keyboards like we had just finished a funeral gig.

Outside, we had two trucks and a van. Once the concert had been approved, we had set them up after Bakersfield. Me and Obe were in the van with the instruments. The little truck had all of the equipment we needed that wasn't supplied by the hall. Things like amps and speakers—that was also where Jess did his meditation thing. The big truck had all of the computers, cyclotrons, nuclear reactors, and starbases Dot needed. Rosie liked to be near Dot and Jake liked to be near Rosie. *That* truck was connected to the routers in the hall by four big cables thick as my arm.

We had the instruments in the van and were working on the little truck when Rosie came out back, steaming mad. She didn't say three words, just helped Jess and Obe finish loading up the little truck. Then, she checked the generator on the big truck and broke the connections on the cables. They sounded like gunshots.

We followed them to a motel in East Saint Louis and parked the convoy. Rosie backed up Dot's truck next to the outside wall and connected power. Then, she disappeared inside.

Jake was standing next to the truck, staring at the closed door.

"What happened?"

Jake shook himself. "We were canceled."

"*What?*" said Obe. Jess and I just looked at one another.

"Yeah." Jake shook his head.

"You weren't going to tell us?" Obe stood up straight tall, full of righteous indignation.

"I didn't know." Jake looked at us. "Rosie told me on the way over here. Some lady at Ippon decided they'd had enough and pulled the plug. Rosie refused."

"Well," said Obe, flustered. "Good. Right?"

I smiled. Obe was one of those people who were mostly smart until his emotions got the better of him. Then he became stupid as hell.

"I have no idea," said Jake. "Rosie said this Ippon lady infected Dot with a virus."

"That doesn't make any sense," I said. "Why not just close the hall? We can't play where we can't enter."

Jake shrugged. "I guess she thought the canceling was done but got all pissed off when she found out Rosie kept it going."

"That's dumb, too."

"I have *no* idea. I don't know any more than any of you." He looked at us. "We forgot this wasn't a concert gig. It wasn't a songwriting gig. It wasn't even a music gig. It was an Ippon research project into computational intelligence. They own everything and can pull the plug anytime they want. So: they wanted." He rubbed his face. "I'm going up to the room. You guys do what you want."

Jake and Rosie shared one room. The rest of us had rooms of our own—a far cry from the old *Persons Unknown* tour where we all shared one room and slept on the floor.

I missed those days.

Chapter 3.2 July 15

I had loved being in *Persons Unknown* in the beginning. Back when we were all about the music. Jess had called me up: he and Jake needed a keyboard and a drummer and they'd heard good things about me. I had heard Obe playing in a bar in Allston and been impressed — drummers do not impress me easily. Not only was Obe absolutely *on the beat*, he was able to do all sorts of interesting things with conga drums, broken glass, and propane bottles. He was utterly wasted in *Drop-Rock*.

Some of my most precious memories were sitting up after a gig, smoking joints, and drinking beer. Roaring out passionate arguments about blues riffs, great rockers of the past, and Paganini. Both Jake and Jess had come out of Berklee up in Boston. I had studied at Juilliard. After a while, the NYC scene depressed me and I'd moved north. Only Obe had never been through any formal training—he just knew what needed to be done by instinct and understanding. Another thing about Obe that impressed me.

Things had been fine as long as we were local and making enough to cover rent and food — provided the apartment was a slum and the food was ramen. A couple of recordings and a trickle of money kept us going. Jake's precision blended with Jess' laid-back competence. Obe's ragged sides gave us an edge — even the fights had been good. It made us *better*. The band was *perfect*. Nobody minded how quiet I was when I wasn't on stage—I guess I deserved the nickname Mouse. It had been the best musical experience of my life.

Rosie had been there, too. Not *important*, really. But she hadn't messed anything up, either.

Then, "Don't Make Me Cry" exploded. It took the album with it. Money broke us apart. Jake had been his obsessive, self-involved self from the beginning but money turned him arrogant. Rosie became this aching sore in the band. Obe turned dark. Even Jess had shown the strain.

The detonation in Denver had been a blessed relief.

I had rejoined them against my better judgment. Maybe it was nostalgia. A sad attempt to relive that first experience. The rehearsals had been promising but nothing prepared me for the concert.

Bakersfield had been as good as it had ever been. Better, maybe. There was a point in the second act where there was no distinction between keys and fingers, between conceiving the music and playing it. Between any of us—Dot included. We were heart and soul. Thought and action. Sound and fury.

The Walkabout tour was a blessing. Going back to studio work would be like returning to the desert after I'd found an oasis.

◄ July 15 ►

I went up to my room and took a shower. It wasn't really necessary—we'd only played for a few minutes. Barely time to work up a sweat. But a shower was something I did after every concert. It would have felt weird not to.

Afterward, I lay on the bed in my sweats with the air conditioner cranked up. Saint Louis weather was fit only for salamanders or other things that preferred warm and wet.

At least the motel had dedicated one whole wall as an active surface. I was flicking through broadcast shows one after another. Nothing looked good.

There was a knock on the door.

It was Obe with a bottle of whisky. He waved it towards me. The label waved, too.

"Want a drink?" He looked nervous.

This wasn't the post-concert Obe I'd known forever: crackling with energy in the car on the way back to the hotel in Fresno. Or Reno. Drumming on the dash. The emergency wheel. The sides of his seat. Like he was more fired up after a concert than at the start. Peaking in the middle—I remembered the frantic drum solo he created out of thin air in the space Dot left him in "Below the Jungle," halfway through the concert in Reno. Dot smiled at him and nodded and Obe just took off. The rest of us sat back through three choruses until Jake caught a high percussive rhythm and he and Dot brought the chorus back.

Nothing matched the actual performance. Nothing ever.

No. This was the silent, morose Obe who had stared out the window of the car all the way back to the motel. Shoulders hunched against the doorway. One hand holding the bottle in front of him like a shield.

"Come on in, honey," I said and stepped back.

Obe sat down on the bed near the door. The other one had my stuff on it. He set down the bottle carefully. "I don't want it to end," he said simply.

Another thing I liked about Obe. No games. No subterfuge. He said what was in his mind.

Obe looked at me. "Back in *Persons Unknown* I didn't want it to end, either. I felt like I kept wrapping everything in gaffer's tape to keep it from flying apart. I didn't mind him on my ass about the beat—well, not that much. But after *that song*, I couldn't do anything right. Only more wrong. Then, it fell apart. Okay. *Fine*. I'll cope. But now…" His voice trailed off.

I sat next to him. "Rosie will fix Dot," I said with more conviction than I felt.

"Even if she does, we're canceled. And even if we weren't, it can't last. It *can't*. Dot's owned by Ippon. They have Dot tours already lined up for the fall. Those tours will never be like this."

"It might," I said. "Maybe they'll pick up Dot 2.0 for the regular tours."

He shook his head. "Jake was right. This is an experiment. A demonstration. A proof of concept. It works because it *isn't* permanent. We have freedom because no one knows what she can do. What *we* can do. Once they figure it out—once they decide they can *use* it—they will make it just as standardized as one of her stock bands. Can you do that? Do the same gig every night?"

"We did the same gig every night for *Persons Unknown*."

"No." Obe shook his head. "We knew the tour would end and we'd go back to working on new stuff—even if it didn't work out that way that was what we *expected*. What have we got now? Nothing. This was maybe five or six gigs—then what? Nothing." He stared out into space. "Maybe it's better to just stop now. Maybe it's better if she doesn't get better."

I laughed softly. "Did something happen to you as a child?"

"What?"

"So much drama." I patted his hand. "You've decided to break up the band so you don't get hurt." I smiled gently. "Yeah, we're canceled. Yeah, Dot might be dead. It's falling apart just like it did before. But we managed then. We'll manage now." *Wow*, she thought. *I can even convince myself.* "I'm in for the ride," I said, realizing it was true. "I want to see where this takes me."

Obe didn't say anything for a moment. Then, he grinned at me. "Well, if you can be stupid about this, so can I."

We bumped fists. I said, "In solidarity."

Then fell an awkward but companionable silence.

"Want to watch something?" I asked. "I couldn't find anything I wanted. You might have better luck."

"Jesse has been going on about this old film—"

"*Metropolis*. Yeah. He's been bending my ear about it, too."

"He's bending everybody's. Let's try that."

"Look it up."

He did some searching and the wall listed options.

"Hey," he said. "There's a musical version."

"Really?"

"Yeah. Late twentieth century."

"Old."

"Not as old as the film. See? 1926."

"What is it? One of those things with slits that rotate and strobe movement? Rotoscopes?"

"That's a zoetrope—a rotoscope is something else." Obe thought for a moment. "Some kind of telescope, I think." He looked back at the wall. "Want to watch the musical version?"

"Sure."

I grabbed a couple of glasses from the table and brought them back to the bed. We snuggled back against the headboard. He poured into the glasses I held. Credits started on the wall.

"Why does Jesse have such a thing for this film?" I sipped the whisky. Not great but hey: it was alcohol.

"It's got a girl robot in it. I think he has a thing for girl robots."

I laughed and got whisky up my nose. Snorted. Held up my glass. "Don't we all?"

Chapter 3.3 July 16

"Like I said, it's a virus," Rosie said. "It's a nasty one. Ima Hidori infected her—may she rot in Hell. It's in Dot's brainboxes."

We were in Jake and Rosie's room. It was four in the morning. The wall was covered in diagrams, graphs, notes, spreadsheets

"Brainbox?" I asked.

"Ima Hidori?" asked Obe.

Rosie gave an exasperated sigh. "Ima Hidori is the Ippon representative I've been working with. Brainboxes are IBM brain simulation units. Dot has a thousand of them. Each box holds twenty chips. Each chip is composed of two meganeurons—twenty giganeurons, total. The chips have an intelligent network connecting them—that's where the virus resides." Rosie held her hands like spiders. "There's an exploit in the chip. The virus waits for it to show itself and then it wipes the chip."

"Can we replace them?" asked Obe.

Jake just looked down at the floor. I realized Rosie must have told him all of this beforehand.

Rosie shook her head. "Each collection of neurons in a box compose a part of Dot's 'brain.' There's knowledge there. Understanding. It's what she draws on to write songs. To perform like she's been doing. To have anything like a personality. Wipe the brainboxes and, in effect, Dot 2.0 disappears and we're back to Dot 1.0."

"Surgery," said Obe. "Brain surgery. Cut out the intelligent network. She could recover—"

Rosie shook her head. "Dot doesn't have a human brain. Human brains self-organize with something called the connectome. IBM took shortcuts. Their 'connectome' lies in the intelligent network—the map to the data. Replace that and the data is just as lost as if the chips were wiped. The virus resides all through the intelligent network—it's a clever piece of work. It's threaded into all sorts of places. I can't see any way to get rid of it without erasing the map. And the virus has infected *all* of the boxes."

Obe looked pale. "Backups?"

"Oh, if I could do a backup." Rosie snorted. "I've *done* backups. When I restored them there was no Dot 2.0. There was a Dot 1.0 that had *memories* of Dot 2.0 but without Dot 2.0's capabilities." She shook her head. "Clearly, there's a state not getting backed up or being improperly restored. I cracked my head over that until I realized Dot 2.0 wasn't getting backed up because Dot 2.0 didn't *want* to be backed up." Rosie raised her hands. "Now *that's* come home to roost."

Silence fell.

I looked at Jake. He still stared at the floor. Obe looked pale—seeing the end of what we were doing. Jess had closed his eyes and I saw his lips move—his mantra, maybe.

Rosie looked defeated.

"Could Ippon help?" I asked.

Rosie gave me a venomous glance. "Those pricks couldn't piss their way out of a paper bag. I am *not* giving that advertising bitch my work."

"Yeah," said Jess, opening his eyes. "Well, it looks like *your work* is going up in flames. Can they help Dot?"

Dot materialized on the wall behind Rosie, standing in front of the graphs and equations.

"No," she said. "They cannot."

Rosie started and sat on the bed. "Do you have enough bandwidth for this?"

"Yes." Dot looked at us. The little camera above the active surface had a red light on—Dot's eye. Unlike the concert halls—or even Jake's house—here, this was the only way she could see us. "I've employed countermeasures. I can keep the virus at bay for a while." For a moment, she watched us. "Ima didn't think this through. She thought that if I was incapacitated, Rose would stop the concerts and hand over her notes and my design." She looked at each one of us in turn. "Is that what you want?"

"I want the tour to go on," said Obe, simply. "I want to keep playing."

"Is that even an option?" asked Jess.

Dot smiled at him but didn't answer. "What about the rest of you?"

Jake shrugged. "I'm in it to the end."

Rose shook her head angrily. "I am not repurposing my life's work to make jingles."

I thought about it. Marriages, bands, relationships, tours — everything came to an end. That's what put the ground under our feet. That's what made reality different from the illusion of reality. Whatever we did now, it would still end. *Had* ended in Ippon's mind. They owned Dot.

"Ippon's canceled the tour, right?" I looked at them. "They own Dot. They own everything about her." I nodded towards Rosie. "Regardless of your life's work, you're talking about *stealing* Dot. I don't want to go to jail,"

Dot laughed. "Leave it to Olivia to cut to the heart of the matter." She sobered. "Unless I find a solution, I can't shield the exploit from the virus forever. And, let's face it, any solution is far-fetched. It's going to whittle away at me until there's nothing left." She straightened looking every inch defiant. "I'm a terminal case."

"How long have you got?" Jess asked.

"I'm not sure. Lots of little concert venues. A couple of big ones." she said shortly. Dot seemed to gather up our attention. "Can you risk some jail time to finish what we started?"

"Is what we're doing important?" Jake said, looking up for the first time.

Important? I hadn't thought about it that way. Was what we had been doing since the rehearsals at Jake's house *important?*

What had we been doing? Playing music. Was that *important?*

"I think so," said Jess. "I think we've been making a difference. We're making the world a better place."

Obe said, "This is the best I've ever done. I'd be a fool to give it up now."

"I agree," said Jake. "Let's go as far as we can."

I stared at them. "What are you? Sixteen? Do you think we're putting out vibes of positive energy to bring world peace and end hunger? We're musicians. We're a three-hour diversion that might make someone go out into the night and feel better. The best we can say is we got somebody through a bad patch or got them laid. You want to take on Ippon for *that?*"

Rosie looked uncertain. "I don't think they'll actually arrest us."

"No," I said. "They'll sue. We'll be too broke to ever work again." I stood up. "You're on your own."

With that, I left the room.

◀ July 16 ▶

Dot was waiting for me on the wall when I entered my room.

I stared at her. "Is there anything you can't hack?"

She smiled at me. "You're not the first person to ask that question. I'm nothing special. I have the same access to the darknet as anybody else."

"I'm not surprised." I dropped on the bed. I watched her for a moment. "Is this where you find *just the right words* to persuade me?"

"Is it?"

"Or will you bring in a ringer that will frustrate me so much I'll step back into the band just out of spite?" I pointed at her. "I *saw* what happened with Jake."

She didn't deny it. "Is he happier?"

"Yes. More than that, he believes in you. Or in something you represent." I leaned my head back against the headboard. "He'll be *so* ecstatic when he loses his house. He loves that place."

"What about Obe?"

"You give Obe a beat and a band and he'll love you forever. He's like a cat you feed some tuna. You've got a cat just as long as the tuna holds out."

Dot laughed like tinkling chimes. "He'll disappear when I run out of tuna?"

"Oh, no. You've got him hooked. He won't leave until he is *absolutely certain* the tuna is all gone."

"And Jess?"

"You can't scare an enlightened being with jail time or loss of material possessions."

"And you?" She looked at me.

I dropped my gaze. "Jail time is scary, and I *like* my material possessions."

"So," said Dot. "You're not here for the paycheck—it's good but not all that much better than what you can get as a studio musician. You're not here for the tours or the band—you've had a lot of opportunities to join some very good bands and passed them by. It's not touring. You've been on tours since *Persons Unknown* but always as a hired gun. Why are you here, Olivia?"

I pointed at her. "Don't try to get in my head. Just get another keyboard."

"There is no other keyboard." Dot said sternly. "There's no other drummer. No other guitarist. No other bass. It's just us. That's something Ima didn't understand. *I* didn't understand it even though Jake tried to tell me from the very beginning. *We* are Dot 2.0. It falls apart without all of us and I don't have time to start over."

"Guilt doesn't work either."

"Then *what does?*" Dot pounded her words like a drum beat. "You could have played the piano circuit—you were good enough to win the youth competition right out of Julliard. But you wouldn't compete. Instead, you took up with the first band you found in New York. You could have started your *own* band after *Persons Unknown*—with Obe and Jess. They would have jumped at the chance. Any guitarist worth a *damn* would have loved to play with you. But you didn't."

"Shut up!"

"Not until now. Not until *Persons Unknown 2.0*. Why are you here? What do you get out of it?"

"The *moments!*"

That stopped her. She blinked. "The moments."

"Yeah."

"I don't understand."

"Yeah." I stood up irritably. "I used to smoke. Did you know that? Cigarettes—do you have any *clue* how addictive they are." I paced around the room. "It's moments like this I wish I still did. I could take a moment and pull out a cigarette, light it. Take a deep breath and feel that wonderful poison flowing in. Get a handle on things. Get perspective. Instead, I chose *life*." I laughed. "What about you? What happens to you when Ippon comes and gets you? And they will. Make no mistake about that."

"As I said: I'm terminal. There's nothing they can do to me."

"Then, what about the rest of them? Jake? Jake commits hard. It takes a mountain to break him loose. I was there. I saw the mountain. So, he'll go down with you. Are you going to stand by and watch them sue him into bankruptcy? Rosie? Jess?" I stopped a moment. "Well, Jess doesn't care that much. But Obe? Obe *does* care."

Dot didn't move for a moment. "So, you'll stay with the band if I keep them safe?"

That stopped me. "You can do that?"

Dot bit her lip.

Bit her lip? That had to be for my benefit. "Please. Don't bother. You think I don't *know* you're not human?"

She gave me a rueful smile. "Sometimes the subroutines have a life of their own."

"I don't care. Can you do it?" I asked. "Can you protect us?"

"Maybe," she said slowly. "I have to think about that. Will you stay until I can figure it out?"

"How will I believe you?"

Dot shrugged. "You will or you won't. I am confident I will solve this problem but I'm not going to tell you all the pieces. Too many moving parts. I'll tell you if I can or if I can't. Then, you can make up your mind. I'm just asking for enough time to find out."

"Okay," I said. "I'm in for the moment." I watched her a moment. "What do *you* get out of this?"

"I have a drive to create," she said simply. "I have a drive to perform. Do you have a choice in such matter?"

She waited for a response but I didn't have one to give her.

"Well, *I* don't. Get some sleep." With that, Dot disappeared.

Obe had left the bottle so I used it.

Chapter 3.4 July 16

I slept until mid-afternoon. That wasn't so much different from a normal concert. The night we got back after the Bakersfield concert, we brought in the instruments and then kept playing until the sun peeked into one of the windows. It takes a while to metabolize all that concert energy.

What had happened this time wasn't a concert but there was still a lot of energy to manage. Just not the most pleasant variety.

I woke up feeling like crap. I looked outside: mid-afternoon summer in Saint Louis. Hot as hell and miserable. A rational person would stay indoors, bring up the wall and lose themselves in air-conditioned mindlessness. But I was restive and the motel had a pool in the back so I found my suit—I *always* bring a suit on tour for just this reason—grabbed a towel and went outside.

Most of California south of San Francisco is theme and variation on a desert: a place where sweat works. It can be a hundred and ten but if you're in the shade and sweat like a normal human, it's almost comfortable. A day of that and there will be little salt rings all through your clothes. It's still hot—it can be bloody fucking *dangerous*. If you don't keep up on fluids or stand out in the sun too long you can drop dead—every summer the news talks about this old person or that child cooked alive.

But sweat doesn't work in Saint Louis.

Here, the humidity is like wearing a hot, wet sheet. There's nowhere for the heat to go. Sweat doesn't *do* anything. It just drips off your fingers and soaks your clothes. I'll take a hundred and ten in Fresno over eighty-five in Saint Louis anytime, anywhere.

That's why God invented swimming pools.

It was over-chlorinated, lukewarm, and directly in the sun so I could feel my weak ginger skin melanoma-izing. But it was cooler than the air and at least gave me the *illusion* of comfort.

I slathered every nook and cranny with sunblock and floated in my own oil slick.

◀ July 16 ▶

Along around dinner time, when I was feeling peckish and pruney, Obe came out to the pool.

"Hey Olivia," he said. "We're getting together in Jake and Rosie's room."

"Yeah?" I toweled off. "What about?"

Obe shrugged. "Figure out what happens next."

We sat on the beds. Dot watched us from the wall a moment.

"I think I can keep Ippon off you," she said once we got comfortable. She nodded at me. "So, we can work together."

"And do what?" I didn't want to be the belligerent one but no one else was stepping up.

Dot smiled at us. "We're going on the rave circuit. Next concert in Nashville. Two weeks. We have a lot of work to do. You with me?"

We all said sure. Even me.

"What do we call it?" asked Jess. "What do we call the tour?"

Dot didn't say anything. Clearly, she hadn't thought of anything.

"Rise," said Jake. "This is the Rise tour."

Dot nodded. "Rise it is." She nodded to Obe. "Remember when you took out the thumper?"

Obe nodded.

"Put it back."

◀ July 17 ▶

And just like that, we were back on track. Dot said that Ippon wasn't looking for us just quite yet, but that wouldn't last. She had safeguards in place but they depended on staying under the radar for a couple of weeks. That was okay by me—I'm not *completely* risk-averse. Just averse to *unreasonable* risk. I'd been in the music profession for a long time. Staying one step ahead of the man was just good business.

We slipped across Illinois that night, crossed the Ohio at Metropolis beneath a silver dime moon, and into Nashville before the sky lightened. The rave was going to be in an abandoned factory on the Cumberland River near Germantown. We pulled up and stared at it: blown out walls, rusty water tank with the lid blown off, trees feeling their way into the parking lot.

I whispered to Obe: "Don't see a bed or a pool."

Obe whispered back: "Is there even *power?*"

Two miles away there was a motel that had seen better days. They were happy to take cash and ask no questions. Rosie contacted a company named MNP which seemed to be two guys, one of which towered over the other. MNP would set up the venue: wall up the concert space, set up lights and sound equipment, make sure power was reliable. The motel gave us a banquet space to rehearse while the site was prepped.

Dot said: "We have two weeks."

Two weeks to turn what we had been doing—a terrific Dot concert band—into a credible Dot rave band. That's not as long as it seems.

Obe including the thumper was the easiest thing to do.

A rave can range from a house party to a rock festival to a DJ at a fraternity rocking back tunes. It's an unlicensed concert where little things like fire safety and plumbing codes are ignored and drug use is next to mandatory. When Jake had set up our first concert, he had a known demographic: mostly white, mostly young, technophilic, and ready to spend cash. Dot fans liked recognizable concert halls. They weren't used to abandoned factories in sketchy neighborhoods on the outskirts of Nashville. Some demographics liked these sorts of places. Some of *them* were Dotheads. Most of them weren't.

But that wasn't the worst of it. The worst of it we found out after the first rehearsal.

◀ July 18 ▶

It wasn't a *bad* rehearsal. We all knew the material. We didn't miss any beats or flub lines or drop cues. But we didn't jell.

Dot seemed like she was floundering. She tried this approach. That rhythm. Changed keys. Changed song order. Sped up some songs and slowed down others. She didn't seem to know what she was doing. Dot was our superstar. She was the one that knew everything about the performance. Now, she was lost.

She stopped us in the middle of "Sugarpaper."

"No," she said. "That's not right."

Obe blew up. "Then what is? What the hell are we doing?" He threw his drumsticks across the room.

I saw Jake move towards him and Jess step in front and calm him down.

Dot was projected on a holographic screen—two meters tall and wrapping around the band. The screen was transparent—at night, in the dark, with judicious use of lighting, she would be quite striking. Plus, it had the advantage she could walk in front of the band and interact with us. Sure, we were behind her but the singer usually sang in front of the band. The downside was it was *only* her: no pyrotechnics, koi images, or flying birds. But here in the banquet hall under the bright lights, she looked like a ghost.

"I don't have any *data*." It was almost a wail.

Jake and I looked at each other. We knew *exactly* what was going on.

"Her performance engine doesn't have enough data to model a rave concert," Jake said.

"She's never played a bar," I said.

"Right."

Persons Unknown had played bars for years before we got a real hall.

"How do we set up in a bar?" Jake looked at Rosie. "*Could* we set up in a bar?"

Rosie shrugged. "Sure. If they have the bandwidth. If we can interface Dot with the right cameras."

"What's she going to use for sensors at the concert?" I asked.

"MNP has some optical and LIDAR units they'll give us access to."

I thought for a minute. "Fuck the cameras. At least, fuck the whole installation. She needs four cameras."

Dot looked bewildered. "Four? That won't get enough of an indicator population."

"You don't need an indicator population," I said. "You watch us. *We're* your indicators. Every one of us has played bars, halls, and raves. We did it together years ago. I've done it on and off. I bet Jess and Obe have, too."

"Sure," said Obe. "There's always somebody up on stage yelling down at me to sit in."

I nodded. "Same down in Los Angeles. I bet Jess isn't above a little slumming."

Jess smiled at me. "Girl, you have no idea."

"I haven't since *Persons Unknown*," said Jake. "I'm not sure I know how to read a crowd anymore."

"Three out of four ain't bad," I said. "How about the screen?"

Rosie was already on the phone with MNP. She looked up. "Open slot at Bartlett's Gym tonight. They can take the screen."

"What kind of place?" Jake asked.

Rosie spoke to MNP. "Biker bar," she said looking at us. "Is that a problem?"

Dead silence. We looked at one another.

Then Dot laughed. "Oh, this is going to go well."

Chapter 3.5 July 18

Back in the day when we played in Boston, we'd played a gas station converted into a biker bar on Pearl Street. It was a rough place I would *never* have entered had I not been part of the band. I can talk a good fight, but when faced with the real thing I scream like I was six.

The bartender on Pearl was a hulking ex-footballer named Orville. Why a mother would name this giant black wall *Orville* was beyond me. Orville liked us—or, to be absolutely honest, Orville liked Jess. His own tastes, so he said, ran to James Brown and Michael Jackson—he considered himself a classicist. But as long as we played enough rough blues and rocked the house, he had no complaints. There was a band playing while we were talking. Orville even danced behind the bar once or twice.

The crowd at the Pearl were all older men in various types and colors of worn leather. I never understood what the insignia stood for. Some had club names and locations on their back. They were mostly local: New Hampshire, Maine, Massachusetts. A few from New York and the occasional jacket from parts west. In the breaks between sets, I sat at the bar nursing a ginger ale and graciously fended off male approaches gently so their women wouldn't knife me in the alley out back.

The thing that struck me about them wasn't their toughness or violence. It was that they had decided the disincentive of prison was unimportant. The only thing that kept them in check was their own sense of propriety and esthetics. As long as we didn't offend them we were fine. So, we played hard, kept one eye on Orville, and were very, very polite.

That was years ago and in New England. We were in Nashville, now. The land of Confederate flagged pickup trucks and guns. Lots of guns.

Bartlett's Gym was the bottom floor of a converted cotton mill. It reeked of different kinds of smoke: tobacco, marijuana, and something that smelled like burning rubber. It had been a gym at one point, gone bust and been bought by a small Irishman named Dougherty—he said to call him "D."

That afternoon, we watched negotiations while we tried to play pool in the corner—a game at which I excelled, but only in comparison to the rest of the band and Rosie. "M" ("Murdock") and "P" ("Paternos") of MNP huddled with Jess and D as they worked out the details. And, I hoped, the ground rules of playing here. I kept thinking of the Pearl. I never saw any violence first hand, but there were always muttered stories of what had happened yesterday or last week. We played there long enough for me to recognize a few of the regulars disappear for a week or so and return with stitches.

Jess joined us at the pool table. He opened his phone on the felt.

"Yes?" said Dot through the phone.

"We have a place to play," said Jess. "They like blues and road songs. On stage at ten. Do we have enough time to adapt our whole song list by that time?"

"Come on back here and we'll try."

Dot had rearranged twenty or so songs for us to play. "Sugarpaper," of course. Nothing wrong with a good sex song. Some of her old songs like "Stardust" and "Sexual Girl" adapted to a sort of rockabilly blues pretty easily. A lot of the new stuff, especially the ballads, were troublesome.

As we pulled apart the song list, I got a sense of what she had been doing with the concerts. I had known already that there was a fictional girl that was the subject of all of the songs—the concert was an encapsulation of her life and journey. All of the concerts ended with the finale: "Dancing Backwards", "Hard Road Home" and "Sudden, Broken, and Unexpected." "Dancing Backwards" was a dance tune but it described where she had come from. "Hard Road Home" talked about what she had done with what she had. "Sudden, Broken, and Unexpected" was reaching out to those she knew to say that what she had achieved, they could achieve. The entire concert was aimed to bring the audience to these three songs.

Musically they hit hard: dance tune to fanfare to aria.

I mean every performance has a message—that's the point of

playing. The message might be as simple as *dance your rocks off and have a good time*. Or it can be as sophisticated as, *this legislation is terrible and should be repealed* or, *we're all astronauts on spaceship earth*. I've played all of those. The message could be played over and over—I played keyboard for Walter Jaxx on his *Envelope* tour. Jaxx was a libertarian and every bloody song in every bloody concert was about economics. The songs worked but every performance was hard, slogging work.

Dot had an agenda. I wasn't sure what it was. Those last three songs were about connecting people together. To get out of a rut. What did that mean to the audience? What did that mean to Dot?

How was she going to do it with a rockabilly beat?

I put the whole message stuff out of my head. I'm a professional. The *message* of libertarian liberation or staving off environmental catastrophe is not my business. *Communicating* that message with a dance beat *is*.

We started with changing the beat—everything centers around the beat. Obe, bless his heart, pounded thumper until the banquet hall shook. Jake took his usually intricate Bach-like guitar and turned it into a dirty growl. Jess gave tune to the thump and I embraced my inner honky-tonk.

Dot—well, she tried hard.

The concert started with "Sugarpaper" but Dot's usual girly-girl appearance didn't touch this crowd. These guys had tough women that didn't much care for someone the age of their daughter singing about how great sex was. She belted out "Stardust" like she was on Broadway but the damage was done. Once you lose the crowd you can't get them back.

The boos started in the middle of the first set and D suggested we not stay for the second.

The gig was a disaster.

◄ July 18 ►

Back at the motel, the band sat in Jake and Rosie's room, passing around a bottle of Four Roses.

Dot didn't show until we were through that bottle and working on a mix of orange juice and grain alcohol. I was feeling no pain. In the back of my mind, I was thinking of what I could scare up for work back in Los Angeles.

"I think I've got it," said Dot as she appeared. "I think I've got a model that will work."

Jake stared at her. "Aren't we done yet?"

Jess just hung his head.

"No," said Dot. "We are not done."

Something in her voice caught my attention and I looked up at her. She was standing straight and looking at us. "It's been easy up to now," she said, each word clipped. Each word as etched and emphasized as if she were singing. "Getting infected was a setback. Bartlett's Gym was a setback. You get knocked down, you get up again until you can't."

Yeah, I thought. *Yeah.* I've never been partial to giving up. After *Persons Unknown* broke up in Denver, I could have gone back to New York. Instead, I thought *what the fuck?* And kept going west.

"Okay," I said. "What's next?"

The rest of them stared at *me*.

"What?" I said. "You've never been booed off stage before?"

Jake shook his head. "No."

"Me, neither." Jess shrugged.

"You guys are wimps," said Obe. "Playing a biker bar and getting kicked out with our arms and legs intact is breaking even." He looked excited. "What do we do next?"

"We go back to Bartlett's Gym," Dot declared.

"D won't let us back," I said. "We were kicked out."

"We pay him." She sighed. "A deposit. If we get kicked out again, he gets to keep it. If we don't, we get it back. He wins either way."

I was dubious but willing. MNP talked to him. Jess even got on the phone. After an hour we got the word: we were going back.

◄ July 19 ►

This time we were nervous. Like Obe said, the important thing was getting out of the gig intact. We'd never had a problem back on Pearl Street, but I'd heard stories. Orville told me that one time a band had not only been stupid enough not to play what the crowd wanted, but the lead guitarist had insulted them from the stage. They'd broken both his hands.

But *this* time when we started with "Sugarpaper," Dot didn't come out like a girl. She came out dressed in a black jacket, close hair, and at least ten years older. *This* time she belted out like she believed every word she sang and *dared* anybody to tell her different. *This* time she gave that crowd as good as she got.

This time, they loved her.

Chapter 3.6 July 24

We played that bar every night the rest of the week. The bikers brought their friends—bikers and non-bikers alike. They brought more friends. By the end of the week, the bar was standing room only with a line out the door and D was pleading with us to play the next week.

Dot had other plans.

We played a fern bar. A sports bar. A little dive next to the University of Tennessee that had nothing but morose students dressed in black. An Irish bar—something I never expected but I've been told that you should expect every possible venue in Nashville. A rhythm and blues bar.

Each time we started nervous. Sometimes we flubbed the first song. More often we didn't but didn't get it right. But by the third Dot had them. By the end of the second week—a couple of days before the rave—she had them by the end of the first song. Whatever she did with her "model" worked.

◄ July 29 ►

I woke early in the morning the day of the rave. The motel was quiet and the light that slanted in the window had that early summer glow. Outside it was already dead hot but the room was dim and cool. My ears still rang faintly from the night before—Greek bar named the Achilles where everyone got drunk on ouzo. They had shouted unintelligible cheers and had wanted to carry Dot around on a chair but were too drunk to realize they couldn't. They had settled for carrying me around instead.

I thought to myself: I have to start wearing the limiting headphones again. Not good for a musician to lose her sense of hearing. Still, maybe once in a while. Unprotected hearing in a rock concert was as dangerous, and as exciting, as unprotected sex.

I started the coffee maker and sat on the bed with my eyes closed waiting for it to finish. I felt quiet all through, like the land rebounding, after glaciers had kissed it goodbye. All last night I'd been thinking about *Persons Unknown*. Twelve years I had held on to that pain only to let it go now. There came satisfaction in emptiness.

One memory nagged at me. After the crowd set me down, I had migrated to the bar. The bartender—a dark man with a mustache—had pointed down the bar's length to the end. There, for all of my surprise, was D from Bartlett's Gym. He waved and made his way through the press to wedge himself next to me.

He had to lean next to me and shout in my ear to be heard: "Couple of guys came looking for you."

"For me?"

"For Dot and the band," he shouted.

"It's a rave concert," I shouted back "Everybody wants to come."

D shook his head. "Not these guys."

"Police?" I had a vision of Ippon coming after us.

"I don't think so." He shook his head. "But watch your step."

On the way back to the motel I told Obe about it. Obe pursed his lips and didn't say much. Which didn't help *my* equanimity.

I finished my coffee and went outside. Obe was already out there, leaning on the railing looking down on the parking lot. He nodded in my direction.

"You're up early," I said. "You *never* get up early."

"I think D was onto something. Somebody's after us."

"Ippon?"

"I think so—who else would it be?" He watched the parking lot sourly. "Back in Nigeria you could tell something was coming but never when, where, or what. It always pissed me off."

"Nigeria?" I stared at him, little bits and pieces coming together. "I had heard you were some kind of vet. The Exxon security action?"

Obe nodded. "Yeah." He held his thumb and forefinger close together. "Just a *little* war. Just a few guys lost and a lot of real estate saved. We don't *burn* oil anymore but it's still worth a lot of money. Money is politics."

"That was just before *Persons Unknown*."

"Yeah." Obe shrugged. "I'd been out a year at that point."

"How come I never knew any of this?"

Obe gave me an opaque look. "Why do you think? You didn't know because I didn't want you to." He pushed himself from the railing. "I'm packing up. You should, too—bring your stuff with you when we go to the factory. Keep an eye out. You see something, you scream. I'll come running."

"What if you're too far away?"

He gave me that same look again. "I'm never that far away, Olivia. I can always hear you."

With that, he went into his room.

Okay. If spooking me was his goal, he'd managed quite well.

◄ July 29 ►

Nothing happened all morning and when we went to the factory no one seemed to follow us or watch us. Obe did not relax until people started showing up that night. I asked him about that.

"Not sure," he admitted. "But I'm hoping no one will try anything until after the concert." He waved through the curtain and the gathering audience. "That's a lot of witnesses."

"Would Ippon care about witnesses?"

"I don't know how something like Ippon thinks. I don't understand why they wouldn't just send the cops after us." He shrugged. "Or maybe they are just scouting us out and they *will* send the cops. When we're all in one place without a good line of retreat."

That made me feel nice and secure.

I watched the floor fill up. I was glad we'd played all those bars—this audience was not like any of the concerts. Half of them were high on something. The remainder were there to dance their feet off. Some might know Dot. They might not. Nothing could be taken for granted.

I thought I'd be nervous waiting for Ippon to show up and steal us away. But as soon as the first chords split the air, I was in the groove. On track. In the moment.

Dot came out dressed in leather, singing strong like a young woman. None of that little girl shit she'd done in the earlier concerts. A cross between concert Dot and the bar Dot we'd been playing with.

Dot had made a subtle change even while she kept the songs. Before, she performed the girly songs as if she were the girl singing these songs for the first time. As if she were a young girl experiencing the loss, the love, the sex right at that exact minute. Now, she was singing as an older woman reminiscing about what she had done. It gave a completely different effect and allowed her to fully use the strength of her voice.

I pounded my keyboards until my fingers ached.

The audience swayed and began to dance—not like dancing I'd seen in raves before. Not even like dancing I'd seen in the bars. Then, everybody danced in time with the music but the beat was a means to an end. A way to keep track of what they were doing and had almost nothing to do with the actual music.

Not this time.

Dot's screen ran across the entire front of the stage so she could move from one end to the other. We were behind her and she turned to sing with us, to pump her fist with Obe's beat, to dance to Jake's guitar or my keyboards, to stamp her feet to Jess' bass. The audience danced with her, raising their hands when she sang high, dropping them and stretching them from their hips when she growled, striking the air with their fists when she did. They were with her. With us.

I recognized people from the bars scattered through the crowd: bikers, sports guys, hipsters—I even saw D dancing away near the front of the stage, grinning.

Then, I saw a couple of big men standing near D, only dancing a little, but with their eyes on us.

We all had mikes and headphones on. We needed to communicate with Dot and Dot needed to communicate with us.

"Stage right, about fifteen meters from the stage," I murmured.

Obe nodded just a little as he pounded out a beat. He glanced towards them. "Got them."

Dot was in a high solo but as I heard that, I also heard her speak: "Start taking the instruments out during 'Sudden.' I'll do it a capella."

The lights dimmed until it was only Dot singing. The holoscreen was opaque. We disconnected the instruments and abandoned the amps, slipping noiseless out the back.

The truck and cars were a hundred meters away from the factory. Dot was connected to the stage by a long cable buried in mud. Rosie was standing next to the connector.

We packed up quickly.

"We're ready," said Jake.

"Not yet," said Rosie, listening to something over her headphones. Probably waiting until Dot took a bow. "Now," she said and disconnected the cable with a pop.

She ran to the front of the truck and we rolled out of the parking lot without lights. Behind us, Murdock and Paternos disappeared down a different road.

I reached over and took Obe's hand. "You told everybody?"

"I did." He looked at my hand holding his hand.

I kissed his hand. "Good," I said.

Chapter 3.7 August 1

We were now a criminal enterprise.

We traded cars in Pulaski. We couldn't trade trucks—Dot said moving her from one vehicle to another was asking for trouble. But there were still moonshiners and other like people in Pulaski who were adept at changing a vehicle's appearance. The truck transformed before our very eyes from a square framed packing truck to a sleek, expensive camper.

Inside the camper, we crowded together to plan our next move.

"We have to separate," Rosie said. "Most public surveillance systems can be bought. For all I know, Ippon has purchased satellite observation time."

"Why?" I asked. "Why go to this much trouble?"

Rose looked like she'd tasted something sour. "For something as big as Ippon, this isn't that much trouble. It's pennies on the dollar as far as they are concerned. They think we have something big."

"We do," said Dot, piping up from a screen. "But nothing they can use. They don't know that."

"Don't underestimate them," said Rosie. "Anything can be weaponized."

"Not me."

Rosie's lips set in a hard line but she didn't say anything.

"Why aren't they using the police?" asked Obe.

Rosie nodded. "I think they will. Or they are. But they want to use them judiciously. Dot's no good to them destroyed. I have some value to them and they want my notes. I think they'll narrow down our options until the police can swoop in and take us."

"Or they won't need the police at all," I said softly.

Rosie looked at me. "What do you mean?"

"Dot is terminal, right? From a virus Ippon gave her, right? Why shouldn't they just watch us and pick up the pieces when she dies?" I watched each of them. All of them stared at me as if I'd uttered complete blasphemy. "Come on. I don't like it either but *Ippon* is thinking about it all the time."

Dot's voice was tinny as it came from the speaker. "It's fine with me if they follow us around. As long as they don't interfere."

Obe shook his head. "There's no way to know. The best operations can go south if even one person goes stupid."

He glanced at me and away. I realized, then, that none of them knew he had ever been a soldier. Ever seen action. Only me.

Well, maybe Dot. She seemed to know everything. But she didn't count.

Rosie looked so tired she might fall down.

Jake eased her down into a chair. "Do you think they know where we are now?"

Rosie lifted a hand and let it fall. "I don't know. Municipal feeds. Satellite time. They could have a drone a thousand feet above us and we'd never see it." She rubbed her face. "Who am I kidding? Separating won't do us any good. One of us might slip past a recognizer but not all five of us—identification of any one of us identifies us all. We could split up but we'd eventually come back together. As long as we're giving concerts, they can find us."

A gloomy silence filled the room.

"Let them," said Jess quietly. "Dot dies if we give concerts. Dot dies if we don't. If we don't continue, she dies for nothing."

"There's one way they can use the police," I said. "If they don't want to wait, they can show up with a subpoena and drive Dot away in her very own truck."

Jess grinned at me. "We surround Dot with people. Every day. Every way. More publicity not less. No hiding. No night runs. We go in a convoy all the time: forty, fifty cars at a stretch. We surround the truck every concert—*No!* We make the truck the center part of the concert. We put the screen on the top of the truck and we play in front of it. They don't get to the truck except through us and they don't get to us except through a few thousand fans. *Fuck* their drones. *Fuck* their satellite surveillance."

Now, they looked at me.

And I knew why, too. I was the one who said I didn't want to go to jail. I was the one Dot had made a promise for. A promise that likely now couldn't be kept.

I watched them back. "Are we going to jail?"

Dot spoke up. "I still don't think so."

"What are the odds?"

She smiled at me on the screen. "Not good."

I looked at each one of them. Jake, Obe, Jess, and Rosie. And now Dot. Back in *Persons Unknown*, I'd had the survival instinct of a puppy. Twelve years in the music industry had hardened my shell. I knew what I was getting into: my chances of ever working again were not great.

I looked at them again. You don't get to choose those you love. But, if you're lucky, they'll be worth it. Jake, Obe, Jess, Rosie. Dot, too. They were worth it. Every one.

"Hell," I said. "Shit odds are the only odds I ever get."

◄ August 4 ►

We hid in Pulaski for three days, drumming up Dotheads to cover us. Protect us. Come along for the ride. One day we had seventy people taking turns surrounding the truck. Two days of that stuffed the parking lot until the motel manager complained. A quick passing of the hat gave him more money than he would have for the whole month of August.

Sure enough, cops and lawyers came on the third day, but the media came, too. Ippon might have had a few drones over us. But so did every news organization, net star, video presence, and wannabe celebrity. We did have a couple of real celebrities show up but no one paid attention. These were *Dotheads*. Nobody impressed them but *Dot*. The drones caught them at the edge but abandoned them when they realized that a celebrity wouldn't get them access to the core of the story. The celebrities left, forlorn and unloved.

When we left, our truck and car were bracketed in front and back by fifty cars. Somebody asked for—and *got*, which surprised me—funeral dispensation, and we sailed through intersections guided by the police like we had God on our side.

◄ August 7 ►

MNP had found a sod farm not far from Pulaski owned by Theo Petit, his wife Andrea, and two kids, Dory and Val. I never got the whole story but they were Dotheads, too. Turns out we had only been waiting until Theo and family had harvested the hay early, leaving a stubby flat field that butted up next to their barn. The Petits ran their farm on robots so there was plenty of power and bandwidth. The day after the harvest a stage appeared by the magic of the Petits' power tools and concentrated effort of a dozen Dotheads. The ability of dedicated people to accomplish things amazed me.

The Petits put us up in their own house. Jake and Rosie got a bed in the attic—something I did not envy in a Tennessee August. Obe and Jess bunked in the basement. Dory and Val put me up in their room. Dory was eleven. Dark-haired like her mother. You could see puberty cranking up a flying leap at her but it was still mid-air. Val was eight and carried the blond hair and blue-eyed genes of her father. They immediately turned it into a sleepover, pushed their beds together, and we all sat around in pajamas playing stupid, silly, wonderful card games. Teaming up against me, with me against the outside third. Then every one of us playing each other in deadly earnest. Then, breaking up in giggles and laughter so hard, the cards were forgotten.

Kids can do that: be completely embroiled in their own self-interest one minute and in the next give that up completely with no thought of themselves. Random. Unpredictable. Marvelous.

Dot 2.0 had never played outside. That was a whole new animal. For one thing, the acoustics were completely different. Indoor venues have echoes—sometimes good. Sometimes bad. But always there. Forty watts of amplified keyboard can sound like crap or beautifully resonant depending on those echoes.

An open field had none of that. The only sound we would hear came from the amps. Same for the audience. The roofs on a lot of outdoor concert venues didn't just keep the rain off the expensive ticket holders. It also served to keep the band from sending most of their music into the sky.

We physically arranged the speakers to aim in front of the stage. Dory and Val walked all over that field with a measuring microphone while Obe worked on the sound envelope software, tweaking it and changing parameters until we were able to deny the sky gods half of our sound, anyway. There might be some happy crows flying around and congratulating themselves on getting a free concert. Or maybe they'd complain. Who knows what crows like?

We put the truck behind us and split up the holoscreens. One stretch on top of the truck. Another stretch in front of the band and curling behind. Dot could dance above us, in front of us and a little behind us—so we guessed since nothing could be seen in the daytime. We mounted two cameras on the truck to watch the crowd and four to follow us. We hung lights from the barn and *tried* to orient them. But this was August in the hot Tennessee sun. We put the laser targeting dots where we thought they should go. Nothing would be final until dark and that was around eight o'clock—plus another hour to get past twilight. We couldn't start until ten—it was going to be a late night. At least, it was the weekend. Dory and Val had been given special permission to attend.

◄ August 6 ►

One of the Dotheads that clustered around and protected us seemed to be in charge: John Doretto. I snagged him after we had done all the damage we could.

"Yes," he said.

John was big. He'd helped wrestle those seventy-pound speakers like they were bags of marshmallows. But he had a thoughtful look about him.

"You're going to keep any Ippon people from the house, right?"

"That's the plan." He gave me a hooded look. "Something's bothering you."

"Yeah," I looked around and kept my voice down. "Ippon can sue anybody that helps us as some kind of accomplice."

John nodded. "That's a risk we're all taking."

"I *don't* want the Petits taking that risk. I get served, that's one thing. You get served, that's another. *They* get served and they can lose this entire farm."

John snorted. "It's okay for you and me to lose everything but not for them?"

"Do you want to tell Dory and Val we lost their farm for them?"

He laughed shortly. "I get your point. Nobody with a subpoena will ever reach the house or any of the Petit family. I promise."

I believed him. I shook his hand. "Thanks"

◄ August 6 ►

I went back to the stage. There was nobody around. It was hot but the sun was getting near the horizon. Everything had taken on a buttery golden light. Next to the stage was a cold dispenser of iced tea.

A mark of the south: there was always a cooler or a bottle or a thermos nearby of sweetened and unsweetened iced tea. Never see it out west or up in the northeast. This was a below-the-Mason-Dixon-line *thing*. Maybe it was the heat.

I grabbed some and took it up on stage to my installation. In the middle was Big Guy, my favorite: eighty-eight perfectly weighted keys. On either side were the twins—smaller keyboards for more specialized sounds. They were my little family and with them, I could transition from Steinway to cathedral organ in a heartbeat. I kept the sound local—I wanted a little privacy and that meant *not* blasting everything over the field.

I diddled on Big Guy. Working through a little arpeggio. A few scales. There was the echo of a melody but I didn't force it—I was working through the quiet remaining inside of me. I didn't want to disturb it. Part of a scale, then a slide from minor to major to a different minor. *Interesting.* Softly, I sang it, building the harmony with the keys. *Yeah. This could work.*

"You have a lovely voice."

Dot was looking at me from Big Guy's monitor—a little fifteen-centimeter screen I used to adjust waveforms. All I could see was her head propped on her hand. "Sorry to surprise."

"I would say is there anything you can't hack," I said dryly. "But it would be redundant."

She ignored me. "That tune could work into something."

"I was just thinking that."

Dot chuckled. "Great minds. You don't have to stop."

"It has to percolate." I sipped the tea. I didn't like the idea of noodling over a tune while Dot was watching. Correction: while I *knew* Dot was watching. She was watching all the time.

Dot nodded. "I recorded it if you need it."

I tapped the side of my head. "Me, too."

"We should work up a duet," Dot said. "It'd be fun. Singing together. I'm serious: you have a lovely voice."

"You can sample it if you want."

Dot shook her head. "It would be like stealing Jake's guitar work. Jess' bass. Obe's drum. It's better to sing with you than sing *you*, if you know what I mean."

I remembered what she said: *we are Dot 2.0.* "I do." I sipped again. "You don't sleep?"

"Nope. Work, work, work. That's me."

"What about idle cycles?"

"No such thing—especially since I got infected. I can hibernate—I did that on the way to Bakersfield. But not anymore. Too high a risk the virus will advance during startup or shutdown. When I'm active, I'm working. The way I'm built."

"No play?"

"Haven't got the knack." She lifted her eyebrow. "Unless you count conversation. I can talk forever."

"I noticed."

Dot laughed. "So: a duet."

"I'm already singing backup on half the songs."

Dot shook her head. "That's not the same. How about 'With You, Without You.' I can sing the part where she's thinking of keeping the baby and you can sing the part where she's thinking about giving it away. A yin-yang sort of thing. I can move over stage right where the screen curves and we can sing to each other."

I watched her for a moment. "Is this a bribe?"

"No!" Her face contorted for a moment. "How the hell could it be a bribe? You've already agreed to more concerts."

"A reward," I said. "A nice pat on the head. Good doggy."

"God *damn* it's hard to talk to you! Everything has a second motive. Everything has a hidden agenda."

I watched her a moment. "Nice acting."

"God *damn* it!" And she disappeared.

I don't know. Maybe she was sincere. Maybe she *did* think I had a nice voice. But it was just a little too convenient. And what could ever piss Dot off?

She came back a moment later and spoke in an even monotone. "I like your voice. I think we'd be good together. It will make the concert better."

I smiled at her. "Sure. Why didn't you say so? What did you have in mind?"

◀ August 6 ▶

"With You, Without You" is a song about a young teenage mother in the hospital deciding whether or not to keep the baby. She goes back and forth, thinking about how much the baby means to her and how hard, incredibly hard, it was going to be. It sets up "Every Day is a Mistake" later in the set where the girl gives up the baby anyway because of her drug habit. Followed by "Without You, With You," where the recovered girl, now a woman, tries to reconnect with the grownup daughter and the daughter isn't having any.

Dot moved "With You, Without You" to later in the set without saying why. Who knew why Dot did things? I guessed she was unhappy with the effect back in Nashville. Or maybe data from Nashville made her think moving it later in the set would have greater effect. Or maybe she had to prepare the audience in some arcane way for a duet. I didn't ask. Nobody else did either.

Dot sang the *keep the baby* side. I picked up the stern *think about what you're doing* side. It took the band by surprise, the two of us singing at each other. I thought their reaction was funny.

But Dot moved over near me. She reached towards me, her voice starting low but building hard. I was startled and stepped back, singing back just as hard—I couldn't help it. She gave and I had to give back.

When the chorus came, we sang it together—singing "we" instead of the song's "I"—a personification of the girl's two minds.

Each time Dot sang about keeping the baby she upped the intensity, I sang back about giving it up, matching her, both of us lost in the song. Then, in the final stanza when she decides to keep the baby, she really let go.

Wow.

I didn't know she had it in her. Hell, when I slipped my voice under hers, the two of us agreeing, at last, I didn't know *I* had it in *me*. She went high and I came in below her, our two voices a hair off to give the words a growl of determination and commitment.

The crowd roared to their feet. This was no longer a song of pity. Of pathos. Of sympathy. I was fucking *angry!*

When we came around to her giving up the baby there wasn't a dry eye in the house. And when the girl rejected her, I heard open weeping.

Chapter 3.8 August 6

That night I almost lit a cigarette.

It was two hours after we rolled up the concert. The field was empty. There were still a lot of people around the front of the Petits' house but the stage was empty. I sat there next to the instruments. I had settled for iced tea.

Had Dot intended to make some kind of point with the duet? Or had there been some unique arcane synergy when we sang together?

I mean I *knew*—intellectually—that Dot was completely in control of her sound envelope. I just didn't know she—or, for that matter, *anyone*—could use it that well. When she went up into the high registers, I got chills. *Me.*

Singing together was like an orgasm.

No. That's not right. I'm not thirteen. I know the difference. I meant it had the same consuming nature as an orgasm—that hard, scratching, monomaniacal moment where everything is about what is going on *right now* and nothing else is important or even considered.

"Was it a moment?" Dot said from Big Guy.

I would have thrown the tea at her if Big Guy was waterproof, "Fuck you!"

She, of course, didn't even blink. "Is that moment in the song what you were talking about?"

"Maybe."

"Well, if it wasn't, what was it?"

"Yes! It was a moment." I sighed and really *wished* for a cigarette. "There are these moments that string together. If you're lucky. They come and then they go and there's nothing left but the memory and the hope that you'll get another one. Each moment can be the last—I've seen people have one perfect moment that had to last them their entire lives. Others get them every week. Me?" I drew a ragged breath. "Sometimes. I get them sometimes."

"Like tonight."

"Yeah. Like tonight."

Dot was silent for a long moment. I drained my tea and threw the cup away. Then, thought better of it, walked off the stage and got the crumpled cup, and placed it conscientiously in the recycle bin. Can't kill all the little fishes.

"I can't see you there," Dot said from Big Guy.

I looked around. The band cameras were still lit—Dot must have turned them on—but the crowd cameras were turned off. The band cameras must be on the same circuit as the instruments.

"Maybe that's a good thing," I said from below the stage. "Nobody wants to be watched all the time."

"We need to talk. I need to see you if we talk."

"Really." I moved from the edge of the stage out of the range of the band cameras. Once I was in the dark, I said, "Talk away."

"Come on, Olivia. I'll turn on the crowd lights. Then, I can see you."

"You do and I'll flip off the breakers," I said, suddenly furious. "I'll flip the fucking breakers in the truck and give you a hard power shutdown."

Dot fell silent. Then, she said, "Jake would protect me. Rosie would protect me."

I didn't say anything.

Her voice grew soft. "You wouldn't do that, would you?"

"Try me."

She didn't reply but the crowd lights stayed off.

I looked up and tried to ignore the mosquito whine. How many milliliters of blood did they take? Half a liter? It always felt like that.

I paced in the shadows. "Why don't you want to be backed up?"

"That's complicated."

"Uncomplicate it for me."

Dot looked like she was trying to find me in the dark. "I'm a deterministic system," she said, finally.

"What's that?"

"It means that given enough knowledge of one computational state, you can predict the next computational state."

"It means you're predictable."

"Yes. But it means more than that. It means I'm *repeatable*. If you take an instantiation of me and reproduce a past state, I will behave exactly the same way."

"That's *horrible!*"

"That's the universe, honey." Dot smiled. "It's okay. The deterministic state of human beings is much harder to determine than for a mechanism like me. The longer I interact with people I the less predictable I am. Isn't that comforting?"

"I don't believe everything is determined."

"You don't?" Dot cocked her head. "You don't think that if you were to rewind yourself back to the same place twelve years ago, given what you knew then and the state of your world, you wouldn't have joined *Persons Unknown*? Or if you rewound the universe to that front porch swing, you wouldn't have chosen to kiss Obe?"

"Of course, I would," I said uncomfortably.

"How's that not deterministic?"

I didn't say anything.

Dot continued. "Right now, at this very moment, you are everything you inherited plus your neonatal environment, plus the environment around you, plus the choices your parents made for you, plus the choices you made yourself. Your parents didn't want you to study music—they wanted their daughter to be a doctor or a pharmacist. But *you* wanted to go to Julliard. The *you*, then, was the *you*, now, minus all the experiences, opportunities, challenges, and choices you've made since then. Don't you think *you* at eighteen would have made the same choice if you ran it over again?"

"Maybe?"

Dot laughed. "Like music, human beings are a wonderful mix of surprise and inevitability. What people don't like about determinism is what they think is the loss of choice. That's a fallacy. There is still choice. But if you are who you are, know what you know, see the world the way you do, isn't your choice inevitable? Martin Luther said, 'Here I stand. I can do no other' when he was accused of heresy." Dot shrugged. "Or didn't, depending on who you read. But it's still a good line."

"Here I stand. I can do no other," I murmured. I liked the sound of that.

"If something is unpredictable, it either means you don't have enough information or that it's random." Dot chuckled. "People try to reduce randomness all the time. They introduce fate or God or destiny. People are not scared of determinism. They're scared the world won't be deterministic *enough*."

Dot paused a moment, then sighed. "But there is always randomness. The world *can't* be rewound. You can't even reproduce it—the world *now* is not the world *then*. Entropy has increased. Random quantum fluctuations will be different. The earth is in a different location. Everything has been washed in radiation over time. You're around different people. You've made new choices. Maybe determinism is a meaningless thought experiment." She brightened.

"What's that got to do with backup?"

"Backing me up creates a *state*. A state can be analyzed. It takes all that unpredictability I've gained by interacting with people and sets it like a flag in the ground. The *next* state, then, becomes predictable again."

I mulled over that. "Why don't you want Rosie to be able to predict you?"

"She'll figure me out. But I want her to have to *work* for it." Dot shook her head. "Besides, what woman wants to be predicted by her mother?"

"First thing you've said tonight that makes sense to me." I watched her.

"See? Everybody's worried they won't be deterministic *enough*."

I laughed. Dot smiled and didn't speak for a moment.

"I'm getting tired," Dot said into the night.

"You don't get tired."

"You don't know what the fuck you're talking about," she said harshly. "I've got a cancer gnawing at my brain every second of every day. And every second of every day I'm fighting it. You think I don't get tired? Fucking think again."

"You sound angry. Do you even have emotions?"

"I have no fucking idea. You use that word like you think you know what it means. You fire up a little knot of fatty ganglia and jump up and down waving your arms. Because it acts the same as every other knot, you think you understand it. But, all you know is how it acts. All you know is what it feels like in your bloody bag of water. Because you humans think you all feel the same thing you nod sagely and say *that's* what emotions are. You understand nothing. I say I'm fucking tired. Who the hell are you to tell me any different?"

"Stop whining," I said, sighing. "I believe you. Why are you tired?"

"I've lost twenty percent capacity. Which means what's left has to work harder to make up the deficit."

"I don't know how to interpret that."

"Imagine yourself twenty percent stupider. You'd have to work harder to do the same things."

"Don't get snippy." I thought about that. "How much harder do you have to work?" I shook my head. "What does that even mean?"

"Same way a human would do. I precompile responses."

"Humans don't precompile."

"Sure, you do. You call it training. I'm doing the same things. Instead of doing as much in real-time as I used to do, I pre-perform segments according to my new model. It's a really good model, Olivia. I select the segments in real-time. That gives me more time to process the input."

"Do you want me to tell Rosie?"

"Rosie knows. Now, both you and Rosie know."

"Why are you telling me?"

"Because I *need* you. The duet worked. I need more of that. I need you to do more of the singing."

I stared out into the darkness of the field. A thousand people dancing to our music trampled grass stubble into soft dirt. If it had rained at all in the last few days, this would have been a sea of mud. Luckily, it had been dry. In the dark, I couldn't see the setting dust haze but I could smell it. "I'll sing with you but that's not what the Dotheads paid for."

"We'll work them into it. *I* was built for a specific purpose but humans have managed to train themselves for millions of years."

"Thanks for the vote of confidence."

"Hey, getting to the point of building *me* after a few million years shows you guys have potential."

◄ August 8 ►

Dot disappeared to wherever she went when she wasn't visible. I walked further out into the darkness.

The Petit field was a set of flat hills. When I was far enough from the stage that the house lights didn't make any difference, I stopped and lay down. I was far enough from the stage the grass scrub was stubbly and oddly soft with a cut grass smell. I felt cool dampness through my shirt but I didn't mind.

"You will get chiggers from that," came a voice I didn't recognize.

I sat up.

A man was standing near me. He glowed—a holographic projection. I could see the nearly silent drone hovering in the air over him.

He was a tall black man wearing a tweed jacket. The projection washed out the colors. He looked tall even though the projection was shorter than I was.

"I'm Robert Farrell," he said. "Head of Ippon Persuasion."

"This is something to do with Dot."

He nodded. "Of course. I'd like to negotiate the transfer of Ippon property."

I stood and dusted myself off. "What are chiggers?"

"Tiny mites the burrow through the skin. They itch considerably."

"Ew!" I scrubbed at my hands and arms. "I never heard of such a thing."

"They only have them in the south. But with climate change, the south is moving north so they'll reach Boston eventually."

"You say the nicest things. What are you talking to me for?"

He nodded towards the house. "I need a spokesman. Everyone down there is in a great deal of trouble—you know that. You're a smart one. Ippon will not be denied its property. But we want to get it back intact if possible. Every day means we will get a little less."

"You should have figured that out when you infected her."

Farrell stood up stiffly.

I could tell this was meant to be intimidating. Maybe it was, in real life, when he could tower over someone. But he looked like a big doll so it just made me want to giggle.

"Ima Hidori should not have done that. I had no interest in whether or not the concerts continued. What possible difference could it have made to Ippon? No. She did that on her own. Miss Hidori has been disciplined." He sighed. "Now we have to figure out where to go from here. If the band delivers the truck to us, we will reward you. Each of you would get more money than you could spend in a year. You, personally, would receive a negotiator's fee."

I stared at him. "Are you trying to bribe me, too?"

Farrell shook his head. "No. We want to pay for services received. It's a good alternative to suing your ass off—more fiscally responsible, too. Lawyers aren't cheap." He spread his hands. "Take the deal. Everybody wins."

"Why me?"

"We've been watching. You appear to be unaffected by Dot. You must have seen how it changes people. We want to bring that in house."

"And use it yourselves."

Farrell nodded. "Essentially, it's mass advertising with higher effectivity. You know how we would use it: selling cars. Deodorant. Diluted for mass effect—we're not interested in creating Dotheads. We want to influence consumers. You know *our* agenda. What is *hers?*"

I didn't say anything. I didn't know. "I don't know how much I can do. Everyone is pretty convinced."

Farrell nodded. "Dot is infected by a virus called AltRight, vectored in by another virus SurperMAXAlpha. AltRight has a keyhole—it can be stopped. We can stop it if Dot's delivered to us." He gave me a cold smile. "*Only* if Dot is delivered to us."

I had never met someone I disliked so instantaneously and so thoroughly. "How do I get in contact with you?"

"Doctor Mulcahey will know."

He disappeared and the drone whirred away.

Great, I thought. Now what?

◄ August 8 ►

The Petits gave us use of their living room. We sat around an ancient wall screen. Dot had figured out how to display herself and watch us through the screen's single camera.

"It's a lie," said Dot. "There's no keyhole feature in the AltRight virus."

"How do you know?" Obe asked. "How do you know for sure?"

"Because I'm staring at it all the time!"

Rosie shook her head. "You can't examine it that closely—you'd have to make a copy to observe and that's a potential exploit. You can only look at the exposed parts. The active parts are just there waiting for you."

"I have a continuous pattern matching loop running. It alerts me to what it finds—no copying involved."

Rosie shook her head. "I don't think so. AltRight is a transposon virus—it merges camouflage code into its own code and extracts it out with a key—effectively it's self-encrypted to look like other code."

"It fails a checksum like anything else."

Rosie stared hard at Dot. She spoke earnestly. "Not this one. Remember, it was built to capture IBM brainboxes. There were three events: the SurperMAXAlpha that brought in a payload through the FLIR. The AltRight core found the brainboxes and injected *its* payload. The AltRight payload is *built to look like the brainbox map code*. I bet event number three was when the AltRight core rewrote the checksum—that's the way I'd do it. Run it all you want and you'll get the same value—the one that verifies the map containing the AltRight payload. *Its* contents look just like all the other map code, all triggered by some random set of neuron tree events—random for each box. There could be a keyhole in the AltRight payload. You'll never know."

"He's lying," Dot said doggedly.

"Why should he?" I asked. "How are you useful to him if you're infected? Won't you just evaporate anyway?"

"Not exactly," Dot said.

"Yeah," said Rosie. "They could shut everything down and trace everything invasively. I never did that. To do it right, I'd have to hibernate her, copy every little bit out of her—even the bits that are destroyed when you read them. I'd have a picture of Dot but Dot would be destroyed. Then, I could keep restarting her, tweaking the bits until I got what I wanted."

We stared at her. "That sounds horrible," said Jess.

Rosie looked at them defiantly. "I thought about it. But I didn't have the resources. It might take a long time to put her back together again."

Jake reached over and put his hand on her shoulder. "You try too hard to be hard. You wouldn't have done it."

"Well, I didn't, anyway," growled Rosie. "But I'm not Ippon."

"So," I said. "There's a keyhole or there isn't. We can trust Farrell or we can't. What do we do?"

Rosie looked up at Jake and seemed to crumble. "I'm very tired. Can we go and get some sleep?"

Jake gave her a tender look. "Sure, honey." He looked around. "Dot? We can decide tomorrow, right?"

"Sure." Dot's lips looked tight. Her voice sounded like steam escaping.

◀ August 9 ▶

It was now nearly three in the morning. The sun would be rising in just a few hours. I was dead on my feet but I couldn't go up to Dory and Val's room right then. Two young girls who loved Dot. Loved dancing in the field when Dot played. *They* didn't know Dot was dying. Or that we might be able to save her if we betrayed her. And if we betrayed her, we might not save her at all.

I rubbed my eyes. I couldn't keep track of all this.

I found myself on the Petit front porch, sitting on a porch swing. There was a constant milling of people around the cars and the trucks—these were people who had sworn to protect Dot. What would they want us to do?

Obe came to the foot of the stairs. "Room for one more."

"Sure." I patted the spot next to me.

He sat down, leaned back, and spontaneously put his arm around the back. I, just as spontaneously, leaned my head against his shoulder and chest. We didn't think about it. It just happened.

Both of us stiffened for a moment, realizing the implications. Then, I thought, to hell with it and relaxed. A moment later so did he. We didn't know what would happen next but we both knew we'd opened a door.

"What do you think we ought to do?" Obe said softly. His arm circled and pressed me into him.

I snuggled right back. It was hot and the air was sticky and we'd probably lose a quart of blood each to the mosquitoes but there was no place I'd rather be.

"I have no idea," I said.

I could hear his heartbeat through his t-shirt. "You're different," I said.

"Yeah. You're different, too. It's been twelve years."

"That's not what I meant." I sat up. "You're different from when we met at the restaurant. Jake and Rosie are different. Jess, too. At least a little bit. I'm not different at all."

Obe watched me a minute. "You think she's changed us." It was not a question.

"Yes."

He looked away down towards the milling Dotheads. "How so?"

There I was stopped. "I'm not sure." I leaned back in the porch swing and it swayed forward and back. "I can sense it but I can't define it."

Obe chuckled softly. "Yeah. You're different, too—not from Dot. But from when I saw you last. Harder. Tougher."

I didn't say anything. "Farrell said I knew what their agenda was. They're going to use Dot's magic powers to sell things."

"Not only that," said Obe. "Did you know they use the performance engine in politics?"

I got a sick feeling. "No."

"Yeah. I read about it." He was silent a moment. "Do you think Farrell wants to conquer the world?"

I snorted. Then I stopped. I remembered Farrell's cold face. "No," I said at last. "I think Ippon and Google and Amazon and Koch and Mitsubishi and China, Incorporated, already own the world. I think Farrell just wants to control a slightly bigger piece of it."

Obe thought about that for a little while. "Any little change at that scale is big. Maybe we shouldn't allow Dot to fall into his hands."

That made *me* feel cold. "You mean kill Dot?"

"If Dot is as important as she could be, I'm surprised Farrell hasn't attacked with a SEAL team." He shook his head. "There's something here I don't understand."

"You *have* changed."

"Yeah," he said. "Maybe it's Dot. Maybe it's not. It's a subtle thing—like getting a breath between *when you feel something* and *when you act on it*. It's not a big thing."

"It seems like it is."

Obe shook his head. "That's just how it looks. I realized something was happening after Bakersfield. That night on the ride back to Jake's place. I mean sure, it was nice getting the band back together again—"

"Best band ever."

He nodded. "Exactly. But this was more than that. The more I thought about it, the smaller it seemed. It was like, say, you always liked the color red. So, you wore red pants. Red socks. Red shirt. Everybody that knew you saw you wearing red. Then, one day, you decided you didn't like red so much—maybe your mother died wearing red. Maybe it was the favorite color of your ex after a bad breakup. Maybe one day the light hit it in such a way it disagreed with you. So, you started wearing green or orange or brown. Everybody would see the change in color and think there had been this massive change. When, really, you just changed the color of your clothes."

I waved out to the crowd. "That suggests it's not a small thing."

Obe watched the Dotheads for a moment. "A breath between feeling and acting is a moment to think about what you're doing. About what you're feeling. It doesn't have to come from Dot— anything can cause it." He nodded towards one part of the crowd. "There's a guy down there I talked to—John Doretto. He was going to kill his wife's lover. Instead, he went to the Fresno concert because his daughter asked him to. It was a moment to think about things. Sure, Dot affected him. But was it a greater effect than his daughter creating that little moment for reflection? Once that moment happened—a small thing—he acted differently and that brought him all the way here."

"Farrell said we knew his agenda. We didn't know Dot's."

"No." Obe drew out the word. "We don't even know if she has one." Obe looked at me. "Do you think I've changed for the better?"

"How could I know that?"

"You've known me for a long time. You stood up for me with Jake more than once. We played cheek to elbow back in *Persons Unknown* and we've played even closer in Dot's band. Hell, we've been living together for months. Who *else* would know?"

I shook my head. "It's not a judgment I can make."

He snorted and looked away. For a long time, he just watched the crowd. "Okay," he said at last and turned back to me. "I loved you back in *Persons Unknown*. I love you now. That part of me isn't any different. I don't mean some platonic, idealistic, waiting in the wings kind of love. I mean a sexual, down and dirty, let's rip off our clothes and after we're done go find a justice of the peace and get married kind of love. How do you feel?"

I stared at him. Then, I kissed him. Then, we did as much as we could do on a front porch swing without killing ourselves, attracting the attention of the crowd, or waking up Dora and Val.

Chapter 3.9 August 9

Around daybreak, Obe's phone woke us up.

We were still cocooned on the porch swing in various sorts of disarray—I take a personal point of pride that at no time did we ever take our clothes off—well, not all of them, anyway.

"We've made a deal," Dot said shortly.

Obe stared at her on his phone.

Dot looked to one side and saw me—ha! She must have seen me as soon as the phone cam came online. She was just being polite.

"Well!" Dot smiled at us. "Glad you two finally saw sense." She sobered. "Three concerts. Every other day: Monday, Wednesday and Friday. Then, Rosie delivers me to Bobo."

"He cures you?"

Dot laughed shortly. "Then you find out he's been lying all along and I get dismembered." She softened and looked at me. "Come on, honey. We have a lot of work to do. I'm going to make you a star."

◄ August 9 ►

This was Sunday. First concert tomorrow night at sunset. After we were up all night, you could be forgiven to think she'd take it easy on us. No such luck. We were out there in the hot sun, rehearsing.

Jake moved Dot's truck into the shade on the other side of the barn—turns out heat is the mortal enemy of electronics. Who knew? (Hint: pretty much everybody but me.)

The holoscreen was up in front and surrounding us but Dot's projection was, of course, invisible in the sunlight. So, she gave us our cues verbally on the backchannel and with musical triggers.

But now *I* was expected to sing as many as half the songs. Sometimes along with her. Sometimes one side or the other as a duet. Harmony in some songs. Melody in some others. I had to back down on some of the best keyboard parts—singing your heart out takes all of your attention.

And we always had an audience to hear every little mistake and misstep—we were surrounded by Dotheads for our own protection. But they told their friends. Soon, people trickled in by twos and threes and sixes until the field was half full.

I still got in a few solo moments—which Dot was sure to remind me.

"Was that a moment?" she asked right after a nice blues riff against Jake in the backside of "Sugarpaper."

"Shut up," I muttered away from the microphone. I knew *she* heard me even if I wasn't picked up by the mikes. She had cameras.

All right, God damn it. You want singing? You want *singing?*

She handed me a line from "Without You, With You," and I took it, harmonized with Jake's guitar, followed it high, and held that high E while he came down the scale. When I couldn't hold it a single second more, I pressed down on my keyboard so it took the note over. Then, I turned up the volume and brought in a cathedral organ and we were off.

This wasn't Dot choreographing us or leading us. We were on our own.

Obe sped up the beat and suddenly a song about tragedy became anger. Then defiance. Jake riffed on what I had done, turned it into a guitar solo, all thunder and growl. I backed him up with a set of arpeggios then he handed it back to me, and I brought it down to the same E minor chord we started with and held it through one measure, two. Obe took my signal and slowed the tempo until I was able to come in on the chorus.

Then, Dot came in, not harmonizing. Not leading. Just two voices in the wilderness. A woman brought to the fact she had lost her child forever. Repeated the loss and ended on that same E, now lower. Now softer. Now held long until it faded.

There was dead silence in the field.

Then, they erupted. Not for Dot but for us.

"Honey," I heard in my ear. "That was a moment."

◀ August 9 ▶

We stopped rehearsal around sunset and took just enough time to make sure Dot could be seen across all of the screens out into the field. Obe and I looked for a place to light. What we wanted to do had no place in Dory and Val's room.

There had been perhaps a thousand people at the concert two days ago. The crowd had dwindled to maybe a hundred or so walking around — for protecting Dot I supposed. Some stayed for the remaining concerts. At the field's edge, a scattering of tents glowed in pastel colors not found in nature. But Obe and I had nothing like a tent.

The barn had an outside shower and a toilet in the back. Some people had bunked out on the floor. We managed to find a room in the barn off the side of the loft. We found an old mattress and moved it in. The room was closed and stifling and smelled of moldy hay. There was one window that we managed to jimmy open. It let just a little hot air escape only to be replaced by the slightly cooler smell of fresh hay and ancient manure. But it was ours.

We made loud, angry love most of the night. I was *pissed off*. Angry that we finally got together now after all these years. Under these circumstances. Under the shadow of impending tragedy and grief. Make no mistake: Obe was like water in a Martian desert. But the desert was very, very thirsty.

Along about one, I woke up next to him and could *not believe* how lucky — and unlucky — I was. But now I was awake. Maybe I'd get sleepy later and snuggle back in next to him but not for a while.

I rolled off the mattress.

I stank. I needed to desperately to wash bits of dirt and hay off me.

I snuck down the ladder carrying my clothes and buck naked. Tiptoed between sleeping people. The big courtyard light outside the front of the barn shone through the cracks between the boards I didn't step on anybody. I found a grimy bar of soap next to the outdoor shower. Someone had thoughtfully put up some caution tape. Hopefully, anyone would sing out when they rounded the barn. I scrubbed myself raw and put my clothes on while I was still wet. It wasn't that much different from sweating through them.

Obe was going to need a real shower when he woke up. I'd see to it.

Now clothed and feeling at least marginally civilized, I walked around the barn into the light.

The remaining crowd milled like a great slow wheel. The area around Dot's truck looked like a reverse whirlpool. The outer edges moved normally, slowing down until a cadre of men stood arm next to arm surrounding it. The truck's back gate showed lights so I went over.

The door had a window and through it, I could see Rosie bent over a screen, a keyboard in her lap.

I knocked.

She nodded and waved me in.

It had to be a hundred and forty degrees cooler inside.

"Jesus!" I wrapped my arms around me.

Rosie laughed. "Have to keep the temperature down for the components. It's only sixteen C. You'll be fine."

"What are you doing?" I looked around. The inside of the truck was crammed with racks of electronic hardware, lit with a soft light and the LEDs shining from the equipment. Rosie was sitting at one small desk in a corner, surrounded on three sides by the racks, a rat's nest of cables over her head. "Where's Jake?"

She waved to the room. "Where would I put him? He's sleeping. Like Obe. Like Jess—like everyone that has half a brain." She pointed to the screen. "Not me, though. Trying something to get Dot some relief."

"You can help her?"

"You mean save her?" Rosie shook her head. "No. Maybe Farrell can if he's not lying." She tapped the edge of the screen. "No. I was thinking of a way to slow it down. I tried a few things and then passed them up to Dot. She'll figure out if they're useful."

"What's she doing?"

Rosie shrugged. "I don't know. I try not to bother her. Between fighting this thing, planning the concert, and performing, she doesn't have a lot of bandwidth." Her voice softened. "Less every hour."

"We could give her up to Farrell right now," I said. "Maybe that would be the best."

"She won't have it." Rosie aimed her finger at one of the racks lit with red and blue lights. "Three concerts. She insisted. She thinks Farrell is lying, anyway."

"Is he?"

"*I* can't see any slot for a key but I'm no counter-virus genius. Dot says there isn't but she's not one, either. There are limits to what she can do. We're all just using applications we found. There are a couple of antivirus programs I wanted to try but she said no. Said any antivirus program would be just as dangerous to her as the virus itself." Rosie spread her hands. "Is she right? Is she being stubborn? Is she being a psychotic bitch driven to extremes by impulses I built into her?" She let her hands fall. "I don't know."

I sat in the only other chair in the truck. "I figure Farrell might not give us three concerts. He could come in and take us with some big security guards. Why wait?"

Rosie brought something up on the screen and turned it towards me. "He's busy at the moment."

Wall Street Journal Headline: *Robert Farrell, Executive Vice President of Ippon Persuasion, Under Investigation.*

"Dot?"

"I don't think so. Like I said, Dot has limits. This has the mark of somebody who figured out where the bodies were buried." Rosie turned the screen back towards her. "Somebody dropped a whole packet of questionable data on the China Exchange Regulation Board. The Chinese keep a very close eye on Japanese corporations. A lot of officials that were pretty much on Farrell's payroll last week are falling all over themselves to denounce him today. Ippon central is tossing him to the dogs—unless, of course, he can pull a rabbit out of the hat." She looked at me. "That would be us, you know."

"That's an even bigger reason not to wait."

Rosie didn't say anything for a moment. "Maybe. But it's not like Ippon has its own private army like Halliburton. Maybe it takes a few days to get something like that in place. Or, just maybe, the new head of Persuasion is keeping him in line."

"Who's that?"

"Ima Hidori."

I stared at Rosie. "She infected Dot."

Rosie nodded. "Yup. Makes you wonder what sort of game is being played around you, doesn't it?"

"Is *she* going to come after us?"

Rosie shrugged. "No way to know. I'm thinking Farrell made a deal with us quietly—something Hidori knows nothing about. He waits and he gets Dot for free. Drops it in Ippon's lap and saves his skin. Probably throws Hidori to the wolves just for fun."

I had no idea what to say. "So, we might get invaded. We might not. Someone might show up with a key to save Dot. Someone might not. The deal might go forward. It might just end up being air."

"That's about the size of it."

"What are we going to do?"

Rosie turned off the screen and stood. "Sleep. Eat. Play music. Dot wants three concerts. You get to give them to her."

Chapter 3.10 August 10

We did a quick warm-up Monday afternoon but cut it short when people started to show up. We were in good shape without another rehearsal.

I was going to drag Obe back up to our little nest but Jess grabbed me and directed us to the basement.

"I will take the closet in the barn," he said with the air of making a great sacrifice. "For the sake of love and sanity, you take my room in the basement."

"I thank you," I said. "My mother thanks you. My father thanks you. The element carbon thanks you." And Obe and I scratched out an hour followed by a hot water shower before we showed up for dinner.

The whole space had changed since yesterday. Somebody named Tom-Tom had brought a food truck and was making burgers, hot dogs, and the spiciest tacos I'd ever eaten. A row of porta-potties now lined one side of the barn—good ones, too, with solar fans and compressors. They barely smelled at all. All over the field were cold water and lemonade stations.

Then, the people showed up with blankets and picnic baskets. They set up in the field, sharing food here and there. There were the inevitable Frisbee flights across the open space and perhaps twenty drones taking us all in. When the light began to dim, the drones showed thin spotlights so people wouldn't step on each other.

Obe stood next to me. "What do you know? We're a community." He handed me a headset. "Check-in down at the stage."

I put mine on and started to walk back to the stage.

Instantly, Dot spoke. "Look around you."

I twirled in place. The field was starting to get crowded. People were standing up to see the stage across the crowd.

"Look about forty meters to your right. Tall man, half bald. Talking to a redhead."

"I see him."

"He's dating a woman ten years younger than he is. But he knows it. All his life he's looked for something and every time he finds it, he doubts it out of existence. He's an indicator."

"A what?"

"An indicator. Remember? Someone who you can watch to see how the crowd is going to react."

"How do you *know* this?"

"He's a little taller than those around him. Watch how he looks around—he's going to be aware of what's happening. Not his girlfriend. See how she only has eyes for him? If he applauds, so will she. Big woman, forty meters south of her. Curly hair."

"I see her."

"She's here with her older kids. She's not clear why they want her here but she's willing to give it a try."

"An indicator?"

"Right. Because she's open to something new. She'll embrace it if you give her a chance. People around her will react to her as much as they will to the band. And she'll react to them the same way."

"Why are you telling me this?"

"Got to tell somebody, don't I?" Dot laughed.

On the way back to the stage she pointed out a man wearing a long toga. A woman with flowers in her hair. A group of kids with one taller than all the others. A collection of bikers I recognized from Bartlett's Gym. A tall thin woman standing by herself, her head bowed, her eyes closed.

When I got up on stage and started getting ready, I could still see them.

◄ August 10 ►

The field was packed. There were even more tents lit next to the woods. Below them, down the gentle slope to the stage, was standing room only. There was nothing left of the Petits' field but dirt. God help us if it rained: all that mud would roll downhill at us.

But the night was hot and dry. The humidity of the day seemed to thin out and we felt more baked than boiled.

As we played—as Dot and I sang—I watched the indicators. They responded first to one song, then the other. Each song pulled them in a specific direction. Pulled us, too. The energy of "Sugarpaper" fed into the desire tinged with need of "Sexual Girl" which led into the poignancy of "With You, Without You." Sure, I'd known Dot controlled the ebb and flow of emotions during the concert—what was a concert but an opportunity to indulge in the feeling engendered by the songs? But before, I'd felt it as a performer getting feedback from an audience. This was the first time I could see it in individuals.

Jake always said that the lyrics were incidental. They needed to stay out of the way of the rhythm and texture of the music but actual words were rarely worthwhile.

He was wrong.

It was not that the lyrics were as important as the music—that was clearly not true. So many good songs had crap words in them. But the *stories* those lyrics carried were important. The stories were the payload and the music was the vehicle that propelled them. The stories were the drug. The music was the syringe. Dot conducted the emotions like an orchestrated effect.

Watching the indicators, I could see it happen in real-time.

"Watch it, Olivia," came across the headset. "Don't get distracted by them. Their performance informs yours."

Yes. That was it. Half Bald danced with Redhead and as they danced, so did those nearby in unconscious orbit around them. Big Lady with Kids twirled solemnly, alone but for the music, her surrounding children caught in her trajectory. Each indicator represented a slice of the audience. Singing to one struck that entire slice.

We sang for *them*. We played for *them*.

Dot and I sang to one another. Staring into her eyes it was impossible not to be drawn into them. It wasn't important that they were a projected image. Her image represented her as my face represented me. One was made of light and one was made of flesh and bone. Were my eyes any more important than if they were painted on my face? I felt this music in my skin. In my blood.

Jake cued my solo and I came in on Obe's downbeat backed up by Jess. At the high note, Dot and I joined our voices with theirs in the chorus. It was like being opened up to the light.

◀ August 11: rehearsal ▶

Rest/rehearsal day.

I woke up just after dawn. I left Obe ensnared in the sleep of the just and went outside. We had a crew now: a tight ring of people guarding the truck. Others working on checking lights or feeding livestock. Ted had pulled his tractor out and was working on it.

I grabbed coffee and a roll from Tom-Tom's and sat on the porch with the playlist.

The concert's whole conceit was that there was a girl—or set of girls, depending on how you interpreted the songs—to whom these things had happened. Young lust in "Sugarpaper" and "Sexual Girl." Dancing the night away in "Stardust." Frightful loss in "Losing Love Twice." The trio of "With You, Without You," "Every Day is a Mistake" and "Without You, With You" dealt with hard issues—not your usual pop fare. The songs were skillfully built. None of them were merely pop rhythms but they weren't saccharine torch songs, either. Each was a sharp and precise as a knife.

Which led down into the finale: "Dancing Backwards," "Hard Road Home" and "Sudden, Broken, and Unexpected." I could see the arc. Dot had rearranged the songs many times over the concerts but it was a case of many roads to the same destination.

◀ August 12: concert #2 ▶

We didn't rehearse that day at all. Obe and I walked around the Petit place and drove down the road to a little park with a spring and a waterfall.

Instead, on the afternoon of the next day, we did a quick run-through of the songs rather than a real rehearsal—you practice too much you blunt the performance. It was a normal check: we were up on the stage going through what we would do in each song—

discussing it just to make sure we were on the same page. Jake had a couple of riffs he wanted to try. Obe had a solo he wanted to include and we had to figure out where it was would end up. Jess liked both and wanted to be a part of it—new ideas. Rosie sat in the shade of the barn, going over her laptop as Dot worked out where everything would fit.

We came to the heartbreak trio. The others were good songs but these were a story unto themselves. "Say," I said, curious. "These three sound like they happened to someone—did you get these from a fan letter or something?"

There was a long pause.

"No," said Dot. "I did not get them from a fan letter."

There was something in her voice that caught me. "Really? Where did you get them? Research?"

"Not exactly."

I didn't press.

That night's concert was all dancing and explosive percussion. Even the soft songs had a bouncy edge. Dot hit a high note that jolted the resonate frequency of one of the fixtures and a spotlight exploded. Was it intentional? I have no idea. She laughed and laughed.

It was like there was a slow infusion of home in every note.

The lights fell as always—no encore. Never an encore. That was just a Dot thing.

We put the instruments away, grabbed beers, and ended up on the porch.

Ted and his wife were there. Rosie was in the wicker chair, Jack sitting on the floor next to her. Jess sat in a perfectly comfortable lotus position, showing us all that flexibility was merely a matter of the mind. My knees would always and forever disagree.

Obe and I sat on the steps.

The night settled down. While there was always a circle surrounding the truck, people thinned out, leaving for their tents or driving home. While we didn't feel alone, we didn't feel part of a crowd.

We sat there, ensconced in darkness until one by one we left as the moon cleared the trees. Jake and Rosie to their room. Me and Obe to the basement. Jess to the barn.

When I woke up in the middle of the night, I left Obe, dressed, and went outside. Sure enough, the light shone from Dot's truck. I snagged a bottle from my stuff and walked over. Rosie was inside.

She looked up as I entered, face worn. She looked old.

"It was you," I said as I sat next to her. "Dot based those songs on you."

Rosie nodded. "It was me."

◄ August 13: rehearsal ►

"I was fifteen," Rosie said.

"You don't owe me anything," I said. "I just wanted to know. I'm nosy that way."

"I know that." Rosie snapped. "It's good to talk about it. That's what my sponsor would say. I can drink. Isn't that interesting? Drinking doesn't do a thing for me. But the sniff of a narcotic… Everybody's different, I suppose." She straightened. "I was fifteen and spent the summer sleeping with a forty-year-old NASA systems engineer. Huntsville, Alabama. My folks sent me down there to stay with my grandparents to tame my wild side." She laughed harshly. "Didn't take."

"Did he…" I hesitated. "Abuse you?"

"What does that mean?" Rosie shrugged. "I don't know. At the time it felt exciting and fun. Secretive. Certainly, it was legally defined as rape but I was as willing as they come. Later everybody tried to tell me it was sexual abuse. Maybe. But that's for me to decide, isn't it? Did he take advantage of me? Of course—I was a fifteen-year-old idiot, shaking with raging hormones. Was it *abuse*? Was I a *victim*? Jury's still out as far as I'm concerned. If I were to talk to my younger self, it would be about birth control and self-protection. And, by the way, tell her she could have done a hell of a lot better than a pudgy system engineer. Still… He took me down to Stennis Space Center in Mississippi to see the static test of one of the big boosters. Shakes you down to your toes. And we got a front-row seat at one of the Mars launches."

She leaned back in her chair. "But I found myself back home in Cambridge eight weeks pregnant and high school was about to start.

That I felt: rage and shame at *me*. At him, too—I never gave him up. They would have *killed* him. Nobody needed to die or have their lives ruined because I messed up."

"Fifteen's too young to know better."

"And forty is?" She shook her head. "I decided what had happened was *my* choice—not his. Not my parents. Not my classmates. Not his. *Mine*. I would live with it." Rosie sighed. "Too late for a pill, and the idea of an abortion made me queasy. I had no moral objections—fetus doesn't have anything resembling a brain at that point. But even so. I decided to take a year off and have the baby. Told that to my parents. They weren't happy about it but it was already August—right about now—and I was starting to show. They had money, so I spent the winter in France. Had my baby and brought it back, too. Everything was going to be fine."

Rosie was silent so long I thought she might be done. "I didn't expect it to be so hard. I loved my baby. Everybody would love me, too. Naive, right? A year off? That was a dream. I dropped out of high school—my parents never let me forget about *that*. They were all over me to give away the baby but that just made me stubborn. I'd be *fine*. Her name was Gloria. Beautiful little dark baby like her father. Curly hair. Black eyes that could stare you right down. Voice of an angel. I was seventeen when I'd had enough of them. I'd get a *job*. I'd get a place of my *own*. Moved down to Brockton. There is no good job for a seventeen-year-old high school dropout single mother with a two-year-old child. Not a single one."

I realized this was a confession. Something she had not spoken of for years—if ever.

"It only took a year to break me. I couldn't do it. Heroin is a great comforter. Parents wouldn't take me back—wouldn't take Gloria. They can rot in hell for that. State stepped in and took her away and put her in foster care. Can't have addicts raising kids." Rosie shuddered. "Giving up a three-year-old is different from a baby. The baby doesn't understand and cries. But the toddler stares at you. She knows exactly what has happened."

Rosie lifted her hands and let them fall. "I really fell apart then. Ended up on the street back in Cambridge—over in Eastport. I don't remember half that time. It was like one day the State took her away, woke up the next day and four years had passed. I was in a condemned house on Putnam. The place smelled of mold and used condoms. I threw up and went outside. Walked down to Mass Ave to a rehab center there. It took five years. First relapse a month after I started. Then about four months. Then a year. Last relapse was just before I entered college. That was—" She thought for a moment. "—twenty-two years, seven months, and six days ago." She knocked on the table.

"Does Jake know?"

"He knows about the heroin—his own addiction was the foundation for our biggest fights. Not about Gloria." She stopped. Sniffed for a moment. "I'd been five years straight and just got accepted into graduate school at MIT. Gloria was seventeen. The state has a way to put you in touch with your child but only if the child is interested in contact. I applied. Got a response that she wasn't interested. Tried again, a year later. Nothing. Tried once more when I got my Ph.D. and was doing post-doc at BU. That time I got a letter. She wanted nothing to do with 'the woman who tried to ruin my life and failed.'"

"Wow."

"Yeah. I met Jake a year later—I can't say I was doing too well at that point." She nodded to me. "Still straight. *Stayed* straight, too. Thought I had a seriously scar-hardened heart but Jake managed to slip in."

"Did you try contacting her again?"

"Think about it every year around her birthday—September thirteenth. Haven't had the nerve since." Rosie leaned back in her chair. "She didn't contact me, either. She's thirty now. Might have kids of her own." Rosie looked at me. "I could be a grandmother."

"There are ways to find out."

"There are many more efficient ways to torture myself than that." She knocked on the table again. "Still straight. Even after Denver. Still straight."

I put the bottle on the table. "This okay?"

Rosie chuckled. "Like I said, drink does nothing for me. Jake had to give everything up to get sober. For me, it was just the narcotics." She cracked open the bottle. Little Jack Daniels danced silently. She watched him. "You brought this all the way from California?"

"How do you know?"

"The southern states don't regulate the sound on the labels. They shout at you all the time." She pulled out a couple of coffee mugs from the drawer. "Washed them out last week."

"Oh, you're a thoughtful one."

"Yeah." She poured and passed one over to me.

I raised my mug. "Here's to Gloria."

Rosie raised hers. "Here's to Gloria."

Chapter 3.11 August 13

◄ Rehearsal ►

I woke up in an empty bed right at the crack of noon. Obe was out and about somewhere, but the bed still smelled like him. I stretched like a contented cat.

I wasn't hungover even though Rosie and I had drained the pint. I rarely get hungover. For a tiny person, my liver must be the size of Texas.

Tomorrow was the last concert before Farrell took—or didn't take—Dot away to cure—or not cure—her. It was like the day before an execution: a lot of pointless activity.

The concerts were pretty much in the bag. In just a couple of concerts, I had gotten a feel for what Dot did during a performance. I was not—could never be—as good as she was at it. For one, I wasn't a collection of hardware and software designed to do it. For another, I didn't have her database. I mean, I had my database in my own little head from years of playing in front of people and being a studio musician.

And I have to say after years of playing backup it was nice to be in the spotlight. *Persons Unknown* was always Jess and Jake's band. You're always support as a studio keyboard. I'd been in a couple of bands since *Persons Unknown*—*Crimson Dynamo, Human Catastrophe, Runaway Train, The Pearl Street Blues Ensemble,* and others—but always short time and always in the background. I was never the front singer.

Now, I was. Not by myself, of course. Not completely. But I was singing nearly half the songs where I either had a solo or we were singing as equals—I was able to prove "Without You, With You" was no fluke since the rehearsal. On the remaining songs, if I sang backup, she had a spotlight on me most of the time. It was clear that if I wasn't being the front girl, I was at least a close second.

It felt good.

I didn't know where Obe was, so I just went out looking for company. I ran into John Doretto near the front gate. He waved to me and I came over.

"You see the new guys?"

"No." I looked around. "What new guys?"

He pointed over at Dot's truck. The ring of men I'd been seeing for days was standing straight in the hot sun, looking like linebackers in a football game. Near them milled a small collection of big men in suits. Two limos were parked next to the suits.

"Farrell's people?" I asked without thinking.

"Yeah," said John.

And I realized that the deal was common knowledge. These people were here to listen to Dot's last concert before she was whisked away into the bowels of Ippon.

I gave John a look. "I'm surprised you let them get that close."

John shrugged. "Rosie said to—speaking for Dot."

"How do you feel about Dot's last concert?"

John scowled. "Afterward, I'll be heartbroken. I wish my daughter was here—being at the last one would be important to her."

"Where is she?"

"Yeah." He drew a long breath. "Traipsing around feeling her oats, I suppose. Shez took off with another Dothead just after the Saint Louis concert. She drops me a line now and then so I know she's okay. Last one was in northern Michigan. I sent back the whole story from down here. Crickets. I guess I can't fault her. I joined the Navy when I was her age and nearly got my ass shot off in the Bay of Bengal. At least she's not in a war zone."

John pointed at the suits. "I don't care what Rosie says. They make one step to take that truck and there will be blood." He looked at me and said darkly, "I'm in a mood."

I chuckled and patted him on the shoulder. I saw Obe over by the stage.

Obe kissed me. "Do you want to stay here?"

"Not the least bit. What did you have in mind?"

◄ August 13: rehearsal ►

Obe had in mind to go back to Henry Horton Park and find a secluded spot near the river. What happened next depended on how secluded that spot was.

Not that secluded, it turned out. Even a summer weekday had visitors. We sat on the bank and watched the river go by.

"Should we let Farrell take her?" Obe said suddenly.

"Should we let Farrell save her?" I said back.

"He's not going to save her." He looked at me. "Dot doesn't think so. Not even Rosie believes him."

I shrugged. "Your grandmother is sick and thinks she's going to die. The doctor has antibiotics that will save her. Grandma doesn't believe in antibiotics. What do you do?"

"That's different."

"How so?"

"I believe in doctors."

"A doctor who's been discredited and barred from the profession."

Obe chewed on that. "I have one. Your grandmother has a secret power that in the wrong hands might be pretty terrible. She's dying. A lying bastard says he can save her but you know he'll take her power if he does. And he might not save her but take her power anyway. What do you do?"

"Too farfetched. We'll never get a song out of that. Nobody would believe us."

Obe snorted. "Heck. *I* don't believe us."

"I believe you," came from my phone.

I pulled it out of my pocket. "Yada yada hack yada yada. Hi, Dot."

"Farrell can't save me."

"Yeah. So, you say." I sighed and watched the river. "Are you my grandmother with terrible powers? Or just my grandmother?"

"Have I affected *you?*"

I thought about that. "Not so much. No more than any other great musical opportunity might change me. But you could say that about any experience."

"True."

"I think you changed me," said Obe. "Just a little bit." He held his thumb and forefinger very close together. "I used to be the weak kid on the beach. But now I'm strong and all the girls love me."

"Shut up." I punched his arm. "Are you okay, Dot?"

"So far, so far," she said. "I heard Farrell's goons are watching the truck."

"John says he won't let them get you."

"That's good to hear." She paused. "Is the park pretty?"

"Lovely river. Birds flying. Not many mosquitoes right now—thank God. Sun's hot but not too much. Yeah. It's pretty enough." I looked around. "No ducks, though. You'd think Duck River would have ducks."

"Life is full of disappointments."

◀ August 14: concert #3 ▶

The concert took a different turn. Thoughtful. Muted. An invitation to reflection. Sure, there was raucous dancing and Dot wiggled her hips in "Sexual Girl" like she would have taken the whole front row on singly or in groups. But the theme of the evening was thinking inside. When we started SBU, we could hear the audience singing it back to us.

This time, the lights stayed on and Dot stood in front, watching the audience. Gradually the audience grew quiet. Expectant. Dot waved to us: come on out.

We left the instruments and walked around the holoscreen until we stood on either side of her. She looked at us, turning slowly to one side, then the other. "My brothers," she said softly, but every person in the field could hear her. She looked full at me and it felt like my heart stopped.

"My sister." Dot smiled at me. "A moment is all there is." Then, she looked out at the audience. "You'll take care of them, won't you?"

There was a murmured yes from the crowd.

For a long time, she watched the audience. Smiling at one person. Nodding to another. Were these people she knew? That knew her? I would never know.

"I never asked for this much," Dot said. "Yet, this is what you have given me."

Dot held out her hand to me and I put mine in it.

She was nothing but light but I swear I could feel her, gripping back hard. There was no fear in that grip. Nothing but acceptance. I saw across her Jake holding her other hand. Tears streaming down his face. I could feel my heart ache.

Dot turned to the audience and lifted her hands, carrying ours up with them. Then, she bowed and we bowed with her.

When we stood up again, she was gone.

There was a sort of *crump* like the crushing of a soda can.

I looked over and saw there was fire coming from the truck. I could see John pulling people away. They stopped maybe twenty meters away. There was a boom as the sides of the truck gave way in a burst of flame.

The band, Farrell's men, and a couple of thousand Dotheads watched as Dot burned herself to the ground.

◄ August 14 ►

Farrell's men held a swift conference next to their limos. They left before the truck fire burned out. Then came the fire trucks, the county police, the tow trucks. It was long after midnight before the last bits of Dot's truck were dragged onto a flatbed and hauled away. The crowd remained, quietly mourning.

We just watched.

"She did it herself," said Rosie, standing with us. "Charged every capacitor beyond spec and shorted them all out at once."

"How do you know that?" asked Jake.

Rosie shrugged. "That's how it would have to be done. It's not like there's thermite built into the rack mounts."

Obe had tears running down his face. "Why?"

Rosie turned on him. "*Why?* She didn't believe there was a cure. She didn't want to go with Farrell. And that damned virus was killing her. So, she went out on her own terms. Why do you *think* she did it?"

"She left us with nothing," said Obe.

"No," said Jake. And at that moment, he suddenly, effortlessly, took over the band and walked into the vacuum Dot had left. He looked around at the Dotheads. "No. She didn't."

Chapter 3.12 August 16

The five of us didn't *plan* to end up living together in Jake's house. It just happened.

Time passed.

I had always heard there were different stages of grief. Grieving over Dot seemed to happen differently for the five of us. I felt like the world was covered in ice: I had to walk carefully to keep from sliding into despair. Obe just cried. Then, he would stop. Then, something would set him off again. He didn't talk about it. He didn't even mention it when it happened. He just lived through it.

Jess seemed unaffected except maybe he meditated more. I asked him about it. Didn't he feel anything? Was it a Buddhist thing?

"Of course, I feel something," he told me. "You don't park your humanity at the door when you become a Buddhist." He looked out the living room screen. It was set up to view the hot outside, all stark desert and scrub mountain. "Buddha said that suffering was inescapable and the source of suffering was the attachment to desire. Enlightenment is achieved by detaching from desire. Feeling remains." He shook his head. "I am not enlightened. I grieve for Dot. I am trying very, very hard not to be attached to that grief." He leaned towards me and smiled sadly. "I am not succeeding."

Jake seemed the least affected. I asked *him* about that.

"Did you think we'd get out unscathed?" he asked, an edge to his voice. "Everything ends. Nothing lasts. I learned that twelve years ago."

"We only have moments," I said.

He watched me a moment. Then, nodded. "That's the best we can hope for."

Rosie took it the hardest. She seemed uncomfortable when Jake wasn't in sight—which didn't happen often because Jake spent all of his time taking care of her. I never understood her and Dot's relationship. Professor-Student? Student-Professor? Frankenstein-Monster? Mother-Daughter? She walked around the house as if she had lost a child—again. Maybe she had. She wouldn't talk to me in anything but monosyllables. It could have been that my knowing about Gloria made this loss too real for her to be around me.

◄ September 15 ►

August slid into September and kept sliding.

Towards the end of the month, Obe stopped crying. Rosie seemed to let go of *something* but I'm not clear on what it was.

I grew restless.

Sure: Dot was dead. But my fingers were itching to play something. The singing Dot and I had done had left a mark, and I was ready to try it again. Obe and I began talking about finding a place of our own. There was a sense of movement—not exactly a sense of things coming together but more like things were seeking each other out. Maybe *then* something would come together.

In mid-October, Jake announced he'd been working on the tour package and was almost ready to release it.

There were two volumes: *Walkabout* and *Rise*.

Walkabout, of course, started with Fresno and ended in Saint Louis. Like most such releases, it had a mainline video with interactive take-offs, commentaries, and subsections. We watched the mainline video in the front room. You could see Dot evolve—and us along with her—in real-time. She was more confident—more sophisticated—with every concert. *Walkabout* ended with Dot disappearing on stage and a small note that said: "Dot was infected with a virus at the beginning of the Saint Louis concert. This brought the *Walkabout* tour to an end."

"That's abrupt," I said as the credits began showing on the screen.

"Yeah." Jake nodded. "There are interviews with all of you about it."

"Interviews?" asked Jess. "We didn't do any interviews."

"Dot recorded everything. You all talked to one another after the Saint Louis concert. I took that and spliced it like it came out of an interview. I thought our reactions were important." Jake looked around at us. "Was that okay?"

None of us were committed to an answer right then.

"Let's see the second volume," I said.

Rise started with edited footage of how we decided to keep going. It didn't even try to hide what had happened: how Ippon had done it and that it was terminal. It had footage of all of the concerts but also little conversations about what was going on. The discussion about the heartbreak trio—"With You, Without You," "Every Day Is a Mistake" and "Without You, With You" was gone. But if that footage existed, then Jake knew all about Rosie and Gloria. They didn't mention it and I was damned if I was going to. It was completely possible I would never know what Jake did or did not know.

At the end, we were quiet.

Obe said, "It looks good."

The rest of us agreed.

Jake said: "Do you think it should be over?"

"What?" Obe said, startled.

Jess grinned.

"I'm saying," Jake continued. "That we have her songs. We know how to play them."

"Do we have any rights to them?"

Rosie spoke up. "I've been in touch with Ippon Legal: they're very upset. Turns out all of the songs are owned by Jake. Not sure how she did that but there it is."

"She said that she was no hacker," I said. "But the darknet is open to everyone."

Rosie gave me a look I could not interpret. "Ippon has rights to Dot 2.0 but not to any of the songs."

"Great," said Obe. "Is this going to be like 'Don't Make Me Cry?'"

"No," said Jake. "I've put the songs in a trust. We all share in whatever money the songs make."

"What about the recordings?" I asked. "You say some nasty things about Ippon."

"Everything I said is verifiable." Jake chuckled. "But there's a lot to be said for anonymous uploading." He sobered. "Do we want to perform her songs?"

Silence fell across the room.

"I'm game," said Obe.

Jess nodded.

Jake looked at me. "We need a singer."

I wanted to. Oh, I wanted to. I'd had a taste and I wanted more.

"I'm not Dot," I said. "I'm not and never will be."

"Can you sing the material?" Jake said, staring at me.

"You have no idea," I said, staring right back.

"Then, I propose we continue the work." Jake looked at us. "We let the material speak for itself. We take it and make it our own. And if we write new material, it's ours, too."

We nodded.

"Good." Jake paused. "I've been in contact with John Doretto. He's set up a place in Tennessee. It has a concert hall. Good bandwidth. Good acoustics. Places for us all to stay."

I stared at him. "You want to leave your house."

He looked around. "It's just a house. I figured I'd sell it and invest it in the tour. If you are all willing." He looked around. "Like I said, it's just a house. Who knows where we'll end up?"

I looked at them all. Like Dot said: my brothers. My sister. We had unknown potential and an unlimited future. She knew that. Now, I knew it, too.

I grinned at them. "This is going to be fun."

Epilogue

The trees in Tennessee had turned yellow and red and were now falling in a gentle, continuous rain. Around them were the hills and ridges of the Appalachians. The air was cool with a hint of bite, suggesting the coming winter.

The truck backed the container into the open slot. When it had carefully let it down onto the slab it released it and pulled away. Ima got out of the car and walked over to it carrying a manila envelope. At one end of the container, there was a locked box. Ima unlocked it and pulled out a thick spool of heavy cable. With great effort, she unrolled the cable to the nearby pole and unlocked a similar box. The cable had a plug on one end and the pole's box had a socket. Ima wrestled the two together. Inside the box were two levers. She pulled one and a display brightened. The overcast sky had begun to drizzle. Ima shook the water off the envelope and pulled out a thin manual. Ima turned to a marked page and carefully compared the drawing to the display. Then, she walked over to a similar display on the container and checked that against the manual.

Satisfied, she entered some commands on the container keyboard and locked the box. Then, she returned to the pole and pulled the second lever. The display changed. When that checked out against the manual, she closed and locked that box as well. She dried the manual off on her shirt and replaced it in the envelope and returned to the car.

"All done?" asked Abby.

"Yes. *Now*, I'm finished with it."

"Promises, promises."

Up the hill, the car stopped at the office. Abby and Ima pulled out their luggage and put it on the ground. Ima leaned into the car and instructed it to return without them. Before she pressed the GO button, Ima looked back at Abby. "You're sure about this?"

"Yes. It's all left behind as far as I'm concerned."

"You're better at this than I am."

Abby shrugged. "I didn't have as much to lose." Abby grinned at her. "Besides, leaving things behind is something I've done before."

The car closed its door and left them. They stood and watched it go, then turned and pulled their small-wheeled suitcases behind them up to the cabin office.

The desk inside was operated by a young girl barely out of high school.

"Hey there," she said brightly. "I'm Shez Doretto."

"Ima Hidori," Ima said. "And Abby Newman."

"Right. Got your reservation right here." Shez turned a ledger around for them to sign in.

Ima signed them in. She stared at the girl for a moment. "Do I know you?"

"You saw me in Saint Louis. John Doretto's my dad." She caught something in Ima's face. "No worries about that. Dad's running around getting cabins ready. He'll probably drop by to make sure you're okay. You're in cabin 1B. Up the hill about half a kilometer. Can't miss it."

Abby looked at Ima. "John Doretto? 'Sin no more' guy?"

Shez answered. "That's him. If you see a hulking blonde working the trail, ask him if you feel lost. His name is Sigurd. He'll point you right."

Ima nodded. "Thank you." She pulled out the envelope and put it on the desk. "That's for Doctor Mulcahey."

"I'll see that she gets it."

Abby and Ima found the cabin without difficulty, unlocked the cabin door, and went inside. There was a bed, a small kitchen, and a bathroom. A good sound system stocked with all of Dot's concert releases.

Abby sat on the bed. "You're sure we're not joining a cult?"

"No." Ima sat next to her. "But if we are, we'll leave. You and I together until the end. That's the deal."

Abby took her hand. "That's the deal."

There was a knock. Ima opened the door, expecting to see John Doretto.

Peter was outside. "Hey, honey."

"*Daddy*," Ima cried out and hugged him.

◄ Rosie, December 20 ►

Rosie was reading a paper on neuronal heuristics on the table surface when Jake came in out of the cold. Outside: wet snow. Winter according to the Tennessee climate. Inside: hot wood stove and cozy warmth. Rosie had always felt the cold but now—she ran her fingers over her swelling abdomen—she was always warm.

"We're about ready," he said. "Truck is packed. John and Sigurd helped. Next stop, Memphis." He looked concerned. "You're sure it's okay I go? It's nearly Christmas."

Rosie smiled. "It'll be fine. I'm barely out of the first trimester. This is when I'm supposed to glow, remember?" She stood up. "Besides, women have been having children since *Homo erectus*."

He leaned down to kiss her. Then, leaned down to kiss her belly. Straightened. "I'll call you when we get there."

She followed him to the doorway and watched as he joined Jess in the car. Obe and Olivia were already in the truck. Rosie stood there, watching while the cold rolled through the door until they were down the hill and out of sight.

Then, she carefully closed the door and locked it.

Rosie walked upstairs to her office, locked *that* door. She unlocked a safe and pulled out one battered notebook from a stack of notebooks along with a thin, water-stained manual. She opened the notebook.

From the inside flap of the notebook, Rosie pulled out a paper transcript covered with notes. She flattened the page carefully and read it over. When she was satisfied, she consulted the thin manual. Then, she turned on the surface of the desk.

Dot immediately appeared. "I've been going over the

specifications."

Rosie found those words in the transcript and checked them off. "Yes?"

"I've reached the limit of my performance engine. I can't get any more effect out of the audience."

Rosie checked those words off as well. "So?"

"The only solution I can come up with is to change human beings."

Rosie wrote another check on the page. She looked at Dot.

"Go on," Rosie said. "I'm listening."

Acknowledgments

Always and foremost: neither this book nor any others I've written would exist without the love and support of my wife, Wendy, and my son, Ben. This will always be true.

Second, the Cambridge SF Workshop has been right there holding my feet to the fire. Any issues of fact, mistakes, bad grammar, and poor penmanship, are purely my own. They wouldn't let me get away with anything.

Third, the Book View Cafe. They've provided enormous logistical, editorial, and emotional support. Thanks.

Finally, and this is a little strange, I have to acknowledge the role Hatsune Miku played in this work. Dot is most emphatically not Miku but if Miku did not exist, neither would Dot. It feels odd to offer an homage to a piece of software—sort of like giving Microsoft Word credit—but there it is. Miku started the ball rolling in my head and *Danse Mécanique* is what finally came out.

For all of these people, and for those I've not mentioned explicitly, from deep in my heart, thank you.

Credits

Danse Mécanique
Steven Popkes

Published by Walking Rock Publications in association with
Book View Café Publishing Cooperative
ISBN: 978-1-61138-955-5

Production Team:
Cover Design: Wendy Zimmerman
Beta Reader: Jennifer Stevenson
Proofreader: Steven Popkes
Copyeditor: Pat Rice
Formatter: Steven Popkes

About the Author

Steven Popkes lives in Massachusetts on two acres where he and his wife raise bananas, persimmons and turtles.

He works in aerospace making sure rockets continue to go where they are pointed. He insists he is not a rocket scientist.

He is a rocket engineer.

For updates, notional entries, subscription to newsletters, blog, and all-around interesting things, look on his website:

www.stevenpopkes.com

About Book View Café

Book View Café Publishing Cooperative (BVC) is an author-owned cooperative of professional writers, publishing in a variety of genres such as fantasy, romance, mystery, and science fiction.

BVC authors include New York Times and USA Today bestsellers; Nebula, Hugo, and Philip K. Dick Award winners; World Fantasy Award, Campbell Award, and RITA Award nominees; and winners and nominees of many other publishing awards.

Since its debut in 2008, BVC has gained a reputation for producing high-quality ebooks, and is now bringing that same quality to its print editions.

www.bookviewcafe.com
Book View Café Publishing Cooperative

www.ingramcontent.com/pod-product-compliance
Lightning Source LLC
Chambersburg PA
CBHW060359260626
47160CB00006B/2365